This book is a work of fiction. Names, characters, businesses, organizations, places, events and incidents are either a product of the author's imagination or are used fictitiously. Any resemblance to actual persons, living or dead, or locales is entirely coincidental.

Published by Griffyn Ink

www.griffynink.com

Copyright © 2016 Griffyn Ink

All rights reserved.

For ordering information or special discounts for bulk purchases, please contact Griffyn Ink at Mail@GriffynInk.com.

LoveSpelled

SAVANNAH KADE

CHAPTER 1

M egan Booker drove out of Hansen, Georgia for the last time in the muddy blackness that was nine p.m. after a massive storm. Fog reached out, snaking tendrils across the road as it seemed to steam in the summer night.

Then again, the shimmer on the road may have been from the sheen across her own eyes, tears she refused to shed. Harsh, hurtful words lingered in her head though they hadn't been said out loud at all. She thought she was immune to that by now. That she'd grown a thicker skin. The pain clenching her chest said otherwise.

It had taken all of an hour to pack everything she truly owned, everything she would take with her. It hadn't been a pretty job. She shoved blankets directly into the trunk of the car, glad she kept it clean. A few small appliances, an insulated mug, and a bag of shoes stuffed the foot wells in the back seat. On top of the seats were several boxes of her favorite books. Never unpacked from when she'd moved home after college, they'd been easy to shove into the car. On top of that lay her hanging clothes. Though she'd rubber-banded the hooks

1

together, the clothes weren't even covered with so much as a garbage bag. The garbage bags weren't hers—despite the fact that she'd paid for them—and she wasn't going to take them.

Next to her in the front seat was a massive pile of her folded clothes. It was shifting each time the road curved, but she didn't care. As long as it didn't get in the way of driving fast and far from here, it didn't matter.

Hansen, Georgia was its own special kind of hell, but she'd stayed anyway. Megan thought of her mother, of her younger sisters—Lizzie and Ari—and wondered what they would do without her. Then she almost laughed out loud. They would do what they always did: defer to her father.

Megan was done with it.

She had everything she owned in the little car, and she owned the car, too. She had money in the bank and some in cash in her wallet because her father wouldn't let her help with the bills. So she only helped with the ones she could sneak in. Now, she had nowhere she needed to be.

Before she unplugged her laptop, she'd logged into the wi-fi she paid for and penned a quick note to her boss. Due to a family emergency, she was taking a week off. She would check email when and if she could. She was sorry.

Megan had almost written 'unforeseen family emergency,' but she should have seen it coming from a mile away. Once she set up her leave time, she canceled the entire phone and TV and internet service, since she'd been paying for that, too.

She wanted to leave it. Let the girls and her mother have cable TV, even if her father didn't let them watch it. They'd been pretending they just got it by accident, they could keep doing that. She wanted them to have access to the outside world, but she didn't know where she was going or how much money she would need, and she was angry at all of them.

Broken branches littered the road, and despite her need to

get out of town and fast, Megan watched carefully for them. The only way this damp and ugly night could go more wrong was if she had an accident and wound up stuck in the local hospital. The local minister would visit her and pray for her rapid healing.

She couldn't have that. The local minister was her father. The same man who'd finally kicked her out of the house earlier in the night. He would pray for her rapid healing, but he would also pray that the demons that inhabited her soul be gone. He would pray that she was anything other than what she was. He would call her evil, suggest she invited it, and then, if she wouldn't denounce her very self, he would demand she leave town.

No, she wasn't going to get in an accident here.

She swerved around a large branch that blocked her lane, fog rising from it like smoke. The storms here could get epic. The humidity only added to the feeling of evil creeping in around the edges. Megan tried to explain to her father that the air vapor and even the storm itself was a scientific act of pressure and weather fronts. He insisted it was Megan and her evil soul that invited the storm and the damage to the town.

She pointed out that storms happened all the time and would happen after she was gone, too. He countered that the storms had never been like this before she was born.

How was she supposed to refute that?

She didn't know. But she'd been trying and failing for twenty-eight years.

Megan took I-75 north into Chattanooga. Though it was midnight when she hit town, she didn't stop. Instead, she hooked onto I-24 and drove several more hours to Nashville. There, she faced a series of forks in the freeway and found herself accidentally on I-40 Westbound and figured that was the best direction anyway.

She didn't stop until the sun was coming up and all evidence of the storm was far behind her. She rented a room in a cheap hotel and slept until one p.m., missing the free continental breakfast. Consoling herself with fast food, she hit the road again, this time sticking to I-40 West and wondering what town she would hit next. Where she might stick.

Little Rock didn't appeal. On a whim, Megan took I-30 and dove southwest toward Dallas. The summer heat beat down on the little car. Where she'd had the air conditioning on to fight the humidity when she left Georgia, she now had it set to the coldest possible setting and could still feel the sun on her arms. She'd expected the air in Dallas to be drier. It wasn't. It felt too much like Georgia, so she headed onward to Austin.

It was a full hour later that she realized the whopping tangle of freeways in Dallas had taken her up into the sky but not aimed her toward the city of her choice. Not familiar with the area, and still upset about everything that had happened the night before, she decided she'd gone too far to turn back. She didn't know anyone in Austin anyway. Maybe this missed turn was serendipity.

She continued on through Abilene and Odessa before being merged into I-10. With no music playing in the car, only thoughts of anger, regret, and her newfound freedom to keep her company, Megan discarded the advantages of every city she saw. Instead, she cataloged the problems.

Too humid. Too dry. Too tall. Too gray. Too many restaurants. Not enough activities that looked interesting to do.

For a girl with a job that was internet portable, she was open to anything and closed to everything. She just didn't want to stay in any of these places.

She spent the night in El Paso. It was cool, sprawling, interesting looking. But in the morning, she hopped in the car and made sure she was still headed farther from home.

Megan stopped routinely for gas, chips, coke, and the

occasional health bar. She ate dinner that night somewhere with salads and service, a book in hand.

She repacked her clothing into the suitcase she'd originally filled with office supplies in her haste to get out of the house. It was hard to organize your life when you suddenly realized you were getting kicked out of your childhood home with no time to plan. It was difficult to do anything the right way when you were being blamed for the storm tearing shingles off the old roof. It was harder still when you heard your father's thoughts and knew that for all the vitriol coming from his mouth, all the foul things he said about you, he was actually holding back.

Megan fought tears again. Her father was supposed to love her. She'd read enough books and seen enough TV, met enough other people in college and through her job that she knew he wasn't normal. Maybe it hurt even more that her mother loved her, but didn't stand up for her. Megan worried about her sisters, but there was nothing more she could do. Besides, her father was already getting to them. How many times could they be told that their older sister was inhabited by demons before they started to question it? And they had started to. Megan heard the thoughts in their heads. When the storm began in earnest, Lizzie wondered if it was Megan's fault, if Daddy was right. Then she'd looked at Megan in fear, knowing her sister heard her thoughts.

That had been the worst.

So Megan drove. Farther and farther away.

It was sunset on the third day when she could go no farther.

Turning around and looking over her shoulder as though she could see all the way back to Georgia, Megan thought about what she'd left behind and what might be in front of her.

There were apartment buildings nearby, she could see them from where she parked. Maybe she could afford one; she was educated, made a good salary. People walked by her, mostly they were happy. She could tell.

5

That was what convinced her to stay.

She could go no further forward, and she wouldn't go back.

She needed a place for the night and tomorrow she would start hunting apartments. Work wasn't expecting her to clock in for another four days. So she turned and looked out at the sun setting over the Pacific Ocean.

CHAPTER 2

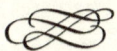

"Excuse me." The woman said after bumping into Megan. The woman was walking backward with her phone up, trying to catch the perfect shot.

"No worries." Though Megan meant it, she only meant it a little bit. She, too, was ogling the scenery. She'd moved here in the middle of August. A heat wave in Hansen, Georgia translated to a merely warm August here, much drier than back home. Though people liked to complain about the humidity here, they really had no clue.

September was starting to bring in cooler temperatures, though they weren't quite 'cool' yet. Within the first week, Megan made up her missed work and found an apartment where she could see the ocean through the sliding doors of her living room. She could sit on the balcony and look out over the waves until they just disappeared. There was often no horizon here, everything just faded into the atmosphere. Though Megan was sure it had something to do with the pollution, it seemed a bit poetic.

She found a grocery store with good brands at decent prices and one with exotic foods at exotic prices. She joined a gym and then canceled her membership within the first week, realizing she preferred to run on the beach. She'd never lived near a beach before. And today, she'd found the weather and the break in her work to be just right, so she came to see Hollywood and act like the tourist she was at heart.

She went to museums and restaurants by herself. She was polite to strangers who tried to befriend her, but always brushed them off. Megan reveled in her anonymity. So she smiled at the woman who had accidentally bumped her and was actually a little bit sorry about it.

Megan walked Hollywood Boulevard, checking out the Chinese Theater and all the handprints in the cement. When she was hungry, she found a local and touched his arm. "Excuse me, are any of these little food shops good?"

"Well . . ." He started. *Not by my standards.*

She'd learned a long time ago not to admit what she heard, but with strangers—people she would never see again—she was willing to act like she was just smart about things. "These are just for the tourists, huh?"

He nodded, glad she understood. "So, there's a great Thai fusion place, but it's on Sunset. About eight blocks that way." He pointed back toward where she'd parked. She was at least headed that way. "Or you can go about four blocks behind you."

She turned with him as he pointed.

"Turn right at that light. Go down two blocks and there's a hole-in-the-wall pizza joint that has the best pizza in Hollywood." He was telling the truth.

"Thank you." She smiled at him and headed for pizza, making a mental note about the Thai place for later.

She enjoyed the walk, looking around like she had no clue what she was doing. Then took the right at the light. She was almost shocked. Despite the big intersection, the street changed dramatically here. Almost as though four different sections of town met up at this point. The theater, up and on her left, seemed very 'Hollywood.' Beyond that the road headed up into the canyons. Across the street, the area became more city-like and less touristy. The glitter embedded in the street dropped off dramatically. Then down Vine, where she was, there was a row of shops and businesses clearly catering to locals. Congratulating herself on a good call, she headed down the street for the pizza joint as the sun began setting beyond the buildings and her stomach growled.

Five minutes later, she had a massive slice of gooey pizza on a flimsy paper plate and a coke big enough to bathe in. She took it out to the tiny metal table chained to the sidewalk and was grateful she didn't have a companion; they wouldn't have both fit. Pulling out her e-reader, Megan settled in to enjoy the food and her book, but found herself people watching instead.

While she ate, she watched in the fading light as a variety of people went in and out of the shop next door. Or at least they tried to. The door was stuck periodically, and she was amused watching them struggle with it. At one point a shop girl came out and tugged on it, even smacked at the frame, though Megan had no idea what that would do.

When she finished eating, she wadded up both her napkin and the plate, and threw all her trash into the small can nearby and checked out the store next door. Standing in front of the big window, she could finally read the gold lettering. *Blessed Be —Magicks, Charms, and everything for the Practitioner.*

Hells bells, she almost *had* to go inside, that was so strange.

Grabbing the door firmly, she yanked it hard, overpowering whatever was sticking and headed into the cool air inside. The bell over the door rang as though it had been smacked hard rather than jostled, but when she turned to look at it, there was nothing there. *Cool trick*, she thought.

"Hi, I'm Yasmin. I'll let you wander then help you when you're ready." The other woman smiled at her and waited just a beat before turning away.

9

No, I'm just looking, almost rolled off her tongue before Megan realized she'd been beaten to the punch. So she strolled the aisles looking at the "magicks."

They had herbs, incense, crystal balls, and velvet pouches for anything you might buy. They had "athames"—witches' knives for rituals apparently. She saw "scrying" herbs and learned that "scrying" meant spells to see something at a distance, like a psychic. She wasn't sure if she was impressed or concerned for their mental health. But while she was admiring the small labels with incredibly high-end prices, another woman entered the shop, then a man.

Who were these people? L.A. was wonderful, allowing Megan to be herself as much as she'd ever been in her life. So she checked out the people who thought they were witches or Satanists or whatever and mentally thanked them for keeping her from being the biggest freak in town.

"Your door is sticking." The man told the woman who'd greeted her.

"Yeah, we got cast on, Frank. One of the intermediates, we think." Yasmin answered him with exasperation in her voice. He must be a regular. Megan enjoyed eavesdropping; she wasn't much into her own conversations.

"You haven't cleaned that up by now?" A new voice entered the scene, but Megan couldn't see him from her position in the center aisle. She stayed still.

"Why haven't *you* cleaned it up?" Yasmin shot back.

"She's your student." He replied in that honeyed baritone. "You're the one who taught her how to do all this."

Megan could almost hear his hands perching at his hips. Instead of looking up, she picked up a little felt doll with no face. It was listed as "poppet—$500.00"

Holy shit. She put it back down in the bin. She didn't think it would break, but that would certainly hurt her budget if she had to buy it.

"You know, Tristan," Yasmin started talking again. "I may have taught her how to do this, but I'm not the one that slept with her and dumped her, and gave her a reason to get revenge on your store!"

Megan actually laughed out loud at that, her hands flying to her mouth to mute the sound. As additional cover, she squatted down and admired the herbs and their price tags. What herb cost *$7,000 an ounce?*

"I'm working on it." The voice—*Tristan*—was angry. Megan heard him walk away then, and heard the other man, Frank, talk to Yasmin.

"That's not your fault." He consoled.

"Don't I know it."

Megan lingered, enjoying the air conditioning and the argument. It was getting dark outside, but the foot traffic was plentiful out on the sidewalk. It was more fun to hang in here with people who believed an amateur witch had hexed their store because of an ill-fated romance. Megan loved L.A.

"Your basket's empty."

Megan looked up as Yasmin came around the corner. At least the witch had a smile on her face.

"Yeah, well . . ." Lingering time was over, since she wasn't buying any of this overpriced crap.

"If you're uncertain where to start—" Yasmin picked up the exorbitantly priced bundle of leaves and tiny flowers in one hand as though she didn't hold the equivalent of a bank stack of twenties, "—you might start with lavender. It's good for general well-being, but it smells good, too."

She held it up to Megan.

"It does smell great," she admitted. "About how many ounces is that?"

Yasmin shrugged. "About five to ten? I don't know." She was looking at Megan oddly.

"So I should spend thirty-five to seventy thousand dollars to make my house smell good? Hollywood prices are way higher than Santa Monica." Megan just shrugged.

Yasmin was looking at her like she was nuts, then she looked down at the tag. "Oh Shit!" Then she looked up at the ceiling. "*Tristan!* Your little one-night-stand screwed with the price tags, too!"

While Megan stood there wide-eyed, Yasmin rubbed at the tag as though the price would just smudge away.

A man who looked like a surfer boy all grown up came bolting out of the back to face Yasmin. He completely ignored Megan while the two verbally duked it out.

"The tag looks fine." He almost glared at Yasmin.

"No, it says seven *thousand* dollars. Per *ounce!*" She countered. After a moment, she stared at him. "Oh, Goddess, it's brilliant. *You* don't see it. I didn't see it until . . ." She looked up at Megan who was sneaking out of the store.

Not fast enough.

She loved her anonymity. No one knew her name here. Not the grocer she recognized on sight. Not even her neighbors, though she waved to the old woman with the dog each time she passed. Well, that was over.

"Megan." She admitted as she consoled herself that she didn't have to ever see them again.

Yasmin turned back to Tristan. "Your ex made it so the customers could see the bad prices, but not us. So we'd never know! Honestly, it's impressive and I think maybe you deserved it."

Megan covered her mouth again to hide another laugh as she set her basket back in the rack and reached for the door. Though she tugged, it didn't give. She tried again. Nothing.

She sighed and waited. Someone was going to have to break the scorned-woman curse on the door so she could go home.

"It was casual. She knew that!" Tristan countered.

"Apparently, she didn't." Yasmin threw back. Then she must

have spotted Megan. "And now our customer who so graciously helped us out, can't even get out the door."

Megan shrugged again.

"I'll get it." Tristan walked away, while Megan frowned.

If he was getting the door, shouldn't he walk *towards* it?

Yasmin held up a finger to her to wait, and what else was Megan going to do? She was stuck.

Then Tristan emerged from the back of the shop, holding some kind of rag in his hand. Or maybe it was a scarf. He was looking down at it, folding it precisely until he was almost on top of her.

Reaching out, he put his hand on her arm and looked at her for the first time. As he made contact, his eyes widened, his mouth opened slightly, and he looked stunned.

Megan yanked her arm back from the sharp sizzle of his touch, wishing he hadn't done that.

She didn't know what he felt, but she knew what he was seeing. The thick black hair that hung in fat spirals she couldn't tame. The wide cheekbones and eyes, her over-sized lips. The right size on an African-American face, they were too big for her mixed race coloring. She was clearly half-n-half. A freak in more ways than one in Hansen, Georgia, but out here, she'd blended in just fine until now.

His eyes trailed down her frame and back up, past her breasts and hips. Not large, she was definitely not petite, either. She'd heard more than one thought about her breast size from men she'd brushed against. She always knew who'd done it accidentally and who was a liar. She almost snapped, "My eyes are up here."

But then she saw herself through his eyes and heard the words in his head even though he didn't speak them.

Oh my Goddess.

CHAPTER 3

Tristan stared, stunned, as the woman finally looked away. He heard Yasmin tell the woman, "Please come back tomorrow. If you come at closing, I'll hook you up with some gifts. On the house." She pushed before Megan could protest.

Megan. He remembered those lush lips saying her name.

He turned it over in his head, even though his brains were still buzzing from the electric jolt of touching her.

"Tristan." Yasmin was looking at him as though she was about to snap her fingers in his face to get his attention. "Get the door."

Megan offered an almost-scared smile at him as he took his mother's scarf with the birch bark folded into it and he rubbed the door frame, silently incanting the removal spell. This time, the door opened right up and he stepped slightly back as Yasmin said a polite good-bye to Megan while his own mouth failed to follow his instructions to invite her back, offer a polite send-off, or say *anything* of value.

He stared out the doorway as she walked up the street under the lights, her purse clutched tightly to her side. She'd jolted him, both with her looks and the zing he'd gotten just from touching her. He held his hand up, wanting to cast on her to make sure she came back the next day, but Yasmin was already slapping it away.

"Oh, no, you don't. I like her." She was pulling him back inside the shop and pushing the door closed, flipping the sign to 'closed' even though it was five minutes early.

Once upon a time, Yasmin nursed a serious crush on him. He'd maintained a carefully professional distance—both because he didn't date employees and also because Yasmin wasn't his type. Since she'd found Luke and subsequently gotten engaged, her crush on him had disappeared as if it had never been and they were able to be friends. He really liked her, except sometimes when she called him on his bullshit. Like right now.

"We have to clean up this mess you made before we let any more customers in the door." She planted her feet and set closed fists on her hips as she raised her eyebrows. "You don't get to start on the next one until you clean up after the last one."

She was right. He tried a different tack. "Maybe we should shut down the beginner's class."

Yasmin called his bluff on that, too. "Okay. You do that. I have two cats and a fiancé who cooks waiting for me. I'm more than happy to be home on Tuesday nights."

Shit. She brought in too much money with her work. Between the classes themselves and the ongoing customers her students became, he couldn't afford to shut her down. And she was right about the classes. "Fine. We have to take care of that damn bell though. Where is it?"

"Non-existent. It's pure spell. That's why we haven't been able to find it." She smiled at him. "I'm a really good teacher. She was a good student."

"Rebecca?"

"No, Courtney, you dipshit. *Rebecca?* That was two girls ago . . . Oh, you think this is because she's jealous of Courtney?" The light flipped on in Yasmin's eyes as she put the pieces together.

"You have no clue which one of them it is! You man-whore!" At least she said it with a smile.

"I'm not a man-whore." He protested slimly. Truth be told, he'd been restless lately and it played out in a faster-than-normal-for-even-him turnover rate.

He liked them girl-next-door-style pretty, smart enough to be fun, and a little bit emotionally over the top. He always wound up breaking it off because they were too attached, too needy, too dramatic, too something. He had to admit it was bit awful that he wound up breaking up with them for being exactly what he'd liked in the first place. The admission, if only to himself, stabbed a little.

Well, Courtney or Rebecca—he truly didn't know—had actually taught him a lesson. No more of that. Then again, the arrival of Megan was maybe a signal that he was done. That thought got interrupted by Yasmin, too.

"Okay, man slut, then." She was grinning at him.

"You know," he countered as he held the scarf up to the door frame again. "You shouldn't pick on me for embracing my sexuality."

He had sisters; he knew how it went.

Yasmin was pulling out supplies from the bins so she could begin a clearing spell. "You're right. That was sexist of me. Just 'slut' then."

Her phone rang and he heard her taking the call from Luke. Yasmin was so much better now that she'd found Luke. They were engaged, happy, solid as a rock. Delilah, his sister was expecting a second child with her husband Brandon. They'd had a bumpy start, but were going full steam ahead now. She wasn't due just yet, but it wouldn't be long.

Maybe it was everyone else finding some kind of domestic bliss. Or maybe just that it was becoming glaringly obvious that they didn't have to introduce their dates at each event; only he did. Maybe it was because they were so stable and steady that he was suddenly starting to feel a bit like a leaf in the wind.

He listened in to the phone conversation Yasmin was having. "I'm staying a little longer tonight. We have to clean up after Tristan. Some girl he dumped hexed the store!" She went on to laugh and praise the girl and take credit for teaching her everything she'd used.

He shook his head. Once, he might have worried that Luke would be jealous of his and Yasmin's friendship. Though Luke Salzone was as straight an arrow as they came, and he still didn't know what to make of Tristan, he never got jealous. No, he knew Yasmin was his and Tristan was no threat. He didn't worry about her being friends with men. Even a man she'd once had a serious crush on.

It got Tristan started thinking maybe he could be ready for something like that. Lord knew he was older than any of the rest of them.

Megan's face swam in front of him as he conjured up the thought of her and the lightning bolt that shot through him at her touch. She sure hadn't seemed to feel it. Or if she had, she'd covered it well.

His mother once told him she'd seen the face of his future wife. So he knew he had one. She said she'd seen her grandchildren. In the plural. So that would happen, too. But she'd said nothing more. Not what this woman looked like, not what she would be like or when she would appear in his life. He hadn't been waiting.

"I love you, too." Yasmin's voice cut through his thoughts. The words clearly were not for him. "Hey, Tristan, quit woolgathering and clean this place up. I have someone to go home to."

Yeah, she did. "You go ahead. I'll clean it. My mess."

She shook her head at him, but took him up on the offer. As

she locked the front door, she pushed tight on it and the stupid little bell went off again. And again. And again.

He sighed at her. "Good night."

She offered only a sharp salute, then headed out the back.

He was left alone in his shop with his mother's scarf, his ex's spells, and his own conscience. He cleaned the spells almost absentmindedly, so it took him twice as long. Spellwork was best when the witch used strong focus and his was shot to hell.

That jolt he'd felt at meeting Megan tonight, that was odd. She was beautiful, too. Stunningly so. And he was struck at the comparisons.

He liked his women a little prim looking. She was lush. He liked them athletic. She was . . . 'full-breasted' was the most polite term that came to mind. Her ass made him check that his tongue wasn't hanging out. He liked women who were worldly. She had a southern lilt. Even her 'p's and 'd's were soft. Not dropped, they just rolled off her tongue like something sweet.

He fought the thought of her while he cleaned up the mess he'd brought onto his store. He finally double-checked the locks because he was being so loopy over a girl that he might miss something, then headed home.

As he pulled out of the back lot and onto Vine, he looked up and down the street, wondering if Megan was still around. He didn't see her. It was a stupid thought; she'd left nearly an hour ago. Yasmin left after that, so if anything, Yasmin would have taken her home and had Luke feed her. Luke wasn't Delilah, but he could cook.

Tristan arrived home, shocked at the empty feeling in the house. He'd inherited the small Hollywood Hills home from his parents. Juliet had barely been out of high school at the time. Delilah was just getting married to that snake David, though none of them had known he was a snake at the time. Maybe he hadn't been. Maybe Juliet brought it out in him.

That was neither here nor there, both were gone now.

Tristan let a sad thought settle into the memory of his youngest sister. Juliet had been skilled, generous, creative, and kind. She also hadn't been able to see past her deep-seated jealousy of Delilah. Tristan had only been able to watch it all unfold. That explosion had burned him, too.

Looking back, he'd become more, um, promiscuous then. Only he didn't see it until now because Delilah had been crazier and deservedly so. He'd been worried about her and hadn't looked at his behavior. Maybe it was time he did.

Only the brief introspection the revenge spells brought on and the jolt of Megan he-didn't-even-know-her-last-name was more than he wanted to look at. He microwaved a dinner, thinking that he didn't mooch food off Delilah much anymore, now that she had a family of her own.

His nuked pasta was lackluster, but his thoughts weren't. They pulled right back to Megan as though she were a magnet.

Something about her had flipped a switch he hadn't known existed. She was shy, sharp, funny, and she was already gone. Maybe that's all it was, a moment's shock to make him get his head on straight. He'd never been attracted to a woman who looked or sounded like her before, but he couldn't deny that he was attracted now. And he'd made a complete ass of himself, staring at her like that. And he'd paid no attention to her while—

Oh, shit.

His heart sank. His head hurt. He was an idiot.

Megan had heard every word of the conversation about the spells being his well-deserved revenge for dating and dumping a woman.

He stood exactly zero chance with her.

CHAPTER 4

I t took Megan a week to return to the store, despite the offer of free goodies. Though the place had been interesting—herbs and voodoo dollies and such—what did she need with free witchcraft fixings?

Wanting to know more about what she'd inadvertently walked into, she googled both the store and the things they sold.

Though the website offered advice and magickal help with any problems she might have, they didn't list the one thing she actually did need. On the other hand, they also didn't offer to help you get your crush to fall in love with you, or kill off your mother-in-law, or even to win the lotto or let some distant relative just slip off to the hereafter and leave you with a whopping, surprising inheritance. They offered general protections for your home, yourself, your kids. They offered general peace in the house—probably for families with teenagers and aged, surly parents, Megan figured. They offered help for couples in which both people wanted it. And they kept spelling 'magic' with a 'k.'

No, there was nothing Megan needed there. Even if it was free.

What drew her back to the store was that listening to the argument between Yasmin and Tristan had been the most fun she'd had since arriving in L.A.

Her father hadn't called and apologized for kicking her out of the house. He certainly wouldn't apologize for calling her demon-possessed or the spawn-of-Satan. He'd been calling her that since she started talking, because that's when they figured out what she heard. What she saw.

She'd been a perfect child until then, or so they told her. Megan thought now—looking back as an adult—that was likely because she heard what her parents wanted. Her communication skills had excelled. Why wouldn't they? Though her parents were often confused by her childish speech, she was never confused by them. She knew when they were truly angry and she wasn't to do something. She understood, innately, when her mother yelled because she was afraid Megan would hurt herself rather than from anger. And she saw her mother's specific fears: the hot stove, the street, the electrical outlets.

But it wasn't enough. No matter how good she was, she still saw things, heard things. As a kid, she couldn't distinguish things she *knew* from things that actually happened in front of her. She'd even been punished for not answering her father. She'd sometimes thought she was only hearing him in her head, so she hadn't responded, not wanting to get in trouble.

No, she wasn't surprised she hadn't heard from her father. But given everything she'd done, all the years she secretly helped her mother pay the bills, fed her sisters when her parents couldn't, she was surprised she'd heard nothing from her mother.

After a month in Los Angeles she still had no real friends. Megan cultivated her solitary life. It was always better than her other options. Sooner or later, she would screw up, and no one liked a girl who knew what they were thinking.

Not boys. Not other girls. Certainly not adults.

Only little kids liked her, but their parents certainly didn't want her around. It wasn't like she could go to a park and hit the playground to get some interaction with someone who wouldn't judge. So Megan lived all alone. Listening to Tristan and Yasmin argue had been her kind of fun. Which was pretty sad.

So she found herself on various websites wondering if there was possibly some witchcraft that could make her normal. After wading through hours of love spells, bad-luck-to-your-boss spells, and even a handful of get-an-A-in-class spells, she'd found nothing.

What had she really thought? Everyone wanted an A in class. Everyone wanted true love. She was the freak. Freak meant they didn't write spells for you. Still, she kept at it. Maybe she wanted a reason to go back to the store.

She found a thread on hearing voices, but it was mostly about hearing snitches of sound that couldn't be placed. Megan didn't have that problem; she knew exactly who each voice belonged to. Things came through when she touched someone, or just from someone being close, and it was always very clear who was thinking what.

Her mouth twisted, Elvis style, as she read about people who thought they were talking to demons and entities. Sad. They would have a good time with her father. Maybe he could finally try to drive the spirits out of someone who thought that was actually necessary. Unfortunately, nothing on that thread or the ones it linked had any information on how to stop it.

Well, one person suggested anti-psychotic medicine. Megan would have laughed it off, but at one point her parents had been so desperate they tried it. Not only had her prescription not worked, it made her foggy, ruining her filter. Instead of being 'cured,' she'd become worse, telling everyone everything in their heads they thought they weren't sharing. She tried a different search.

Eventually she found it: a spell for quelling the voices.

Megan frowned at her screen.

To quell the voices in your head.

Was it for schizophrenics? Or people who had negative self-talk?

She sighed. She had no clue.

There it was—her excuse to go back to the magicks store. She copied the list of supplies, the webpage assuring her that the spell was perfectly safe and wouldn't trigger worse problems.

Because *surely* she should believe everything she read online. Megan tucked the list in her pocket anyway and looked out the window. The sun was shining, and despite the day being still a bit overwarm, she stood up and opened the sliding door to the balcony. She left the air conditioner on. She was wasting energy, money, and more. She felt good. Alone. But good.

Her salary was excellent and while she could easily blow it in L.A. she didn't have enough friends or hobbies to do it. So she enjoyed the sound of traffic on the street below her. She could hear the noisy birds at the beach three blocks away, though not the waves as the rolled in. She could see the Pacific stretch to the edge of nothing. Bigger than her. Bigger than her father. Bigger than her entire hometown of Hansen.

She could smell the sea on the air. For once she had plans for tonight. But first she had to schedule the training classes for her company. Then she had to double-check her training slides for the online management training she was running the next day. She would be on camera for part of that one, which was as close as she got to interacting with people. Every now and then a stray thought leaked through online, but it wasn't the constant barrage of noise and anger and desires and more like, say, dancing in a club. Or going to a busy restaurant.

Hungry after her morning of avoiding work, and realizing the day had already passed well into the afternoon, she headed downstairs. She rarely took the elevator—it was more likely she'd bump into someone in there—and she was surprised today to find the stairs had two different tenants climbing up them. She got nothing from the first one, but the second one was an older gentleman who was upset about his cat that had passed the night before.

There was nothing she could say or do. Anything that let him know she understood his thoughts would likely upset him more than it helped. At the lobby, she saw the elevator was getting worked on and she accidentally touched the ladder, which yielded information that the elevator wasn't broken, just getting an upgrade. They expected it to be running again within five hours. Not that she cared. It was just more of the detritus that filtered into her brain on a normal day.

The sandwich shop yielded a toasted turkey on wheat. It was piled with crisp green peppers, tomatoes, provolone cheese and a light layer of Dijon. It also came with the knowledge that the sandwich maker had just been accepted into Wharton, her top choice MBA school.

Megan wanted to congratulate her.

She, too, had been accepted to Wharton, but decided to get an online MBA instead. She'd barely survived college on campus. Her online classes had been much easier to deal with. But Megan held that in, too.

She took her lunch down to the beach and sat in the warm sand. Her coke was melting in the heat, but it kept her just barely below threshold to break a sweat. She watched the waves and enjoyed her sub and chips.

The beach was generally a good place for her. People were almost always happy at the beach. Not that she interacted with anyone, but she still got impressions. Someone bumped her or she touched something in a store and it would have some *energy* clinging from the last person who touched it, or someone would just be broadcasting.

She watched the waves roll in until she found her sandwich

was gone and her chips bag empty. Though the soda was all watered down by that point, she sipped it for the cold and liquid and made her way the three blocks back up to her house.

Pulling her key from her pocket, she marveled again at how unencumbered she was. Many times she didn't even carry a purse, just her key and a twenty in her pocket for lunch. She was alone, utterly alone in life, and it felt good. But she had to get back to work and pay for that great view somehow.

So she walked up the stairs and into her apartment with the sliding glass door still standing open. She pulled her laptop out on the balcony and got to work.

It was hours later that she'd designed the program to poll the trainees on their preferred schedule, then assign them and her to the proper training times. She was hoping to group them by how long they'd been with the company and even by what previous trainings they received.

When she was finally satisfied, she looked up to see the sun was low over the ocean and the day had passed much later than she expected. It was almost eight o'clock. If she ran, and if she didn't encounter too much traffic, she could make it to the shop before they closed for the night. She nearly slapped her laptop closed in her haste. Once she made a plan she didn't like to vary from it. She'd buy some herbs and see if she could quell the voices.

Wending her way across town, Megan took surface streets until she arrived at Hollywood and Vine, then hung a right. As she pulled up she prayed for parking, surprised at how quickly prayers came to her when they weren't forced. She would have thought she'd never pray again, even for something as simple as traffic.

A spot opened in front of her and she thought of all the unanswered prayers that had been so much more important than this. But she took the spot anyway.

She walked into the front door and into turmoil.

CHAPTER 5

Once she was inside, Megan realized she was the only customer. The tall, disturbingly good-looking blond man couldn't be a customer. He was behind the counter with Yasmin and Yasmin was arguing with him.

Though Megan only met the woman once, she had the right talents to be an excellent judge of character, and she couldn't imagine Yasmin flat out arguing with a customer. So Megan pulled her list out of her purse and this time when she perused the aisles, she had a goal.

She managed to gather three items on the first aisle before Yasmin came around the corner and greeted her.

"Megan! I'm glad you came back." The smile was genuine and Megan found herself smiling back. She did that a lot more these days and Yasmin made it easy to like her. "You have a list?"

Megan nodded in response, though she didn't show her plans to the other woman. "Last time I was here, I literally wandered right in. This time I came prepared."

Yasmin seemed to notice that she wasn't sharing, but that didn't deter her friendliness. "Remember, it's all on the house."

"Oh, that's not necessary." Megan countered. She'd not expected to find such open generosity in such a large city.

"Yes, it is. We've got you covered." She smiled again as she left Megan to her shopping.

Growing up, Megan was told that large cities were harsh and unfriendly. Small towns were better. They were where all the good people lived. Then again, she'd been told a lot that proved not to be true in the end. Why should this be any different?

She found herbs from her list and a little flat burlap cut-out that resembled a gingerbread. The prices were much more reasonable tonight and Megan thought again about last time. She still hadn't quite wrapped her head around the moment when Yasmin rubbed the tag and the exorbitant number faded away, revealing the real price.

Megan found herself in the last stocked aisle, but she hadn't found two of the items on her list yet. She was about to round the last corner when she heard what Yasmin and the blond man were arguing about.

"You can't do anything?" He was asking.

"I can't." She sounded sad. For all the raised voices, it wasn't actually an argument. "I keep running up against a wall on this one. A bad one."

"No way around it?" He asked, sadder, but his tone was understanding.

"I can do it anyway. But the last time I did a spell I wasn't supposed to I ended up in the middle of a gang war."

Wow, Megan thought.

"Yeah, I guess that's enough to convince me not to ask again."

Megan turned the corner, braving breaking into their conversation, and saw Yasmin swat him on the arm playfully. She turned to Megan. "What can I help you with?"

"I need these two last things." She held up the list this time. It was embarrassing, maybe. Yasmin would probably know what she was doing. However, once Megan had the things for the spell, she never had to see the woman again.

"You're doing a *quell*?" Yasmin frowned.

"Mmm-hmm." That was all she was willing to say.

"You'll need . . ." She looked at the list again, then turned down another aisle. She handed Megan a small bundle of tiny white flowers. Before she dropped them in the basket, she shook them slightly at Megan. "Do not eat these."

"That was not my intention. It's not part of my spell." She grinned as the small buds plopped into the bottom of the basket and Yasmin frowned.

She pulled out one of the other herb bundles Megan had chosen. "These are the cheap Farshade. You want the other ones, we import them from China. I don't know what they do to them, but they are potent."

In a moment, the cheaper ones were exchanged and the better version put in her basket. Then Yasmin pulled the last item off the shelf handing it over. "This is all for a generic *quelling*. You may want to do something more specific?"

Megan frowned at her.

"If you want to quell something in particular. Generic *quells* aren't anywhere near as potent." When that didn't work, Yasmin flat out asked. "If you can tell me what specifically you're trying to stop, I can get you a better spell."

Megan scrunched her mouth, trying to figure out how much she could give away. If she said *the voices* then she'd sound crazy, and she might get a spell for schizophrenia—which she didn't have. Having been treated for it previously, she wasn't about to do it again.

Yasmin saw her hesitation and accepted it. For that Megan was grateful.

"I get the feeling you aren't an experienced witch." Though it was a statement, Megan recognized it as the question it was.

She shook her head.

"I can do it for you. It will probably work better." Yasmin shrugged with the offer.

It was sincerely given, but Megan wanted to do it herself. Now that she had all the stuff, she wanted to give it a try. *Thou shalt not suffer a witch to live.* The words reverberated through her brain. Maybe she *was* a witch in some way, just like her father had accused.

"I want to try it myself first. I won't light my apartment on fire, will I?" When Yasmin shook her head no, Megan continued. "Then I'll come back and have you do it if my try doesn't work."

"I like it." Yasmin smiled and led her to the check-out area. She rang up each piece and at the end zeroed out the whole transaction despite Megan's protests. "It's on the house. I told you."

Megan smiled as Yasmin excused herself to duck into the back for something extra. The man behind the counter stepped forward to introduce himself.

"Hi, I'm Luke."

Megan didn't like to shake hands, but his was extended and she was the only person in the room. His lack of smile concerned her. There was a very good chance that all his worry would flow into her. Megan surmised it was like having a panic attack or an anxiety disorder—she was flooded with feelings that didn't belong to her. She hesitated, but he didn't notice.

She didn't even have the bag in her hand, Yasmin had left it perched, open, on the counter. So, with no excuse she could readily find, Megan reached out and braced herself.

His hand clasped hers and his love and concern for Yasmin flooded her. But she'd been ready. "Oh! You're the fiancé!"

"Yes." He nodded, but the second wave hit her before she could let go. This was what he'd been thinking about. His feelings for Yasmin must be some amazing core he built everything around, because that hit her first, let her think he had sunny, happy thoughts despite his frown.

No, he was thinking about a woman. She was beaten badly, tied to a chair, bleeding slowly from a gunshot wound. A man stood over her, holding a gun and sneering. He didn't shoot her again, didn't let her die quickly. She wasn't worth the bullet to him.

Megan yanked her hand back as she looked up at Luke to see him stare at her.

She was staring back. Did Yasmin know what her fiancé was involved in? Megan told herself she didn't know the woman and didn't owe her anything. She also reminded herself that she didn't have the whole story and that this Luke clearly loved Yasmin very much.

Which didn't automatically make him a good person.

"Are you okay?" Luke's voice cut through her thoughts, splintering the image lingering in her brain.

"I'm fine." She turned away, not wanting anything more.

"You don't look fine."

Just then, Yasmin came out from the back. "Here!" She singsonged, "This is a beginning Wicca kit that we made up a while ago. It's—"

She stopped dead when she saw Megan and set the box on the counter without even looking. She was around the edge and standing by Megan just as the world swirled.

Hands reached out and caught her though she fought them. It would feel better to hit the ground. They didn't let her.

"Megan?" She heard Yasmin's voice punching through all the images and words coming at her. There was something behind it, some hint that Yasmin had a clue, but Megan couldn't put her finger on what it was.

"Yasmin?" She reached up, not knowing why she did it. Megan didn't reach for people. It didn't help; she got hit with more crap that wasn't worth it. But she held her hand out to Yasmin, and Yasmin clasped her tightly.

More flooded in. More than she could handle. Even stronger than the vitriol that came from her father. Almost as if Yasmin was pushing her thoughts into her.

She saw Luke, smiling, the badge at his hip. She saw Yasmin's house and Luke getting lost trying to find it. She saw the shop, and a blond woman with a toddler, pregnant with another. She heard names. Luke, Delilah, Luke, Tristan, Luke, Luke, Luke.

She saw Yasmin, and a parking lot. Bullets and a circle of blue light. She saw folders, the woman in the chair, some weird board with pictures of horrible-looking people.

"Stop touching me." She managed to choke out.

Yasmin and Luke laid her out carefully on the floor and obliged her. When she managed to get her head straight, sort out what was hers and what wasn't, Megan sat up.

"Are you all right? This happens a lot?" Yasmin was looking in her eyes.

Yeah, Yasmin had things pretty much figured out, but Yasmin didn't know what Megan did now. And neither did Luke. He was just the link. Megan nodded. "All the time."

"Is it new?"

She shook her head sadly, noticing that Luke was not following the conversation. He understood they weren't talking about vertigo and passing out, but he didn't know what. Megan told the other woman, "All my life."

"Jesus. That was the strongest I've ever seen or felt." Her gaze turned sad, somehow without being pitying. "You can't control it?"

Megan shook her head and Yasmin responded. "The *quell*."

This time Megan nodded. She stood, brushed herself off. Her head hurt. That was massive. She had not been prepared, but she turned to Luke.

"Your informant is dead. They beat her, wanting her to turn her husband over to them." Megan paused. "She didn't."

Luke turned ashen and she realized her mistake.

"They shot her. She died knowing she'd gotten herself into it. She wanted the money. Didn't tell her husband. It wasn't your fault."

He took minimal comfort in that. Megan had none to offer. In fact, she had worse. "They want the husband. They're going after the boy to control him."

"Shit!" Luke burst out, not apologizing. He turned, reaching for his phone. He was barking orders to someone before Megan turned to Yasmin.

"He's police, right?"

"DEA these days." Yasmin watched his back, his soft teal shirt wrinkling, the pop of color at odds with the mood. "You helped him. I couldn't find her."

Megan felt better knowing he was an officer, not just some random guy who was connected to a dead woman in a warehouse somewhere. She felt her hand going to her head, the pounding worsening rather than fading.

Luke turned back to Yasmin. "I have to go. I won't be home tonight." Then he turned to Megan, "Thank you. I'm so sorry it cost you, but you probably just saved that little boy and his father's lives."

He kissed Yasmin hard and disappeared out the back of the store. He spoke to someone else in the hall as he left, the back door slapping in his haste.

Yasmin took it all in stride. She watched him go before tuning and locking all the doors, flipping the signs to "closed" before she focused back on Megan, "Do you want me to work on your headache?"

"She has a headache?" The new voice popped into Megan's head, but she knew it was real. She recognized it. Tristan.

"Did you just get in?" Yasmin asked him, frowning.

"Wanted to get the books taken care of." But he turned back to Megan, "You have a headache?"

Megan nodded at him, her expression pained. "I'll take a Tylenol."

"I can take care of it for you." He offered a small smile at her, believing he was hiding his thoughts.

Desire flooded her. He was working hard not to look at her chest. He wanted her. He also believed he could get rid of her headache with a spell. "Yeah?"

Yasmin watched the exchange with raised eyebrows.

"Just come back into my office. I'll take care of you." He smiled again at her and she could almost feel his heart thudding as he wondered if she'd say yes.

She wanted to. It had been so long since she'd been with anyone.

Yasmin interfered. "Let me ring her up. Go take care of your books. I'll send her back later if she wants to take you up on that."

His smile only faltered a bit, but he nodded at her and disappeared into the back.

Yasmin stared at her. "You can do that with anyone?"

"Anyone I touch. And lots of people who are just close by." Megan shrugged.

"So you know what he's asking?" There was nothing to ring up. She'd already been rung up. So this was just Yasmin watching out for her.

"Oh yeah." Megan smiled. "I can handle Mr. Humpy Dumpy."

Yasmin's eyes widened for a split second before she started to laugh, then put her hands over her mouth to try to hide the sound. It took a moment to get herself together. "Okay, then. I'm going to leave."

Then she paused a beat before laughing again. "He has no clue. This is going to be the best thing ever."

CHAPTER 6

Tristan looked around his office, thinking that he'd done a piss poor job of making the place suitable for a woman to come into. Well, make that a woman he was interested in. Almost three-quarters of his employees were women and the place suited them fine.

That was when it hit him he'd never brought a date in here. Never a woman he was interested in. Even the two women he'd dated from Yasmin's class. As he thought of that, he shuddered. The damage done to the front of the store could have been catastrophic to business. Had whoever-she-was known what was back here and how to screw it up, he could have been in trouble with the IRS or worse. But he pushed that feeling aside, wondering if Megan would actually come back.

Quickly, he closed the accounting program on his computer. He closed the leather check ledger that he still kept for a few of his employees and vendors who preferred good old-fashioned paper checks. Then he surveyed the place.

Tugging on the minimal furniture, he swapped his chair for the guest chair. His was practically a recliner, while the guest chair was no more than a spare seat, not intended for anyone to sit in it for long. It was no easy feat getting his chair out from behind the desk, and he charmed it a little to help it slide.

He looked again. The small couch—love seat really—that sat pushed against the wall was covered in crap. Folders, magazines from the trade, mail, his jacket, and more all littered the surface. Quickly, he gathered them up. He hung the jacket on the peg behind the door, already overwhelmed with three jackets he'd left behind in the past weeks. He stacked the folders on the old wooden file cabinet and realized it was nearly pointless. The files it held were often a decade old, but now was not the time to purge.

Tristan went a little too Mary Poppins on the place, wanting to give it a general buff and shine, in case Megan came in.

She didn't. But it seemed she hadn't gone home yet either. She was lingering out front, talking to Yasmin.

With the general detritus cleared, he decided he should do *something* so she didn't find him sitting here, lurking shark-like. He couldn't remember the last time he'd been this nervous, but he decided that purging the old files would be something useful and something he could stop on a moment's notice should Megan appear. He'd pulled two files when he heard the back door shut.

Damn.

She was gone. Probably taking that unnecessary headache with her. He could have fixed it, but he'd learned a long time ago that he couldn't and shouldn't fix people who didn't want it. Guilt burrowed deep. Should he have fixed Juliet anyway? He'd wanted to, and he hadn't done it. He'd bided by the rules and now she was dead. So was David.

Brushing that thought aside—there was nothing he could do about it now, it had been a handful of years ago—he got to work on the files. He pulled the entire bottom drawer out and piled folders haphazardly around him. Nothing deserved to stay. One group would get shredded, one taken to storage, and the last tossed, because who cared? It occurred to him that he should have started at the top, instead of removing all the weight from the bottom of the cabinet. Well, live and learn.

Most of the tall furniture was bolted into a stud in the wall. That was normal in California, but the file cabinet was considered too heavy to fall. So he put his hand flat on it, closed his eyes and spelled it to stay regardless of the size of earthquake that might come.

"I'm sorry. Are you and the files having a private moment?" Her voice popped his eyes open, spell unfinished.

Of course, Megan walked in right then. He shrugged, then was surprised at the words that tumbled out of his mouth. "My files and I have a long and deep relationship."

Yasmin would say that was about right, but he looked at Megan again.

She wasn't anything like the women he usually preferred. But as he looked at her now, he realized maybe Megan was more All-American than what he'd been thinking of. Clearly of mixed race, she was stunning. She was in great shape, but maybe it was the size of her breasts that kept him from thinking of her frame as 'athletic.' He'd never been the kind of man to stare at a woman's chest, but he was having to forcibly drag his gaze away as she spoke. And there had been that undeniable zing when they'd touched.

She seemed amused by his befuddlement. "You said you can take care of my headache?"

"Oh! Yes." He'd been a dipshit and forgotten she was in pain.

She shrugged at him as though she didn't know what to do. Why would she? "I've never had a . . . spell remove a headache before. I've always just taken something over the counter."

He grinned, finally on solid footing. "This is better than over the counter. And it won't come back."

Her eyebrows raised as if asking him how he could know that.

He didn't give her time to ask. He was at least a twelfth generation witch. Before that, they didn't have records. He'd been born with the skills for something as simple as wiping a headache.

"Come sit over here." He motioned to the chair he'd pulled out from behind his desk, then swiveled the chair so he could stand behind her.

Megan's expression was wary, but Tristan understood. What his family did was unusual, no doubt about that. After she sat cautiously, he settled himself in, leaning against the edge of his desk, just the way he'd planned it when he pulled the chair out. "Lean back. I'm going to put my fingers on your head, okay?"

She leaned back, but held her hand up. "I have clips in my hair."

"Not a problem." But he couldn't see them. They must be tiny, must match the color of her hair and be buried in those unreal spirals. "I'll pull them out if they're a problem?"

She nodded and leaned back in the chair, though she still seemed untrusting and a little stiff.

Tristan put his hands on her temples, once again unprepared for the jolt that assailed him. Good Goddess, his heart tripped as though someone had run jumper cables between them. Under his sensitive fingertips, Megan twitched, too. Tristan tried to act as though nothing had happened.

Running his touch up to her hairline, he looked for the source of her headache but couldn't find it. He pulled his hands back through her hair, assessing it when he should have been doing spellwork. He liked women with silky smooth hair. Then again, most of them put all kinds of crap in it and killed the idea that it might ever be silky. When had he last touched soft hair? Megan's wasn't silky, but it was soft. It sprang up, teasing his touch, begging him to linger.

This wasn't the time. He pushed his fingers through the mass of her hair, ignoring another jolt to his system, the desire to play with it. His fingers tangled slightly, and he realized he'd run into one of the clips. He plucked it and watched the hair fall forward. Another clip stopped him and he undid it, too, leaving it on the desk by the first. "Is that okay?"

"Mmmmmhhmmmmmm." She was leaning back into his touch now, her voice somehow a hot shot to his groin.

Nope, he told himself, *not the time.*

But he looked down and saw that her shirt was more unbuttoned than he'd noticed when he first came in. He had a straight line view down her shirt at those magnificent breasts.

Oh dear lord, he blinked. He had to stop looking.

As if she knew what he was thinking, she took a deep breath, pushing her head back into his waiting hands, reminding him to move his fingers, to do something other than stare. It also moved her breasts up in slow motion.

Oh, he was fucked.

By sheer force of will, he concentrated on finding and plucking the rest of the clips, amazed at the way her hair moved around his hands now that it was free.

Even when he focused, he couldn't find the source of her headache, couldn't discern muscle tension, an injury, sinus pressure, or anything else he normally found. So he began trying to relieve what she was obviously feeling even if he couldn't find it.

His fingers massaged her scalp and her breath pulled in.

Shit. He reacted to the sound, wondering if it was a noise she would make in bed. Tristan tried again to concentrate on the spell.

As if she knew what she was doing to him, she made another noise.

"Mmmmm." Her head tipped even further back into his hands. He could see her face, her straight nose, her inky eyelashes laid against her cheekbones. Her full lips inspired more untoward thoughts and he worked hard to squash them until, with perfect timing, she let them fall just a tiny bit open.

His cock twitched. His chest froze just watching her. At some point he realized he'd stopped moving, breathing. He shook it off, grateful she was in the chair facing away from him and couldn't know his reaction.

Just then, she slowly opened her eyes and offered half a seductive smile. "That feels good."

Yeah, it does, he thought as her eyes fell back closed. But he shouldn't be thinking that. He'd offered help; that was all. Sure he had hopes, but normally he controlled his thoughts so much better. As a witch, he was trained at it. His thoughts helped create his spells and couldn't run wild. So why was it so hard to focus with Megan? Why did it seem she just did everything right at the exact right time?

Her chest heaved with another deep breath. The slightest sound of pleasure hummed from between her barely parted lips.

Tristan almost fell to his knees. She was killing him.

Instead of begging her to put him out of his misery, he forced his thoughts once again back onto track. "How do you feel?"

"Really good." Her face moved as though she were close to orgasm, and he couldn't decide if he should stop or keep going.

"How's the headache?" He asked a more pointed question this time, trying to ignore the pressure in his jeans. The tug in his chest. The overall zing of primal lust that coursed through him at the very touch of her.

"It's gone." She blinked quickly and smiled up at him. No guile this time. She even sounded surprised.

His own return smile was easy, genuine, and he almost laughed at her shock. "Good."

Then her expression changed. "Have you been looking down my shirt, Tristan?"

His mouth opened but nothing came out. He didn't want to lie, but he sure as hell didn't want to admit the truth either.

Her head rested lazily against the back of the chair, her hair still in his hands. Lust shot through him again and she gave a subtle arch of her back as though she felt it, too.

Smile gone now, she stared him in the eyes from her seemingly upside down vantage point. "You like looking down my shirt, Tristan?"

Again, he couldn't answer. His mouth worked and he realized he must look like a damn fish. So he forced out sound. "I wasn't trying to."

As he watched her watching him, Tristan saw her hand snake up the front of her shirt. She began plucking her buttons open, one by one. "Shall I make it easier for you?"

All his blood shot to his dick. He couldn't form words.

"Do you want me?" Her voice was coy, almost too coy. She adjusted it to a more honest tone. "Just tell me if you want me, Tristan. Say no, and I'll leave."

She moved so slowly, unbuttoning her shirt. The top was falling open, revealing a red bra cradling those magnificent breasts. She hit the bottom button and ran her hands up the edges of the shirt. She wasn't touching herself, but she was sending a clear message. When she hit the top, she pulled the shirt slowly open revealing dark, unblemished skin. More of it than he'd ever thought he'd see.

"Tristan?" She asked again, since he was unable to operate his basic functions such as speaking a single syllable.

Somehow, he managed it, breathing out the single word of a gush of bone deep lust. "Yes."

CHAPTER 7

Jesus, it felt good to have a man want her like that.

Megan could read him like a book. She didn't even have to touch him; he was broadcasting all over the place. For a moment she wondered if there was anyone else nearby who might overhear his thoughts. Then again, she'd never met anyone who could hear other voices in her head like she could. Tristan's voice was simply clearer than the rest.

He wanted her. His feelings gave her power and fed a need to be touched. She hadn't been touched in so long. Over a year. Since the last time she'd gone off her rocker and done something like this.

Standing and turning to face him, Megan let her shirt slide down her arms and fall to the floor. His breathing kicked up. He was considering turning her down and being a gentleman, despite the fact he was nearly in pain. She could feel it radiating from him.

She knew what to say. She knew exactly how to be his fantasy—at least as best as she could. So she waylaid him. "If you want me, this is your one chance."

"One chance?" He asked.

He wanted to know why only one. Megan wasn't going to explain. She walked slowly around the chair, turning it aside and giving her room to stand in front of him where he still leaned back against the desk. He was in a t-shirt and old jeans, less professional than the first time she'd seen him. And sexier.

She stood so close, rose on her tiptoes and whispered in his ear, "Now or never." Then she ran her hands around the sides of his waist, fisted them into his shirt and began pulling upward.

Immediately, Tristan complied. He chose 'now.' Not shocking.

She understood that she wasn't his usual type. It came through loud and clear that he didn't understand his attraction to her, but it was there all the same. She caught snapshots of his thoughts. Visions of the two of them on the couch behind him, naked, joined, writhing. She saw another quick flash of her undoing her skirt, unhooking her bra, peeling her panties. She could do that, too. He wanted to make her scream in pleasure. Which was exactly why she'd picked him.

With his shirt off, he braced his hands against the edge of the desk as though stopping himself from doing something. Megan couldn't tell what. Still she knew what he wanted.

She reached to the side, catching the zipper on her skirt and slowly lowered it exactly as he'd imagined, before dropping it in a puddle around her ankles. Her underwear was pink and didn't really match the red bra. Tristan did not care.

He was having trouble breathing.

For a woman who spent much of her life afraid of what people would think of her, this moment was heady.

Though he wanted her naked, she wasn't quite ready. He hadn't even kissed her yet. She hadn't pushed it. Between the flashes of images Tristan was inadvertently sending her, Megan felt her own nerves. He'd shocked her when he touched her the first time. Kissing him concerned her, but she wasn't going to do the deed without it.

Make it or break it time, she thought and stepped back in close. "Kiss me, Tristan."

She didn't have to ask twice. He didn't even think it before he did it, so she had no warning. His arms were around her, skin on skin. His mouth covered hers, primal, needy, and demanding before she even saw it coming.

It was like a thousand volts coursing through her.

Her brain fried.

Her body melted.

She was a live wire, arcing whichever way the current took her. His hands held her while his mouth explored, hot and vivid. The images he unwittingly showed her lost form and substance, unraveling into a nebulous but overwhelming feeling of need.

Or was that her?

Striving for something she couldn't define, she moved with him. She was no longer anticipating his moves, just reacting. Megan reached for him, not realizing until now just how starved she'd been for someone to touch her, want her, need her in any way.

His hands roved her back while their mouths fused and fused again. His fingers found their way into her hair, which she was self-conscious about. Pulling back a second, she looked into his eyes and saw that he loved the feel of it. He was fascinated by her, and she had to admit she was fascinated by him, too. His hands tugged her close, not demanding but asking, and Megan didn't say no. She pressed against him, her mouth on his again, reveling in the sensation of his hands on her shoulders, splayed broad across the bare skin on her back, tugging her closer and closer still.

With one hand in her hair, cupping her head, Tristan moved the other to her waist. Then up. Then he was testing the weight of her breast and brushing his thumb across her nipple, making both their mouths open in a soft gasp.

He did it again before she realized her bra was missing. He

was touching her, fondling her, sending bolts of lightning through her, but she hadn't peeled her bra like he wanted her to.

It took effort, but she refocused on him. He wanted her hands on him.

So she gave him that. First, she stroked his chest, then his back. When she arrived at his jeans-clad ass, she stuck her hands in the back pockets and curled her fingers. His muscles clenched involuntarily. She loved that it jerked his hips forward, into hers. That it shot another bolt of lust through the already clouded corners of his mind.

Megan moved her hands and pushed his hips back, enjoying the disappointment in his thoughts. He worried, was she pushing him away?

No, she thought. *Not that*, and she reached for the button, snapping his thoughts back to where she was going. She slid the zipper down and let her hands slip inside, trailing over his boxers and along the hard length of him.

His mouth fell open. He stopped moving and stared at her.

She was in control again.

He didn't just like it, he was completely unable to move.

His voice came to her in her thoughts, harsh but desperate rather than demanding. *Again.*

She acquiesced.

This time his voice did escape his mouth, a guttural groan of pure pleasure. Megan touched him a third time, only this time she pushed her hands down farther, pushing his jeans down with them. Time to get him out of his pants.

As if he had read her thoughts, Tristan hooked the waistband on his boxers and managed to kick his shoes off as he peeled the last of his clothing. It couldn't have taken him a whole second; he was a man on a mission. When he stood back upright, his clothes were tangled on the floor beside him and he was completely, gloriously naked. Fully erect and breathing hard.

Megan stepped back and Tristan simply stared at her for a

moment. His mind didn't—couldn't—form actual words for her, but he was asking again, yes or no?

She hooked her thumbs in the sides of her underwear and slowly peeled them down while watching his face. He was mesmerized. His breathing somehow managed to become more labored.

Suddenly, he dove for his pants, scrambling in them with one thought slashing through all the others. *Condom.* Megan fought a smile.

He emerged with a foil pack and tossed the pants aside. One pant leg was now inside out. His wallet was out and open, a twenty and a credit card scattered in his haste. He didn't care.

Knowing what he wanted, she took his wrist, shocked again that he could jolt her still, and led him to the couch. She saw his eyes widen with recognition and a flash of him being grateful he'd cleaned all the crap off it earlier. She was grateful, too, but she reached for his shoulders and pushed him gently down to sitting. Then she carefully straddled his lap, his nostrils flaring at the scent of her and with surprised that she'd put them exactly in his fantasy position.

Tearing open the condom, she situated it, lined it up, then kissed him hard while she rolled it down and he bucked upward into her hand. She kept kissing him while she positioned herself and slid onto him. But then she couldn't kiss him any longer. Her mouth opened on a forced sigh at the feel of him inside her. Her head fell back at the need racing through her, both hers and his.

Tristan rocked up, watching her through his own hazy gaze, watching for her reaction. That sweet, sexy boy wanted to know if she liked it.

Megan nodded at him. Then when he didn't move, she breathed out, "Again."

Tristan complied. And complied again.

His hands found her breasts and shot more arcs through her.

He kissed her, and she let her head fall back the way he wanted. Then she was glad she did it. He ravaged her neck, sucked on her earlobe, and traveled his mouth down to the peak of her breast. He didn't stop moving inside her the whole time.

She heard him every step of the way. He wanted to do those things. He wanted to lick her and suckle on her and touch her. And he wanted to please her. Still wanted to make her scream with pleasure.

She couldn't stop the mews and whimpers that fell from her mouth.

He lavished one breast then the other. Then he joined his mouth to hers, his arms anchoring her flush against him, rubbing her nipples against the soft smattering of hair on his chest, against the hard pecs beneath that, with every thrust. He tripped something in her, building the tension in her, until he pulled back and looked her in the eyes.

For one lust-shot second she thought he could read her, that he knew what she was doing. But he thrust into her again and again, until he gritted his teeth and she knew he was getting close.

Something in him bloomed open to her and she felt everything. Overlaying her own heat and lust was his. The exquisite feel of her wrapped around him, of the electrifying rub of her skin on his, and she lost it.

Her head fell back, breaking the eye contact if not the connection. He waited her out, pulse after pulse, while she lost herself, not sure if she screamed as he wished or not. She felt him tense as she finished and finally let go himself. He held her in a vise grip while he reveled in his own release even as she slowly came back around.

They sat that way, his arms around her. Hers were around him, too, in a death grip she'd had no idea she'd done. She didn't know how long they lay against each other. His skin was slick with sweat and so was hers. His breath a steady rasp in her ear, the smell of him a taste in the air where her mouth lingered so close to his neck. She was languid, almost liquid. She'd needed the release.

Slowly, her breathing headed back toward normal. Clearly exhausted, Tristan started to lean back against the couch, his rigid position finally melting away. He tried to bring her with him, to get her to relax over him, still joined, but that was definitely her cue.

Pulling back, Megan carefully moved her legs and extracted herself delicately. His face was shocked for a moment that she'd stood up, separated herself from him. She heard as he searched for a plausible explanation. She needed a drink? She was uncomfortable?

He was reaching out with his hands and his voice, despite his sapped energy, trying to figure out what she needed. "Megan, can I get you—"

She held her hand up to him and grinned. The grin seemed to help him feel better, but she felt the tide turn when she reached for first her underwear then her bra. The undies slid right on before he got his thoughts together. But her bra was a work of architectural genius. For a buxom woman like her, it had to be. It took her a moment to shimmy in and get everything in place.

He was almost enjoying the show, but she felt the worry running in from every side as he started to stand, still naked. "Megan, you don't have to go. Please, don't."

She nodded at him as she pulled her shirt on and only hooked every other button. She was tucking it into her skirt before she realized what to do. She stepped into her sandals, wiggling the straps into place then stood on tiptoe against his still-naked form. She kissed him on the mouth. It was intended as a thank-you, but Tristan was having none of that.

He grabbed her, pulled her against him, pushed her mouth

open with his and joined them almost as intimately as they had been during sex.

She slipped under the tidal wash of feelings between them again. Kissing him back, she clung, not controlling her own thoughts or worrying about reading his.

Don't go.

His voice was clear as a bell in her mind. A big, big cue it was definitely time to go.

She pushed against him, stepping back and out of the kiss. Then back a little farther and out of the office.

He followed her, naked and unconcerned. She'd already grabbed her purse and bag of goodies from Yasmin and was at the back door by the time he appeared in the lit doorway. "You don't have to go."

"Yeah, I do." She smiled and turned the lock, letting herself out to the sound of his voice calling behind her.

"Where do I find you? Megan? Megan?"

CHAPTER 8

The next morning Tristan was in his office before time to open the shop. He was in earlier than usual because he knew Yasmin was opening. Sitting in his office, he waited in the big comfy chair he'd put back in place behind his desk.

He'd fixed it last night. While he was more than perplexed about Megan's screw-and-dash, he was not perplexed about Yasmin's powers of deduction. So he put everything back exactly as it was, including the crap on the love seat. He did leave out the piles of files he'd purged, he wasn't going to undo that work, but if she saw the big chair out of place, the love seat cleared, she'd figure everything out. Real fast.

Last night, he'd headed home for not enough hours of confused and relatively useless sleep. Now, he managed to purge more files before he finally heard the click of the back door and squashed the urge to attack his employee for information.

Just barely, he held it in check. She usually came in and said hello to him if he was in here. He'd hold out for a bit. Besides, he knew Yasmin once had a crush on him. It had taken his sister Delilah telling him flat out about it for him to see it, but he finally had. Was it wrong to ask her now for information about the woman who'd caught his eye?

No, he decided. Yasmin had Luke. She'd left any feelings for Tristan far in the dust. She'd smiled at him about Megan, made fun of him with her expression and her laughter. No, things were okay with Yasmin. Now could he get them squared away with Megan?

He pulled another file and didn't even recognize the name of the vendor. The writing was his mother's feathery scrawl, and the folder a shade of manila that either wasn't produced anymore or had colored over the years. He was setting it on the 'toss' pile when the small knock came at his open door.

"Morning, Tristan. How goes?" Yasmin's voice held a hint of curiosity.

"It's good."

"You're in early. I thought you might be sleeping in, all snuggled up at home with your cell phone and Megan's number on speed dial." Her grin told him she harbored no remaining feelings for him that way.

Now, what to tell her? "Um, no."

She was surprised. "Did you help her with her headache?"

"Yes." He wouldn't tell her the details. It took a moment to work around what to say and what not to say. "She said she felt better. We talked a little—" Okay, that was a lie. Talking was not what they had done. "—then she ran out the door and . . ."

"What? You ran her off?"

"No!" It wasn't like that. He knew because Megan had screamed her head off. Even after she was dressed, she'd smiled at him and kissed him like there was no tomorrow. "No. But I didn't get her number."

"Oh." She seemed genuinely surprised. "What did you talk about?"

"Um." He shouldn't have said that. "Stuff." Goddess, she had to see right through him! He was a terrible liar.

She nodded thoughtfully. "Oh. Then . . . no number? You asked?"

"Kindof." He shrugged. This hurt worse than Megan dashing out the back door last night. He desperately wanted to find her. "She was already out the door. I asked, but she didn't answer at all. No *yes*, no *no*."

"Well, she lives in Santa Monica. Use her last name to do an internet search." Yasmin smiled for a moment, then saw his expression, then sighed at him. "You don't know her last name, do you?"

He had to shake his head. When had he ever slept with a woman whose last name he didn't know? Never. Not before last night, that was for certain. Then again, he did know the last names of the last several women he'd slept with and he still couldn't tell who'd hexed his store. *Crap.*

Pity shone in Yasmin's eyes. She could tell he really liked Megan, and honestly, he more than 'really liked her' now. He craved her. Wanted her body naked next to his like she was heat or air or food. He wanted a full night, in a big bed, moonlight in the window and no cares in the world. Instead, Yasmin was staring at him sadly, because despite how much he wanted that, she was going to make him ask. He bucked up and did it.

"Will you please tell me her last name?"

"I can't."

He blinked at her. Had Megan told her not to tell him? Had she planned to seduce him and bolt? Had she—

"I don't know it." Yasmin confessed before the train of his thoughts completely derailed.

"But you talked to her. You . . ." didn't ring her up, didn't get her last name. *Double crap!* "So what do I do?"

He was thinking a *compel*—make her come back. Get her to call the store, her number would be captured. He could scry for her apartment . . .

"Leave her be." Yasmin offered the terrible idea with a kind look on her face.

He couldn't just sit back and wait. For some reason he felt a need to find her.

"Maybe she actually didn't want you to find her." Yasmin offered with a wry twist of her lips and a shrug.

He had to consider that possibility. He'd asked and she'd been out the door. Tristan told himself that was because she hadn't heard him, but probably she had. *She* peeled her shirt and came onto *him*. When he thought hard about it—without letting his breath catch in his chest or his imagination run wild —last night couldn't have been the first time she'd done that. She was too smooth. Too much his fantasy. She must have done it before. Known what every guy wanted. And left on purpose.

Only this time, he didn't want that.

"Maybe she'll come back." Yasmin offered, leaning in the door frame now. He realized he hadn't moved from his position on the floor amongst the files. He stood up now, hope surging.

"You think?"

Yasmin nodded at him. "She headed out with our old starter kit and the makings of a *quell*."

He frowned at that. "A starter kit means she didn't have anything of her own. Right? And a *quell* is hard to screw up royally, but that's because it's hard to get right, too. You let her go out the door that way?"

Yasmin shrugged. "I couldn't really stop her. She wouldn't give me any specifics about the *quell*—" She paused for a moment, her eyes looking up as though putting something together. Before he could ask, she continued, "Anyway, she said she'd come back and have me do it if hers failed. I'm pretty sure hers will fail."

"So she'll come back."

"And she'll come to me." Yasmin offered him a small smile.

"And you'll get her number or name or something of use for me?" He pushed at the glimmer of hope he was starting to feel.

"I'll ask. If she says no, then it's no."

"Of course." He spoke just as his cell phone rang. A voice intruded into his head as he considered ignoring it.

It's me. Delilah! Pick up. I'm having the—

Even the thought broke off. That was odd. Tristan pulled the phone from his pocket the name showing that it was his sister. He answered it. "Li?"

She huffed for a moment before finally speaking. "Sorry. Contraction. I'm having the baby. Get Yasmin here to babysit? You come get me. We'll meet Brandon at the hospital."

She hung up on him and Tristan's eyes widened even as he figured out his sister had gotten through to him first. Brandon was only just now becoming better at hearing her. He was great if he listened, but he wouldn't be listening. They were five weeks before her due date.

"Yasmin!" He yelled it only to find she was still in the door, wincing at the noise. "Sorry. Delilah's having the baby. Can you—"

"On it." She rushed into the store, presumably to put a note on the door. She was back as he was frantically scoping the room, trying to decide if he needed anything other than his wallet. Deciding he didn't, he led Yasmin out the back door and locked up with hands that were surprisingly shaky.

"Hey," Yasmin consoled him, "She's done this before. It will be fine."

"It's too early."

"Nah, lots of babies are early and do just fine. Five weeks is just at preemie status. No big deal." She laid a hand on his arm and he thought for a brief moment of Megan touching his arm the same way and how it shot through him so hard he thought he would see sparks. Then he turned his head back to the task at hand. "Ride with me?"

"Nope. I'm going to follow you so we each have a car. And I'm calling Libby while I drive so I can get her to come in early, or find someone who can." She was already sliding into her coupe in the tiny back lot, the warm day posting a ray of sun on her face. For some reason it made him believe in her confidence and he felt better.

Sliding behind his own steering wheel, Tristan turned and headed out to his sister's. Delilah and Brandon lived in West Hollywood, not that far from the shop. He cursed every light he hit until he got to Delilah's house and found her out front, standing with Yasmin, the go-bag in her hand.

He needed to spell the traffic lights, turn them green. Didn't know why he didn't think of it earlier. So he did, and arrived at the hospital to find Brandon already there and waiting.

His brother-in-law smacked Tristan on the shoulder and grinned. "What took you so long?"

More than a week later, Tristan was exhausted. He'd been running the shop like normal, visiting his sister, and running errands between the hospital and her home and his. He was helping Brandon manage a family in two locations. The older child, named Ethan after Brandon's father, couldn't go to the hospital. The new baby, Juliana, was a preemie in the NICU, so no children were allowed. His sister and the new baby would be in the hospital for a while.

The name Juliana was as close as Delilah was willing to get to touching their sister's name—Juliet. Tristan thought it fitting. After all the things Juliet had done, it was surprising his sister had it in her heart to forgive even that much.

He, it seemed, was left with the same tangle of emotions he'd always had about the whole situation. The smack of old feelings, the scrape of sharp knives in old wounds weren't things he wanted to deal with this week.

And he couldn't sleep.

Thoughts of Megan Whatever-her-name-was plagued him. Sometimes he woke up hot and tangled in his sheets, sweating, groaning. Other times, he woke up cold and wooden, dreaming that he searched for her and never found her. Once, he woke up content, having dreamed he was older, with children and Megan beside him.

Though his dream feeling in that was peaceful, his waking feeling was beyond confused. He wasn't sure he was ready to settle down and get married. And if he did, would hell-on-heels Megan be the one? She seemed pretty experienced at seducing men. He didn't discount that as wrong, just not something he was sure he wanted forever.

It took a handful of days for Tristan to admit that he was struggling to accept that he was someone else's one-and-done. It took a few more days to realize he simply wasn't accepting it. Had it been any of the women he'd recently dated, he would have easily let them go, but for some reason, he couldn't shake Megan.

He let the back door to the shop slam, a sure sign of just how tired he was. When he heard Libby out front talking to someone, he tried to casually head out that way.

It wasn't Megan.

Of course, it wasn't. If Megan came back, she would talk to Yasmin. Even though, according to Yasmin, Megan didn't know her schedule. He said a polite hello to everyone, then watched as Libby looked at him strangely when he headed into the back toward his office.

He didn't usually come out unless a rush was coming. So Libby saw him head out, expected a slew of customers to come in, then was abandoned. He wanted to care, but he couldn't.

Instead, he cleared his desk. He knew full well it wasn't his smartest move, but did it anyway.

Tristan pulled out a wide paper map of L.A.—it was the easiest way to scry. Digital didn't work the same for witchcraft. Digital witchery existed, but one of the main tenants was the connection of everything. The paper the map was drawn on held an elemental connection to the place. The digital representation didn't hold the map all the time, thus didn't create the connection a solid map did. He sighed; he would have to deal with the vagaries of the modern age some other time.

He pulled a pointed stone from his desk drawer. It was mounted on a chain his great-great-grandfather wore his wedding ring on for years after his wife passed away. Both had been powerful witches, and the chain had absorbed a lot of that. Tristan held it now over the map. Long practiced at this, he first asked if Megan was in Santa Monica, California.

The process was often very literal. If you asked the universe to bring you a cute chick, you might very well wind up with a fluffy, yellow, baby chicken. If he asked if she was in Santa Monica, she might be in the resort in Florida or somewhere else.

Sure enough, his first answer was yes, Santa Monica, California. He divided the town into quadrants, checking each for a yes/no answer. Was Megan there?

"Crap!" Tristan realized he said it out loud. He looked around, grateful he'd closed the door to his office. It wasn't that anyone couldn't see him scrying, it was that he liked to not be interrupted. Though normally he was doing accounting, orders, real business.

He'd asked "Where is Megan?" That was a bad question for a literal answer. She might be at the beach, or a sandwich shop, or somewhere she wouldn't still be by the time he arrived and he'd have to start over. So he had to start over now.

His eye twitched. If that was from his rookie mistake or

from the fact that he probably shouldn't be doing this, he didn't know. He was too tired to figure it out.

Thirty minutes later, he'd pinpointed her apartment to a building he'd probably driven past at some point, but certainly couldn't identify. He jotted the address, told Libby he was leaving, and barely remembered to put away his map and scry crystal.

He headed to a toy shop just three doors down from Blessed Be and went inside. Then, thirty minutes after that he was parking his car and walking to Megan's building.

CHAPTER 9

D eeply involved in her spreadsheet, Megan twitched at a noise from the street below, but it didn't really penetrate her thoughts. Not until it came the third time.

That was when she looked up and realized the noise wasn't from the street, but from her balcony. Something pinged the sliding glass door.

A bird? A large bee? She wouldn't have thought there could be anything bigger or meaner than the bugs in Georgia. A good palmetto would fly right at you and was heavy enough to make a dent if you didn't duck.

She didn't see anything at the window, so she dismissed it. Standing from her position on her maybe-too-comfy couch, Megan stretched. She headed into the kitchen for a glass of ice water. As she moved into the tiny space, nicer than her parents' home, but nowhere near what she could afford in a different town, she realized she was approaching two months in L.A.

She liked it. Stresses she hadn't realized she carried were lifting. There was something about knowing she never had to deal with her father again that allowed her to finally unwind.

Even almost two months after her flight from Georgia, she was still feeling as if she was shedding her old life, layer by layer.

There had been stresses that were obvious—worrying about her mother and her sisters. Worrying that her father would come after her physically again. It hadn't happened in a long time, but with him you couldn't tell. It was like living in a war zone. When she first arrived here, not knowing what was happening with her family was another stress. But when her mother hadn't contacted her, and neither had either of the two girls—who knew perfectly well how to work a phone—Megan shed them, too. If they needed her, they would call. She couldn't worry about people who were glad to get rid of her. She hadn't realized she'd feel better when she let go.

She'd cried at the unexpected loss. Picked up. And moved on.

Now she poured water into a green glass she bought at the local 99c Store. The price didn't change how much she loved it. She poured from a filter in the fridge, like she'd tried to get her family to use, but they'd brushed off for one reason or another. Maybe just because the idea was hers.

The water tasted better because it was hers. It tasted better because the ocean beckoned outside. She'd worked all day. She filled her time with errands and the slow, deliberate decorating of her apartment with bargains she loved. She had no one to tell her no. No one to impress. No friends to call. No parties to attend or crash. And none of the worries from the old days.

Megan polished off the water and put the glass into the cream-colored sink embedded in the fake granite counter that marked the building as trendy about ten years earlier. She could see the sea through her large windows. Floor to ceiling, they spanned the apartment. The dining area, the living space, and her bedroom each had one, and each slid open to step onto her narrow balcony.

She was contemplating heading down to watch the water for

a break, when she heard the noise again. She was looking out the dining area window when she realized something was on her porch. Something small. Something that buzzed.

Had a bird. . . ?

She frowned and went to look. She found a small plastic drone ramming into her window. She sighed. Some idiot kid was playing with it and had lost sight of it.

It took a moment to decide if she should slide the door open or just let it die there. If it came in the apartment it could cause damage. If she went on the balcony and grabbed it, the rotors might cut her. She stared for a moment before realizing a sheet of paper hung from it.

She squinted as she realized the paper said, "Hi Megan!"

She was stunned. Who did she even know out here? A neighbor kid maybe?

Without thinking now, she opened the sliding door and stepped out to pluck the page from the moving target. She grabbed it once, jerking at the page that was too well stuck, so it tugged the drone out of its flight pattern causing an odd whirring noise. Startled, she let go and it buzzed away.

"Megan!"

Startled again, she looked over the balcony, thinking as she did that it made sense the person was below.

Tristan.

Wasn't he supposed to dump her? What was he doing here? How did he even know where here was? Her frown must have said all of that for her.

"Megan!" He said it again, his smile blooming on his face and somehow also inside her.

She grinned back, even knowing it wasn't smart. "Are you stalking me?"

"No. What's your last name?" He grinned again, his neck craned up to see her three stories up.

Though she could clearly discern his answer that he wasn't

stalking her was honest, she countered with her own question. "What's yours?"

"Goodman." It was sharp and clear. "Look me up."

If he was stalking her, he was doing a relatively poor job of it. She headed inside and grabbed her tablet, then came back out on the patio. Watching him over the rail, she typed in his info and found a handful of articles about the shop. His name also popped up in conjunction with a handful of other bits of interest dating back a number of years. He wasn't hiding anything.

She'd gotten no bad vibes from him. And she'd had them before; she knew what they felt like. She always listened to her gut instinct along with the words that rang from a man's thoughts. No foul thoughts or even just angry ones had emanated from Tristan Goodman in the time she'd spent with him. She gave him what he wanted. "Booker."

He grinned at her again, but she asked a question before he could do more than just try to get control of the drone he was no longer paying attention to.

"Why are you here?"

"I wanted to see you again." He landed the toy—poorly—at his feet on the sidewalk, his thoughts scrambled. "I, uh, I wanted to ask you out to dinner."

That was last minute. He was broadcasting all his jumbled thoughts to her now. Though he'd had no clue he was going to ask her out, it was sincere. She laughed.

He frowned, and she heard him wondering if her laugh was because he was scrambling or if she was being mean. She smiled even though she wasn't ready to agree to anything.

"Say yes to him!" A voice down the street shouted up at her, but she couldn't hear the thought of the person who'd shouted it. Once upon a time, she might have wondered if that person was angry or being silly or whatnot and she would have taken it upon herself to make it okay. Not anymore. She couldn't even fix anything in her own family.

Instead she looked down at Tristan, still holding the drone remote. "Your mother named you after the wrong literary character. You should have been Romeo."

He shook his head. "That would be gross. My sister was named Juliet."

Something dark passed behind his thoughts, something sad and confused. It didn't escape her that he'd said 'was named' as if Juliet was no longer around. To break the subtle tension, she offered a whim of her own. "Yes. Dinner. Tonight. Now."

"Okay!" His answer was fast even though he hadn't been expecting it.

She leaned over, speaking before he could suggest something different. "Give me five minutes and I'll be down." Then she pulled back and practically slammed her way through the sliding door.

What was she doing? She didn't even know why she'd said any of that. But she was in it now. She stepped into her bedroom before she stopped to ask herself why she felt giddy.

She'd been on dates before. Not many and not often, but she'd been out. Megan lived in the same damn town almost all her life, and people knew what she could do by the time she was in kindergarten—when she was too young to know to hide it. More than one boy had wanted to test himself against her skills. She turned those boys down flat out, but three made it at least partway into the first date before she figured it out.

Another boy was crazy in love with her. He always thought about how beautiful she was and how much he wanted to be with her. It had taken four months and her virginity before she realized he had no clue who she actually was. He just liked the looks of her. Loved touching her and really liked having a girlfriend in a picture in his wallet to show to his cousins. The picture didn't show that no one but him would speak to her. Or that when she talked, he didn't care.

There had been others. Some made it to three dates. Some were only useful for sex, though those mostly didn't know what she could do—it just made things easier. Megan reminded herself that she'd already put Tristan into the second category. But even so, she was excited to go out with him.

She pulled off her sweat shorts and slid into a skirt before strapping sandals onto her bare feet. She traded her tee for a nicer shirt, swiped a colored lip balm on and spent the rest of her five minutes applying product to her hair and trying not to pass the tipping point where it would look like she'd made close friends with a vat of hair oil.

Seven minutes later, she trotted out the front door to find Tristan talking to two little boys who'd come up to him. He was showing them the drone and how to work the remote. At least he wasn't just tapping his toe, waiting on her. She smiled at the boys who were crazy excited about the drone—they were going to get one—and they wanted Tristan to teach them how to use it.

It was cute, she thought, as Tristan molded the older boy's hands around the remote and started the model up into the air. Then he looked up and noticed her. "Oh! How long have you been standing there?"

"About eight seconds." She smiled at him as his eyes wandered up and down her. He thought she looked better than he remembered, and she fought a blush.

"So let's go." He held his hand out to her and she took it, ready this time for the sizzle of contact.

They made it three steps before she stopped. "What about your drone?"

He'd left it behind with the boys.

"Oh, it's theirs now." He tugged at her hand, pulling her

along to the beach. "I just got it to deliver a message to you. I don't know what else I would use it for."

"How will you ask me out next time?" The words were out of her mouth before she even thought them. *Megan!* She chided herself. Most men don't make it past the first date. Your decision, not theirs. She shouldn't have insinuated there would be another before she knew.

Tristan took a deep breath in, disturbingly happy about what was essentially a slip. She was going to tell him that, but he answered her.

"I was hoping to use a phone for that."

Well, she'd gotten herself into that mess, hadn't she? Megan only smiled and nodded. "Where are we headed?" She knew he didn't have a plan.

But he surprised her.

Pulling his phone out, he showed her three different places. One was swanky, which she was underdressed for, and honestly so was he. She appreciated that he was willing to go for it, though. One was a bar that served food, and the other was a restaurant that had tables open to the beach. She knew of them all.

He surprised her again, interrupting her thoughts and asking, "Are you good to walk?"

"Huh?" That wasn't graceful. "Yes, these are comfy shoes." Which was true, even if they did make her legs look a mile long and an awesome color. Tristan appreciated it, too.

For the first time Megan found she was telling herself, *I will not sleep with him tonight. I will not sleep with him tonight.*

She picked the beachfront place, and they walked in relative silence. Her thoughts, pinging all over the place, occasionally ran smack into one of his. She wondered what she'd agreed to; he was happy she was there, glad she'd said yes. He thought about their fingers still laced together, and now so did she.

They reached the restaurant quickly, and she was grateful it was less crowded than it had been when she passed by before. She hoped she wouldn't get a headache from all the thoughts flying by.

Instead of dwelling on it, she turned to Tristan and asked, "So, I got the feeling that—" that was always a way to start when she'd read someone but didn't want them to know, "—you hadn't planned on asking me out."

"I did, but it wasn't going to be the first thing I said. I just kind of stumbled over my own words. I was afraid you weren't even home. So it just popped out." He readily admitted the error. She liked that. He wasn't afraid to be imperfect.

She smiled while the waiter brought them water and menus.

"So what were you going to say?" She took a sip of the water.

"I was going to tell you I was doing a customer satisfaction check."

Megan almost spit the water all over him.

CHAPTER 10

Tristan watched in horror as Megan choked on her drink while staring at him in shock. He tried to help, but she held her hand out to him, warding him off while she watched him, stunned.

Finally, she gurgled out the words, "Customer satisfaction check! Do you always follow up with your dates?"

He started to realize what she thought and he could feel his face turning beet red, but she continued.

"Is there a survey?"

"No!" He held his hands out to stop her train of thought before it derailed the whole evening. "Good Lord. No."

Then he took a deep breath and started over. "I meant about the *quell*. I wanted to see if it worked. God, no, not that."

"Oh!" She caught on and took another sip of her water as Tristan wondered if he could make himself into any more of an idiot tonight.

First, he'd nearly taken her window out because he'd bought a drone and they weren't as easy to handle as he'd thought. Then he'd almost clipped her in the head with it. That had petrified him. Honestly, the toy was safer in the hands of the little boys he'd given it to. He was a menace, apparently.

Then, he'd asked her out, obviously on the spur of the moment. Not very smooth. Now he'd been unclear and made her think he was doing a customer satisfaction survey on his bedroom skills. He should call a do-over, make her go home and pretend this never happened. Then again, maybe he could order something that would give her food poisoning. That would really top this date off well.

The server came back and they ordered. Somehow Megan got it together and was no longer actively choking. She even managed to smile at the waiter and place her order.

When the waiter left, Tristan finally spoke again. "I guess I'll be more direct this time. Did the *quell* work?"

Scrunching one side of her lip, she shook her head. "No. I'm sure I screwed it up."

He nodded back at her. "Not to be rude, but you probably did. *Quells* are hard. On the upside, they don't mess up anything else if you do screw them up."

"What do you mean?" She frowned at him. It looked like she hadn't considered the possibility.

"It's like medicine."

"It has side effects?" She tipped her head, thinking about it.

"That's actually not what I meant, but yeah, it can have side effects." He hadn't thought about it that way. Delilah and Yasmin had both suffered some serious side effects from spells, from spells gone wrong and gone right. "What I meant is that if you screw up the ingredients or the dosage you can get real problems."

Megan was nodding at him, but he continued before he did something else just awful, like telling her she'd screwed it up, or that it would poison her. "On the upside, *quells* don't have any real side effects. So they're hard to create, but if you screw them up, nothing bad happens either."

"Well, that's good to know." She sighed and took a sip of her water again as the conversation stagnated.

So, maybe this had been a bad idea, Tristan thought. He'd wanted her to come back and be as interesting as she'd been the first time he'd met her, when he'd been stunned. He wanted her to make him feel as interesting as she had the second time he'd met her when he'd been prepared, and he'd still been stunned.

He was surreptitiously watching her, thinking how badly he was botching it if he couldn't even make first date conversation. He opened his mouth to fix it, but she beat him to it.

"I'm sorry. I'm so bad at this."

"Why?" Again, not his smoothest move. He should have said 'No, you aren't.' And she probably wasn't, but it wasn't all moon-eyes and anticipation either.

She didn't seem to take offense. "I don't get out much. Seriously, you and your store have been the highlight of my interactions since I got to L.A."

"When was that?"

"Almost two months ago." She grinned as the food showed up and she inhaled the scents.

"I've been here before." He told her. "The place is worn and has metal chairs on a cement patio, but the food is to die for."

She smiled at him now and his heart tripped a beat. "So this is going to be the best grilled tuna sandwich I've ever had?"

"I can't promise you that. It depends on where you've been eating." He waited though. Watching her rather than eating his own food. Even when she was quiet, she was fascinating.

"Hansen, Georgia." She said, then took a bite of the sandwich and gave him a thumbs up as she chewed. Definitely the best grilled tuna sandwich she'd ever had if her expression was anything to go by.

Tristan took a bite, too, his loaded fish burrito calling to him. But then he said, "Hansen, Georgia?"

"No one's ever heard of it. It's in the middle of the state and about the size of your thumbnail." Then she paused. "My whole family still lives there."

She'd said it just before he could ask and he scrambled for another question. Until she turned the tables on him, he was going to keep her talking. "Why did you leave?"

Every bit of glow in her expression faded suddenly and he regretted asking. He was holding his hand up to tell her, *You don't have to answer that*, when she shook her head.

"It's fine. It's the truth, so I'll tell it. My father kicked me out."

"Because you're an adult?" Tristan didn't understand. She had to be in her mid- maybe late-twenties, so why was she getting 'kicked out'?

"Twenty-eight." She said, "And I was living with them and paying most of the bills. My father is a preacher." Then she paused as if searching for the words. Tristan felt there was a deeper story there. One she wasn't going to tell him.

She took a breath. "He didn't like me. We were always at odds, since I was a small child. It finally came to a head and I left. And that's all I'm going to tell of that story." She took another bite and shook off the melancholy as well as the topic. "I've never lived near the ocean before. And I feel positively rich paying only my own bills. But I don't get out a lot."

"What about the people you work with?" His burrito was half gone.

"Online. I work in my pajamas, often over texts or messaging. Sometimes I'm on camera, but I only put on a shirt and do my hair. I mean, mostly I'm still in my fuzzy socks and jammie pants." She shrugged at him. "I don't talk to people a lot and I haven't dated in a long time."

"Preacher's daughter, huh?" He was trying to put all that together with the woman who'd ridden him on his office couch the week before. Was it in spite of her upbringing, or because of it? Did it really matter? "Well, I'm glad you're here."

"So how did you find me?" She finally turned the

conversation to him, and the rest of his food disappeared while he told her about scrying over the map and making sure she was really in California. Then getting the drone on a whim.

The server came by just then, and Tristan watched her face, assessing dessert. He was of the mind to just get it, then she could eat it if she wanted or ignore it. But he wanted to pick something she liked.

Seeming to see his indecision, the server suggested the three mini-desserts and Tristan placed the order before turning back to the conversation. No time like the present.

"I had no clue how to fly it." It hit him this was a good time to explain about being such an idiot with it. "I'm really sorry. I only realized after I got it too close to you that I could catch it in your hair. I was being dumb."

"Yeah, this hair is an ecosystem unto itself. Don't mess with it."

He laughed. "I was only afraid that I would tangle it and mess it up."

"No one would have known." She shrugged, setting down her sandwich in a way that clearly declared her done.

"It's gorgeous." He checked his hand first, then reached out across the small table to finger one thick spiral that managed to drape by her collarbone.

He wouldn't have been so forward on a first date, but he'd been inside her. He'd had his fingers in her hair before. Flashes of the two of them together in his office turned his blood hot.

She pushed his hand away then. "Careful, loverboy."

Tristan frowned at her. He wasn't coming on to her, just touching her hair—something he'd already done before.

"You were supposed to be a one-and-done." She informed him, shocking him to his core.

"I was supposed to be what?" *One and done?* Who told her that? She just admitted she didn't get out much.

She was opening her mouth to reply when the voice burst through his thoughts. *I'm sorry to bust up your date, but I need you, Brother.*

His phone buzzed in his pocket. *It's me. Pick up. Emergency.*

The tone of Delilah's voice in his head was calm, but the message wasn't. Tristan held his hand up to Megan, "I'm sorry. It's my sister."

"Dee?" He answered on a worried note.

He barely had the word out before she talked over him. "I'm taking Julie to the hospital. Brandon is waiting with Ethan until you get there."

"I'm on my way." He was standing and signaling the waiter, ignoring Megan for the emergency. "What's the problem?"

"She has a cold and she's not breathing well. I'm worried."

If his sister—the witch who would just 'see' everything—was worried, she was probably right to be. Brandon would be worried, waiting at home, unable to do anything until Tristan arrived. "I'm in Santa Monica. I'll be there as soon as I can be."

"I'm sorry about your date." He heard the noises as she was clearly getting into the car. "I have to go."

And she was gone. He hung up the phone and turned back to the table. He saw now he'd caused a small scene with the other patrons on the patio. Luckily, they were few and far between.

"Here." Megan handed him a bag. When he looked inside, the dessert was boxed and ready to go.

"The check?"

"I paid it."

"No." He shook his head. He'd just ruined the whole thing and she'd paid when he'd asked her out. "Let me—"

He was reaching into his wallet, but her hand was up, palm out, stopping him. "I'll walk home. You go get your sister taken care of."

Had he told her that? Had the conversation been that loud?

Instead of wondering, he grabbed her hand. "Come with me."

Tristan started walking to his car a few blocks away, still wondering where Megan had gotten the idea that he was 'one and done.'

CHAPTER 11

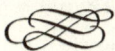

Somehow, Megan wound up in the car with him. He was parked just few blocks from the restaurant, apparently where he'd finally found a space so he could walk to her place. All the parking on her street had been taken.

He wasn't angry, or pushy, just firm. She was coming with him. Would she help with his nephew?

What else could she do? He was holding her hand and pulling her along. Sure, she could break away and walk home by herself, but he was holding a bag of dessert, and she liked kids. Tristan wasn't assuming she was good with children because she was a woman, he just wanted her to come along.

Megan couldn't remember the last time someone just wanted her along.

On top of that thought was his confusion about her saying he was supposed to be "one and done." As if Tristan didn't know he had that kind of bad-boy reputation. She frowned as he pulled up to a small house in West Hollywood.

Brandon was holding the door open for them even before they got out of the car. "Come on in. Ethan's in his pajamas and he's had dinner. It's bedtime but he's a little shaken up."

"Shall I calm him down?" Tristan asked.

"Yes. Please." Brandon looked at his brother in law, imploringly. Then, just as quickly as he appeared, he disappeared.

Megan heard him talking to Ethan, telling his son he was headed to the hospital, but it was going to be okay. She also heard Ethan, who didn't ask what was going on because he was afraid because his father was afraid.

Brandon brought the small boy into the living room holding his hand and trying to walk calmly. He wanted to be out the door, but he wanted to be a good father to Ethan, too. His kids were tugging him in two different directions.

Megan stepped forward, realizing Brandon didn't even worry about who she was. "I'm Megan. Megan Booker. I'm a friend of Tristan's." Then she knelt down to Ethan's level and smiled at him. "I'm Megan. You must be Ethan."

He nodded solemnly and reached out to her hand, taking it before he let go of his father's. The soft skin and small size of his hand felt right in hers. Kids were honest, and they accepted her as she was.

Brandon had hugged Ethan twice already and she heard his internal debate about a third hug before realizing the oddity of it might upset his child more. With as normal a good-bye as he could muster, he was out the door.

"Do you want to play a round of Candy Land before bed? Or read a story?" Tristan offered. He knew his way around the house just fine. He spent plenty of time here, Megan knew.

But she wasn't surprised when Ethan shook his head and solemnly pointed at her.

"You want to talk to Megan?" Tristan asked, smiling and seeming to understand. Before he even finished the question, Ethan had pulled her to the couch, climbed into her lap and curled up.

Her heart flipped at the feeling. Her sisters had done this

when they were small. Before her father convinced them their older sister was bad. Before he said what she could do must have been a gift from Satan.

But Ethan was still young and trusting, and she wasn't bad. Besides she'd only interact with him this one night. He looked up at her and asked point blank, "Is baby Julie okay?"

He was confused, she could feel it. Everyone had been skirting the issue with him. So she answered honestly. "No, she's not."

Tristan startled and she heard his, *No! What?* from across the room, but she ignored it. As far as she knew he didn't know she could hear him. She'd spent a lifetime training herself to not react, to not let people know she heard. It was her only hope of any human interaction.

She stayed focused on Ethan. "Baby Julie is sick. Not just regular sick, extra sick. She was having trouble breathing."

Across the room Tristan marveled at her memory and that she'd picked up that much. He figured she must be paying attention. She needed to be more careful what she spilled. He'd figure things out pretty soon if she babbled anything more she couldn't otherwise know.

She kept talking as Ethan nodded, glad for the real scoop. "Baby Julie had to go to the hospital because she was having trouble. But your mom and baby Julie are already there, and they've already given her medicine. And she should be just fine. You know how you take medicine when you're sick, and a few days later you feel ready to play again?"

He nodded at her, finally having a grasp on the situation.

"Well, it's the same for baby Julie. Only there was no medicine in the house for her. She needed medicine from the hospital." Megan waylaid the little boy's next question because he was only debating about asking it. "Your mom and dad were really upset, huh?"

He nodded again, and Tristan came and sat on the couch

beside them. He was marveling at how good she was with kids. Which was funny. Kids were easy when you could really hear them!

"Well, your mom and dad love you so much that they get really upset any time you're sick. And having to go to the hospital can be scary, but the hospital is a good place full of doctors who will help baby Julie. Your mom and dad will feel better in no time, too." She hugged him for a moment until his breathing was steadier.

He was thirsty, and she asked, "Do you want a small cup of juice or milk before bed?"

He nodded again and hopped up, pulling her hand along and pointing in the fridge. Between his gestures and his thoughts she could put together what he wanted, what cup he usually used, where Delilah and Brandon kept the sippy cup lids.

It was a good ten minutes before she and Tristan were tucking the little boy into bed. She was feeling how tired he was, about to crash after finally letting go of the worry and fluster of the evening.

Tristan hugged him, then Ethan held his arms out to Megan, again making her heart flip. She'd really have to look into a sperm donor and just have a kid one of these days.

She hugged him tight, surprised when he kissed her cheek and whispered, "You're like my mom. You can hear me."

Startled again, she pulled back to look in his eyes.

I love you, Megan. It came through her thoughts as Ethan grinned.

Can you hear me?

He nodded.

I love you, too, Ethan.

For a moment, she just stared at him, stunned. She'd never met anyone who could do what she could do. Ethan could hear her? She really did love him. Just for being a kid, and for being the first one to ever listen.

She smiled at him as she fought tears. Then she felt Tristan's hand on her arm, tugging her out of the room. Ethan was already snuggled under the covers, drifting off.

He could hear her?

"You're really great with him." Tristan whispered as they walked down the hallway and away from the door. His voice returned to normal as they turned the door to the living room. "I didn't even have to cast a calming spell on him."

"Is that what Brandon was asking you?" She only asked it because it would be normal. She'd heard the idea—nebulous though it was—from Brandon's thoughts as he'd left. Sometimes words or pictures were clear. Sometimes fuzzy. Asking for clarification only helped her tone down looking like she could do what she could actually do.

Tristan nodded and didn't let go of her hand or even sit on the couch. He kept heading right toward the dining room. "I wouldn't have answered him the way you did. But it worked."

Her attention snapped back to the conversation and away from the amazing little boy in the back bedroom. "But he knew everyone was upset and even afraid for the baby. He thought she was going to die." *Okay, shit. That was too far.* "I mean, that's the impression you can get when you're a kid and your parents frantically whisk the new baby to the hospital."

Tristan was nodding as he pulled the plastic container with their desserts out of the bag he'd brought along. He plucked the lid as she watched. "That makes sense. So if I'd said, no, everything was okay, he'd have known I was lying."

Megan nodded, thinking the little boy flat out knew when they were lying. He didn't have to wonder. She changed the topic. "Is that creme brulee?"

Tristan nodded then disappeared in the kitchen for a moment before asking in a musing tone if she needed a separate spoon for each dessert.

"One will do." She hollered back to him, looking at the trio which also included some rich chocolate cake and a fresh peach tart.

He emerged through the doorway, holding two spoons and looking good enough to eat. Megan smiled. She was actually having fun.

Tristan held a spoon out to her and settled their chairs side by side at the table. His leg pressed against hers, and he slung one hand across the back of her chair, tugging her closer, in case eating from the same dish wasn't intimate enough.

She used the edge of her spoon on the tart, slicing through peaches, a thick pastry cream, and ultimately the crust. She was lifting it to her mouth when a shot of lust hit her from the man next to her.

She ignored it.

People broadcast their thoughts all the time. The closer they were to her, the easier they were to read—or the harder they were to ignore. Him sitting pressed against her, his bare arm brushing hers from where he rested it across the back of the seat, and the strength of his feelings all seemed to add up to her not being able to ignore his thoughts at all. They weren't loud, per se, but they were overpowering.

It was the spoon at her mouth. Something vague and primal about her lips. She chewed carefully thinking what a normal action it was and how Tristan smiled beside her while his thoughts careened from her mouth to her breasts, then to a vivid picture of him taking her across the table.

Lord. It was his sister's *dining room table.* Then again, people thought all kinds of weird, awful, lustful, mean, wonderful, crazy things that never showed on their faces.

She smiled almost blandly back at him and took another bite. By the fourth bite, when she was choosing which dessert to go back to, she couldn't eat normally anymore, so she scooped out a chunk of creme brulee and slowly slipped the spoon in her mouth, using her lips as she dragged the utensil back out. Tipping her head back, she let her chest heave in a sigh. Then she looked up at him with heavy-lidded eyes, turned the spoon over and sensuously licked it while she stared at him.

"Jesus, Megan!" He jumped up too quickly, then huffed his breath out as he stalked awkwardly off to the kitchen, thinking about the pressure in his jeans and hoping she didn't realize what he was doing.

Despite her mind-reading capabilities, his thoughts admitted that it was obvious he was adjusting himself, and she heard his frustrated sigh with her ears this time. "Tristan!"

"What!" He barked back as she laughed.

"I couldn't enjoy it with you staring at me that way." She shrugged even though he couldn't see her and dug into the chocolate cake this time. God, it was good. She took a second bite, scraping at the sauce that tried to escape her spoon. She sighed as she ate it.

Only as she opened her eyes did she see Tristan standing over her, hands on his hips. "Well, if this is how you eat it when you think I'm not watching, it's almost as bad as you messing with me."

She shrugged.

"If you weren't so damn hot, it wouldn't be a problem."

"Oh, so this is *my* fault?" She asked him, even as something bloomed inside her at the knowledge that he really thought she was. She knew all the words in his head.

Beautiful. Intriguing. Mysterious. Hot. Sexy.

And never Freak.

He said it out loud. "You're beautiful, Megan. But more than that, I really like being with you. You're killing me here."

She laughed at that. Then shook her head, not wanting to destroy the moment. It was fun. She liked him. He didn't think she was a freak. Neither did Yasmin even though Yasmin knew what she was.

For a moment, she considered telling him she could hear what he thought.

Wondered if he could handle it. Handle her.

Then she thought about what it would turn to. Could she hear everything he thought? Yes, even when he didn't want her to. Could she hear him even when he didn't think in words? Yes, she could read his emotions, feel them pass through her, or linger if they were strong. And yes, she could see pictures from his thoughts, too. Sometimes, if she touched someone or something, she could even pick up information about something far away, like she had with Luke's informant.

As soon as Tristan understood the extent of her abilities, he would call it quits. She didn't want that. This was a fun adventure, the likes of which she'd never had. She'd come to L.A. to find herself. And she liked having a man interested in her.

So she smiled at him, "I will try to eat more carefully and less like a siren."

CHAPTER 12

Tristan let his breath out, felt the tension in his dick shift if not really diminish. "I think it's just something you do. And just something I like."

He watched as she took another bite and chewed robotically. By the second time she did it, he was laughing at her. By the third bite, he grabbed his spoon, realizing he wasn't going to get any more of the sinful desserts if he didn't get to it.

They ate in companionable silence, and in just a few minutes he was scraping the last of the thick chocolate sauce from the textured bottom of the container. He looked up just as he did it. Megan watched him. Though he'd planned on eating it, he decided it would be more fun to feed it to her.

Sure enough, where he'd held it in check for a little while, it turned him on. He only smiled blandly and pulled his spoon back before plucking hers from her fingers and taking everything away. Away into the kitchen. Away from where she could see him and probably right through him.

He rinsed the container as he corralled his thoughts.

He liked women. He'd thought Rebecca was pretty. He

hadn't had any trouble performing for anyone, so obviously he'd been turned on. But it hadn't been like this.

When he was around Megan, his skin felt like a low level current ran through it. Like it felt when bass music made all your cells hum. When he got actively turned on by her, it was as if every cell in his body shifted and aimed her way.

In the past—and he only saw this now with the comparison —he was turned on by the idea of having sex with an attractive woman. That's why it never mattered which one of them it was. He understood fidelity and that it was good, reasonable even, in a relationship, but he was never upset when things were over.

He loved Yasmin as a friend, his sister as family, he liked Libby who worked in the shop, and had no trouble seeing other women for themselves. Still the women he dated had been entirely interchangeable. He listened to their stories because it was interesting at the time. But he never thought about what they said.

Shit.

He'd been such a prick.

Here he was with a woman who practically lit him on fire. He wanted to hear what she had to say, and this time he wanted to listen. Wanted to puzzle together the pieces of what she said and build a picture of her. He wanted a part of her that she gave to no one else.

And he was completely blowing it.

Or he wasn't blowing it. Maybe he was doing fine and she simply didn't feel the same way about him. He'd told her he thought she was beautiful, but he understood how that must sound like a line. If he said he'd never felt this way before, she surely wouldn't believe that either. So he didn't say it.

He'd just said he really liked her and wanted to spend time with her. She hadn't responded with the same.

Shit, again.

He realized he'd been standing at the sink, holding the quite clean plastic and running water for no good reason. *Way to save the earth and recycle, Dickhead*, he thought.

He turned off the water just as he felt Megan's arms slide around him from behind.

Her voice was soft but clear. "I really like you, too, Tristan." She paused and he thought about how she was almost too good at saying the right thing. Maybe she had some Wicca in her background? Her voice cut his thoughts.

"I'd like to spend more time with you. So what if I asked you out this time?"

He dropped the container and the spoons he still held, and quickly wiped his hands on the towel Delilah left at the sink. "No." He turned around and faced her, wrapping his arms around her so she couldn't go anywhere.

He continued before she got the wrong idea, but her expression didn't falter. "I asked you out this time, but you wound up paying for dinner. So I get a do-over. Then you can ask me out the next time."

She nodded slowly, looked off to the side as if thinking. "You really think we're going to make it to three dates?"

"Oh." He breathed out the worry he'd worked up. "Yes."

Then he leaned down, only a little because she was tall. His hands reached for her without him thinking about where to put them, about what was best. Reaching for her just *was*. One hand wound up in her hair, grabbing the mass in a fist and tugging ever-so-softly to tip her head back to him, so his mouth could take hers.

It wasn't like him. He didn't usually act that way.

He was a thoughtful lover, kind and clear. This—the fist in her hair, the other hand gripping her shirt, his arm tugging her to and up against him where his hips bucked forward—was primal. Needy. Pure lust.

His hips moved again. Megan lined up against him, her full breasts pressing into him where he could feel the almost corsetlike construction of her bra. At that sensation, he thought about taking it off her, about getting her naked and hot and writhing under him or over him or . . .

Her mouth pulled back. Wet and open, it formed an "O" while she looked up at him with a hazy stare.

Too much, too fast. Never mind that they'd already slept together. He was not one-and-done, thank you very much. But he was going to have to get some of his smooth moves back or he'd scare her off.

She didn't pull back far enough to remove her hips or her breasts from where she pressed flush against him. Each harsh breath she sucked in moved her closer against him, heating him up further.

He stepped back. Time for something a little more subtle. Maybe some real seduction. Without ever breaking contact, he slid his hand down her arm and took her fingers in his. Leading her to the couch, he walked backwards, offering a small smile and trying to think his way through things.

Not too much.

Not too little.

He sank into the deep cushions and tugged her down beside him. With their legs facing each other, he couldn't pull her up against him, but that was fine. He wanted to kiss her for a while.

He slid his hands up her arms, feeling her skin under his fingers. Watching the play of his pale hands against her darker arms. He loved the feel of her. She was both foreign and known. His fingers traced along her neck, to the soft area under her chin, then along her face.

Now, he watched her eyes, watched her watching him, almost confused.

He was almost confused, too. He'd slow things down, set her at ease. He meant to put some known moves on her, and he was. But it was having maybe too much effect on him. He liked touching her this way, couldn't stop. So he tugged her forward and saw her eyes drop slowly closed as if she was falling under a spell he cast.

When his mouth met hers, all thought—rational thought having already fled—disappeared from his mind. He was a ball of pure sensation. Her soft mouth moving against his. Her fingers fisting into his shirt and holding him as if she wouldn't let go. Her leg pressed against his as they tried to get closer.

He breathed slowly, reveling in the sensations that spread everywhere. His hands moved as if this was a dance they both already knew. Their heads turned, taking the kiss another direction, taking it deeper, harder.

Her breasts brushed his chest again, then pressed fully into him. He wished his shirt away, then took a stutter breath thinking he shouldn't actually put spell energy into that. What would she think?

But her hands tugging at him pulled him closer. Her hips were moving against his again, her body undulating against his.

He knew how it felt to have her move naked against him. But last time, she'd been on top. So when he felt her leg along his hip, his mouth opened on a heady gasp at the sensation of having her legs wrapped around him for the first time.

Megan pulled away and sucked in air and only as she did it did he realize that he'd tipped her back and was laid out across her, pressing her into the couch.

He was lined up in exactly the right way, moving against her, her legs pulling him closer. Tristan ran a hand up one long, smooth leg, thinking that if they weren't fully clothed, they'd be making love on the couch.

"Oh!" Megan sucked in another breath on the sound. This time her hands pressed flat against his chest as if she might push him away instead of pulling him closer. He hated that, but the feeling of her underneath him was too right to move.

"We can't do this." She whispered.

"Yes, we can." He whispered back on a grin, his hand now

sliding up under her skirt and cradling her ass. He tucked his fingers under the edge of her underwear and squeezed slightly.

"What if Ethan wakes up? What if your sister comes home?" Then she did push on him gently.

Reluctantly, Tristan pulled back. "You're right."

This time, when he stood up, he adjusted his pants without being embarrassed. She'd already felt what she did to him. Throwing a smile her way, he pulled out his phone and headed down the hall. He was back a few moments later.

"Ethan is out cold. And Delilah just texted back saying the nurse is about to come show them how to use a nebulizer and then the doctor will give them the prescriptions, then they can check out and come home." He waved the phone at her as if she might read the text for herself.

As he watched, she absorbed that information and he picked up the remote control. "We should watch some TV."

He sank back on the couch, flipped through some stations trying to figure out how he could make this work. "How about this?"

"You know, I can call for a ride." She was reaching for her own phone now.

His attention turned to her. "It will be a while before they show and I can probably take you back in about an hour. Stay."

Shocked at how nervous he was, how afraid she would say she should just go, he was happy when she said, "Fine," and sat back down.

This time, he shoved himself back into the corner and tugged her down between his legs, wrapping her up almost so she couldn't get away. He gave her the remote and told her to choose something.

She flipped a few more channels and decided on something along the lines of a Hallmark movie of the week.

"Oh God, really?" He asked her even as he tugged her back to where she was relaxed against him. He could feel her laugh and he liked it.

"You told me to choose."

"You really watch this?"

This time, a shrug. "Sometimes. This one is one of the better ones."

"They get worse than this?" He clasped his arms around her waist, thinking she felt right there.

"Oh, now you have to watch it." She set the remote down and snuggled deeper against him, making the awful show worthwhile.

He tried to pay attention, but it didn't work for more than five minutes. Her hair was in his face and he was burrowing deeper into the thick spirals rather than listening. When his mouth found the side of her neck, he hadn't planned it, but he wasn't surprised.

Her head tipped, so he smiled and did it again.

A few minutes later and his hands slid up under her shirt, only to be stopped by that bra. He worked around it, tracing her ribs, the tops of her breasts, the seam where skin disappeared behind fabric. Then his thoughts went rogue and he followed the fabric around to the back and popped the clasp.

"Tristan!" She protested, her hands flying up to hold the cups in place.

"Shhhh." He whispered against her neck and pulled her hands away. "Watch the show. Aren't you enjoying it?"

"Um. . . . Yeah." The second word came out on a sigh and his hands slid under her shirt, this time finding her breasts with no impediment.

She made soft noises as he touched her. Megan tried to look like she was paying attention, but she didn't seem to have any better grasp on the show than he did. He wasn't watching the show at all, he was watching her back arch her breasts up into his touch. Watching her mouth fall open as he fondled her, enjoying the feel of her on his hands. Watching her chest move against his touch.

Then he slid one hand down, past her skirt, over her thigh and back up. He traced her thigh, up over the band of her underwear, then down and in. He felt her soft and wet against his fingers.

His heart stuttered as she gasped.

CHAPTER 13

Megan sucked in her breath at Tristan's touch.

She thought about telling him to stop. Ethan was down the hall, but . . . her thoughts rolled away for a moment as Tristan found the exact right spot.

When she opened her eyes she was staring at the ceiling, her body undulating under his expert touch. His breath was warm and soft on her ear.

"You feel so good."

Yeah, I do, she thought, but he couldn't hear her.

Even with her thoughts rolling over and getting churned under, she could still hear him. He was turned on just touching her. His feelings swept through her, leaving her with heady ideas. But under it all, she could feel his concern.

Was she faking it?

Could he get her all the way to orgasm?

"Mmmm." She'd tried to speak, failing miserably at just making words. Megan tried again. "More."

It would have to do. Because yes, he could get her to orgasm, in just a few more . . .

She clutched his arm involuntarily, as though she could hold his hand there and keep him doing what he was doing. Her hips moved, grinding against his touch, and her breath came in shorter and shorter gasps. As she hit the edge, he stilled, holding her tight against him as she rode out the waves.

She was still breathing heavily as her thoughts became coherent again. She was looking at the ceiling, her fingers dug into his flesh. She let go. "Sorry."

"I'm not." There was a smile in his voice, a thought backed by contentment.

Megan was confused.

Didn't he want to finish, too? She listened carefully, and he didn't. She blinked into space as his hand slid out from her underwear and he kissed the side of her neck, still satisfied despite the need she could feel in him.

Jesus. She liked him. If she wanted to keep seeing him she should try to keep him happy, right? She liked being with him; it wasn't as if it was a hardship. She waited, but nothing more came from him. No requests, wants, or needs hovered in his thoughts. Megan found herself in the awkward situation of having to ask him what he wanted.

"Tristan. Are you okay?"

"Oh, I'm more than okay." *The truth.*

"Don't you want to . . ." What were the right words? She couldn't offer up a BJ here. If Ethan saw Tristan's hand under her skirt he probably wouldn't put two and two together, but if he saw a BJ in action? Well, they'd traumatize the kid for life. Or, God forbid, Delilah came home and Megan met Tristan's sister while she had Tristan's cock in her mouth. In the woman's living room. No. That could not happen. That was bad juju forever and ever.

"No, I'm good." His words whispered next to her ear, riding on the reality of his statement. Just because she heard his thoughts didn't mean she wasn't confused by them.

Generally, she was good with people. Which was ironic. She

understood when people operated from fear instead of real anger. She understood when they had past incidences that led them to be or do things one particular way. She could rarely see the incident itself, but she could read the underlying emotions left from it. She understood the mark that left.

It was other people who weren't good with her. They felt violated by her presence. She was a threat, and they defended against her whether she deserved it or not. Between what she could hear and her general lack of meaningful human interaction, it was rare that she was confused by someone.

As Tristan sighed and wrapped himself around her, he breathed out the words, "Why aren't you watching this hideous show you picked out for us?"

"Because you distracted me."

"Mmmm-hmmm." He pulled her up tighter against him, the feel of his arms, his words, his emotions a wonderful cocoon that she found she wasn't willing to give up. Not yet.

Maybe he confused her because he was the first person she'd done more than scratch the surface on in a long, long time. Megan knew her family, probably better than she knew herself. She knew a few of the kids from her high school, but it had always eventually turned sour.

This hadn't turned sour yet and the thought made her happy. She considered keeping Tristan as long as she could. Los Angeles wasn't Hansen. When things were over, she wouldn't have to run into him or probably ever interact with him again. He was in Hollywood, she was in Santa Monica. They might as well be in different states.

As she sat there, enveloped in his arms, Megan made a decision. She would hold onto this—to him—as long as she could. Eventually, he would figure out what she could do and that would be the end of it. It always was. Or else he would tire of her or get angry at her or whatever and that would be the end of it. He would end it. But in the meantime, she might just have the closest thing she could have to an adult relationship. Because the only person she'd ever met who could do what she could do was Ethan, and he was four.

She didn't get to dwell for too long. The movie was nearing the end when Tristan straightened behind her. "Delilah's almost home."

That was weird, she thought. How he just knew that. Then again, who was she to judge?

He was scooting her out from in front of him. Whether that was because he didn't want his sister to see them together or just to get up, she wasn't sure. As she stood in the living room trying to ascertain if all her clothing was back in the right place, Tristan headed down the hall.

A moment later, he came back out and smiled as he found her in front of the mirror. "Don't worry. No one can tell."

No one can tell that you just got my rocks off? She thought. *Good to know.* But she smiled back at him.

He hardly noticed as he walked around the house and checked the locks, the kitchen, the table where they'd eaten dessert. "Ethan's still sound asleep," he told her.

He was a good brother, not leaving crap behind for his sister and her husband to clean up. Coming at the last minute to watch her children. He hadn't even balked mentally. Megan hadn't found an ounce of resentment in him. He'd simply jumped to help.

She heard the car pull into the driveway then. A few noises then a key came at the door. A petite blonde woman came inside. She looked tired and haggard and wrung out. Until she looked at Megan.

Then her eyes narrowed just a little before she smiled. "You must be Megan." But there was an underlying thought too, *You don't look anything like my brother's usual type.*

Megan just smiled back and shook her hand. "Delilah, right?"

Delilah nodded, then turned to hug Tristan, her wariness showing through again.

"Where's Brandon? Julie?" Tristan asked of his sister's head as she leaned on him.

Standing back on her own two feet, she sighed. "They aren't long behind me. Brandon sent me back so I could get some sleep. We have to wake her up and give her treatments every four hours now." Another sigh. "And we just got her to sleep through the night regularly."

"Is she going to be okay?" Megan asked before she thought better of it. What if the answer was 'no'?

Delilah nodded. "Just mild asthma. Not that unusual in L.A. apparently."

"You go to bed then. Megan and I will let ourselves out." Tristan volunteered.

Delilah hugged him again, said goodnight to Megan, and went down the hallway on weary feet. Megan noticed she was rubbing her fingers against her palm, as though she had gotten something on it. And she heard Delilah thinking some tired, nebulous thought about Megan.

She didn't need Delilah figuring her out. That wouldn't help her keep Tristan around for long. Yasmin at the shop already knew. She'd probably spill the beans to her boss one day, but there was nothing Megan could do about that. Still, something about Delilah, rubbing the palm on the hand she'd used when she shook Megan's hand spoke of her figuring something out.

Megan didn't get to dwell on it too long. Tristan had her by the hand and was pulling her behind him, locking the door, and hoping his sister would get some real sleep. Ever the gentleman, he opened the passenger door for Megan and closed her in.

Only then did it hit her how late it was, how tired she was. She couldn't fight the yawn that hit. Despite not having a regular schedule, she didn't usually stay up this late. What was there to do until two in the morning most days? Even in L.A. she didn't know of much.

Tristan smiled over at her as he started the car. "I'm sorry I kept you out so late."

"Not your fault." She offered a smile back, knowing he was worried about the state of the evening. She just didn't know how to put him at ease about it.

They rode back to Santa Monica in relative silence. Well, the car was silent. Tristan's thoughts were pinging around the place like stray bullets, occasionally hitting her.

He was worried she wouldn't want to go out with him again. She couldn't just say so. That would be too odd. He was sorry he'd kept her out so late. He was trying to think of something spectacular to make up for this date, which he was chalking into the 'disaster' category. Again, though, there was nothing she could say that wouldn't reveal her ability. Since doing so would be the end of anything, she didn't speak.

What she didn't find in all his mental wanderings was anything concerning about her. He wasn't upset or even the slightest bit put-out that he was driving her practically to the coast in the opposite direction of his own home in the dead middle of the night.

She kept her mouth shut, wondering what to do and not having anything to say until they were pulling up by her building. The spot in front was an illegal spot.

"Do you want to move your car? You could come up with me." She offered. He'd gotten her off, but she hadn't been able to return the favor.

His first answer was to shift the car into park. Then he shook his head. "Don't take that the wrong way." His eyes wandered off as he thought about the right way to say it. "It's not that I don't want to. But that's not all this is about and I don't want you to think that it is."

He was trying to make sure she saw him as one of the good guys. That she understood he wasn't just using her for sex.

She let out a little sigh and a breathy laugh at that. "Don't worry, Tristan. I know you're a decent guy. You can still come up. I owe you one."

His thoughts turned as rapidly as his words, hitting her almost like a physical force. Then he reeled it back a notch. "You don't owe me anything. I didn't do it for a return."

He sighed and looked out the window, no longer facing her. "I touched you because I wanted to touch you. It wasn't an investment on you doing something for me."

"I'm sorry." She whispered. They weren't words she said often. She didn't have to, she didn't often misread people so badly.

He nodded but didn't look at her. He waited a beat and when neither of them moved to get out of the car, he sighed a little. "If I call you, will you go out with me again? Give me a chance to get this right?"

"You didn't get it wrong, Tristan. Things happen. You were being a good brother. And it wasn't even bad."

He nodded, his thoughts still worried. But he got out and walked her to the front security door at her building. He waited a beat, unsure what to do and she hovered, wondering what to do for a moment before she gave up and offered a small smile, then stuck her key in the door.

His hand on her arm shot sparks through her again. Before she could react, or even understand what he was thinking, Tristan had her in his arms, his mouth on hers. Megan was disappearing under his touch, losing herself in the electricity of the moment.

Then he pulled back, his thoughts re-forming. He wondered if she was avoiding the question. So she answered him outright.

"Yes. I'll say yes when you ask me out." She paused, then

addressed his other concern. "I do know that you're one of the good guys."

"Sure." He didn't believe her, even though he was looking at her now. He held her door open for her as she walked through, his last words following her into the stairwell. "Somehow you got the impression I was 'one and done.'"

CHAPTER 14

Tristan bided his time calling Megan. He didn't want to seem too eager. He even managed to put off calling her for seven whole hours.

So, at two twenty-three the next afternoon, he cracked. He found himself smiling as he dialed. She'd already told him she would say yes. So, without any real plan, he was asking.

"Hi, Tristan." There was a grin in her tone, too, and it only made his smile broader. *When was the last time he'd felt like this?* He couldn't remember.

"Hi, Megan." It was unnecessary, but it felt good just to say her name. He was glad he'd closed the door to his office; he was behaving like a fifth grader, passing notes to the girl he liked. "So, I was calling to see if you'd go out with me tomorrow night?"

He wanted to see her again tonight. The buzz in his chest at just the thought of her made him want more. Even though he hadn't managed to hold off calling her, he was going to hold off on the actual date. Besides he hadn't thought of what to do yet.

"So, you have no plans yet, huh?"

Damn. She was too good at that. "Of course, I do," he blurted out, but he could feel in his bones that she knew he was lying.

The silence from the other end of the line reinforced that.

His mother's voice rang to him in the back of his head. An old phrase she loved to tell her kids. He could hear the cadence of her words clear as day.

Begin as you intend to go on.

"What?" Megan asked, startling him.

"I—what?" he fumbled back.

"Sorry, I thought I heard something." She was confused, and well, so was he.

"I didn't say anything." He thought about his mother's words though. *Begin as you intend to go on.* Tristan did not want to establish anything with Megan in which he was a liar. He was getting vibes that she knew it, too. He wanted her trust. He wanted her to want him. He wanted her, period. So he fessed up. "Actually, I haven't decided yet. I'm still in the planning stages."

"Okay." Her tone returned to normal and he breathed out a sigh of relief that he'd done the right thing.

Note to self: do not ever lie to Megan. She's onto you.

Her voice popped over the line, breaking his thoughts into pieces. "Thank you for not lying. Even little things. It means a lot to me."

"Good. Then let me work on it and I'll call you with a time once I've got it?" He was leaning back in his chair, relaxed by the sound of her voice, by the agreement to go out with him again.

"Sounds like a plan." She paused a beat, then laughingly asked, "Is that why you didn't ask me out for tonight?"

"Well, I wanted to let you get a good night's rest in between me keeping you up all night." He grinned.

Then it fell off his face as he realized what that sounded like. "Oh shit, Megan, I'm sorry. I didn't mean that I was going to . . ."

His head fell into his hand, full face-palm. His chest caved at the thought that he'd just issued this woman he really, really liked about the dirtiest insinuation he could. It would only be worse if he'd said he was going to 'ride her all night.'

Her voice came through the line, a laugh, then another. "I understand what you meant. You can get your face out of your hand now."

He lifted his head, wondering how she could know that. Then, instead of wondering, he flat out asked. "How did you know I had my face in my hand?"

"You sounded embarrassed and a little muffled. You did it last night, too. Just a guess." Her words were easy. The explanation made sense. Tristan ignored the tickle at the back of his neck.

"Well, I'll text you when I figure out times. And right now, I'm going to get off the line before I say anything else that might incriminate me."

"Like asking me about a customer satisfaction survey?" Her voice was bright, not angry, upset, or anything else that might be bad.

Tristan felt his lips curving into another smile even as his face turned beet red. "Yeah, just like that."

A knock was the only warning before his door opened and Yasmin stood there, leaning against the jamb. An amused grin played on her mouth as she watched him. Tristan waved a hand at her to go away. The last thing he needed was Yasmin watching him get all stupid.

She didn't leave. Just crossed her arms and waited.

"I'll talk to you soon." He waited for Megan to sign off then he hung up the call. With a sigh, he looked up at his employee. "What do you need, Yasmin?"

"I need to watch Megan Booker make you blush again. That was fun."

He fought the urge to sigh audibly and roll his eyes. Yasmin spoke before he could demand a reason for the intrusion again.

"So, I'm glad you like Megan and all, but I'm happier she's not a practicing witch." She motioned him out of the chair. "You have to come see this."

Tristan stood and followed, the sudden change in Yasmin's expression bothersome. As he hit the front room, he didn't see anything amiss. Nothing warranted Yasmin's dour expression. A handful of people milled about the shop looking for various items. That was good. People shopping was what kept them all going.

Just then an older man, one of the regulars, stepped up to him. Tristan worked at knowing everyone's name and encouraged all the employees to do the same. "Hey, Bob, what can I get you?"

"I don't know why, but I can't find the jimson weed today. Did you move it?"

"No worries." Tristan walked the man over and even reached into the basket. "Do you need one bundle or two?"

"Let's do two." Bob held out his basket and let Tristan drop the ribbon-bound dried plants in it. "I must have looked directly at it three times."

Tristan sent Bob on his way, helped another customer, and didn't catch on until Yasmin glanced at him over a low display and said. "Here it is, Mrs. McNeery," and pointed right in front of where the woman was standing.

Shit. No one could find what they were looking for.

Crazy Ex-Girlfriend—whoever she was—was at it again.

Yasmin smiled at the woman, but as soon as the customer looked away, Yasmin pointed at him then pointed him into the back. Tristan read it plain as day: *you, go fix this.*

With a sigh, Tristan began grabbing things off the shelf. He was supposed to be selling this stuff, not using up his own stock to keep the store running. But he did it anyway, pulling feverwort and black salt from shelves. He took a set of saw palmetto berries which were also for protection, and then on a whim grabbed dogweed for love, sex, and faithfulness. He ducked into his office, pulling his black velvet pouch of tools from his desk, and continued into the back.

Closing himself in the beginners classroom he stepped carefully around the pentagram painted into the floor. The soft, blue-gray lines were thick enough to show on either side of the white salt line that ran roughly down the center of the outside circle. Fat candles sat in pillars at almost the exact centers of each wall, lining up with the compass. They waited at the ready for any witch to perform a spell. In the center of the floor sat small vessels for wine, salt, water, whatever was needed. Two small quartz statues, one sun and one moon, occupied the dead center. They weren't *his* altar pieces, but they would do.

He opened the pouch and pulled a felt roll full of pockets. Each time he saw it he thought about Delilah. She'd gotten him the piece from a cooking outlet, recognizing that the same thing that held her kitchen knives so cleanly would work for her— and his—Wicca supplies. He slid his athame from the pouch. Again, the ritual knife was not his personal one, but a spare he kept here at the office. He then pulled a willow wand his great-great-grandfather had owned, letting it sit across his palm for a moment.

Then he got to work. He was casting a barricade this time.

His gentle *no more spells on the store, please* that he'd cast last time had not been enough. This time he was keeping the bitch out. Using a break in the salt to enter the circle, Tristan carefully sealed it behind him.

Then he stood in the center and whipped the room into a frenzy. Using his anger as a focus, he put everything he had into the barricade. With a palm faced to the candles, he lit them almost like a conductor at a symphony. They whooshed to life, then calmed to begin their work. The air inside the circle crackled and shimmered with life. Once he had the barricade formed, Tristan sat in the center of the circle and drew the power into himself, then with a quick motion, sent it outward almost like a shock wave.

Suddenly going still, he stopped the ripple where he wanted it.

A perfect circle of magick now surrounded the shop. It would cut into the neighbors' shops. But no matter. All it meant was that the employees most liked to hang out on the wall attached to his store. More patrons would choose to sit at the tables on that side, though they wouldn't know why. The clothing store next door already sold more off the wall attached to Blessed Be than the clothing on the other wall. He didn't care. He just wanted protection from the meddling little witch. He wished he'd never let Yasmin teach her anything. Whoever she was.

He didn't check.

Though he considered scrying to find out who she was, Tristan figured in his current mood that might be dangerous. So he grabbed the dogweed and started a second spell. He was casting outward, searching for the woman who'd hexed the store. With a finger, he swirled the salted water in the wide, shiny black bowl until it abruptly stopped. Though a face began to swim, Tristan shut down the image.

Still he cast on it. His best spell to bring love, hope, and fulfillment. May she get everything she wanted.

This was the harder spell to cast. His focus was shifted by his anger. He didn't really wish her the best, but he put a solid effort into it and, because he was a stronger witch than most, he was pretty certain it would take effect. If she found something else, something real, maybe she would spare him this crap swishing around his store.

Just as he finished, a soft knock came at the door. Even from the other side, Yasmin had known and waited. He called out, "Come in."

As he stood and picked up the water with one hand and

grabbed his personal tools out of the pile, he looked up at Yasmin. She followed him down the hall to the sink where he dumped the water and she smiled.

"Good work. All of a sudden, everyone went, *Oh, there it is.* So we are back in business." She looked at him closer. "You didn't just clear the spells like last time, right? You did more?"

"One of my best barricades." He smiled. "Then I cast a universal dream-catcher on her."

Yasmin frowned. "Why would you do that?"

"If she finds something else, maybe she won't latch onto this anymore."

"Ooooh." Yasmin sucked in a breath. "That's got to be sketchy. Not very pure emotion, I'm guessing."

Tristan shook his head. Not at all. Now if Megan needed something, he'd be able to conjure that up easy. He turned to Yasmin. "Is there a spell for dreaming up the perfect date?"

She only looked at him oddly, as if she were trying to figure something out.

CHAPTER 15

Megan sat back, her hands resting on the blanket as she watched the sun set beyond the waves. The light was too bright, but she loved it anyway. Sinking back, she listened to the sounds of the evening unadulterated by thoughts coming from every direction.

Watching her, Tristan laid back, too, his hands laced behind his head.

She'd once thought life might be easier in the big city, that all the voices would blend to white noise. They didn't really. They were still just as clear. The advantage, it turned out, was that she could be anonymous. She could pass people, hear a single thought, like a note on an instrument, without having to get the whole story.

She watched the sun turn from yellow to a blazing orange as it sunk. Still it cast plenty of light into the small cove of white sand Tristan had found. Back home, the sun set faster, trees and mountains gobbling light before sunset was official. Here, it went forever and Megan thought—when the water was still—she could see the curvature of the earth. Even better, she could lay back and listen to what was mostly silence.

She could hear her own thoughts bouncing around in her head. She could sort out that she didn't really know anyone but Yasmin and Tristan and that was okay. Her neighbor—the older woman across the way—missed her son. He'd died overseas as a soldier. The woman was proud, but lonely and sad. That was it. That was the only story Megan knew in LA, and it was awesome. Not the story, but that she didn't know the butcher's wife was cheating on him and he knew it. She didn't know the banker was hiding funds from his boss, or that the man three houses down was having an affair with the college student in the house on the other side of Megan's home. She didn't know that the woman at the nail salon was beaten by her husband, but she'd never speak against him because she loved him so much. Megan didn't want to know these things.

She no longer had to. She sighed in deep contentment.

The sun sank at last, orange rays showing over the water though the edge of the orb had sunk beyond the horizon. The late summer weather was perfect. The beach had always made her happy; in general, people were happy there. But this? The beach, almost entirely alone? It was wonderful.

She turned to Tristan. "How did you know I would like this?"

"I had three options." He grinned. "Something told me you'd like this one best."

"Something? Or witchcraft?" She arched a brow.

"Witchcraft is something. Was I right?"

She didn't sit up, too comfortable where she was. "What were the other options?"

"The observatory and a swing dance class in Los Feliz." He was looking at her, really wondering if he'd gotten it right.

"Nailed it. I love the beach." It felt odd to tell him what she liked. She had to speak things out loud even though others around her didn't. But honestly, no one had really cared what she liked much. Her mother sometimes wanted to know what she liked for dinner or if she needed her laundry done. Her little sisters wanted to know what Megan liked on TV. But that was it. She suppressed a shudder at the thought of her family but pushed it aside.

"What?" Tristan asked.

She shook her head. He'd seen the spark of resentment and worry as it worked its way out of her system. "Just pushing aside bad memories."

"You can tell me, you know."

He meant it. Still, she didn't want to talk about it. "Maybe later."

He nodded and looked back out over the water. The tide was coming in but was still a good ten feet away from the edge of the blanket. They could stay. She meant to ask him how he knew about the hidden cove in Malibu even though she'd already picked up that his sister had once lived in the area and told him about it a handful of years ago. She also knew that while he visited the spot he didn't bring dates up here, though she couldn't tell if that just wasn't the norm or if she was the first. But the sound of the ocean creeping closer in its rhythmic surge and fall was lulling her back into relaxation. She didn't know how long she lay there just listening. But the sun was gone and the light came from the full moon now.

"God, you look beautiful in the moonlight."

She smiled even though she didn't look at him. He meant it. He really thought she was beautiful.

He wanted her, there on the blanket, he told her. Even though anyone could come up and find them, he didn't think they would. Leaning over her, propped on one elbow, he pressed soft kisses to her lips, then along her jaw. His fingers trailed down the front of her shirt, popping buttons as his tongue worked magic in her mouth.

By the time one hand found its way under her bra, he was half on top of her and her arms and one leg were wrapped around him, holding him close. His mouth found the side of her neck and she tipped her head giving him better access even as her hands snuck under the hem of his soft t-shirt. She needed to touch skin, to feel the heat of him, to absorb something from him.

"I brought a condom." The words whispered along her neck and she almost didn't register them. "But only one."

She breathed in, out, absorbing the feel and smell of him, of how much she wanted him, before she pulled back. "It doesn't matter if you have one condom or twenty, it's illegal to have sex on a public beach."

Even as she pulled back, she arched up into his hand, loving the way he touched her. He managed to work his magic without exposing her to the world—or even anyone who would come along the beach. But then she realized he wasn't touching her anymore. He hadn't pulled his hand away, but he wasn't into it. He was staring at her.

"What?"

"I didn't say that." Now he was frowning. "I didn't say it out loud."

Shit. Megan fought to cover her blunder. Ironically, she decided her best defense was lying. "Yes you did. You said you only had one condom."

"No. I didn't." He'd pulled back and his eyes narrowed on her.

She could practically hear the gears clicking in his head. And she could actually hear his thoughts as he put the pieces together. Lying wouldn't save her. He'd hate her forever. Megan couldn't have stood that.

Her heart pounded loud enough she thought he could probably hear it. But if he did, he wasn't paying attention. Tristan was cataloging every conversation they'd had.

Shit. Shitshitshit. She'd known it couldn't last too long. But he'd been too nice to her, tried too hard to get her to like him.

He didn't deserve for her to lie and run away. So she would tell the truth and run away.

"You probably didn't say it out loud." Megan sat up and scooted back away from him. When she hit the corner of the blanket, she began buttoning up her shirt. Looking down at the task she was performing with shaking hands she said, "Sometimes I can't tell."

Tristan didn't answer. He just sat and stared. His shirt was pulled from the waistband of his shorts, loose from where her hands tugged it free wanting to get to him. His shoes lay abandoned-looking in the sand beyond the corners of the blanket. He breathed heavily as he wondered what to do.

It didn't matter. Megan understood. It had always been this way. She could only keep friends, lovers, anyone, if they didn't know what she could do. Standing, she slipped her own shoes back and on reached for her bag.

"Thank you." Her voice wasn't as loud as she wanted, so she tried again. "You've been wonderful. Thank you."

Then she turned and tried to make a graceful exit through the sand. Sadly, it grabbed at her feet, sucked her movements away, and basically added insult on top of rejection.

"Where are you going?" He asked from behind her, but he didn't get up.

"I know you didn't say that out loud, but I'm going to get a ride. I'm going home. I'm sorry." She started walking away again.

"No."

Megan stopped. Had he just said 'no'? She didn't buy it. "I'm going to the parking lot and I'm going to get a ride."

"No." He was definitely speaking out loud now.

She wanted to tell him to stuff it. She was done. On the other hand, she felt she owed him. She'd basically lied to him for the whole time she'd known him, but she felt she owed him, too. He had been the best relationship she'd had. He actually liked her.

Or at least, he used to. So she turned and looked at him. "Why not?"

"I don't want you to go." He was kneeling on the blanket, shoes not on. Though he was solid in his not wanting her to leave, he still hadn't figured out quite why yet.

"I should go. You'll be mad soon, if you aren't already."

"I'm not mad." He paused and so did she, waiting while his thoughts came together from the incoherent jumble in his brain. "Why didn't you say anything?"

"What would I have said?" She shrugged and started walking away again.

This time she heard him behind her. Still she kept walking away. He would give up.

But he didn't. His hand came down on her shoulder, his larger size and better control in the sand effectively stopping her. "I'm your ride."

They were almost an hour up the coast. Traffic might be better now, but she didn't want to stay in the car with him that long. Megan sighed.

"What? Afraid to try and figure it out?" He didn't remove his hand, just looked at her, almost daring her.

The word that passed through her lips was entirely unplanned, but the cold forming deep in her chest was something she knew well. She'd faced it numerous times before: the loneliness, bullying when she was a kid, her father's wrath. She didn't need this.

Was she afraid?

"Yes."

CHAPTER 16

Tristan could almost feel the silence. It sat between them like a breathing thing. Megan looked out the passenger window as if she couldn't care less about what was going on inside the car.

He'd convinced her to wait, packed up what had been an amazing picnic on a small secluded beach. She'd been happy. He'd been proud of having an evening in which he'd *not* suggested she was easy, suggested he was easy, or generally insulted her. So, now, this.

At least he'd stopped her from calling for a ride. Who would she have called anyway? By her own words she didn't have many friends and actually preferred things that way.

"I would have called a service. It's L.A. There are at least three, plus your general taxis." She sighed softly, still not looking at him.

Okay, that was unnerving.

"I'm sorry." She turned and looked out the window again.

Tristan still hadn't said a single word.

He stilled his thoughts, figuring they were leaking. That was easier thought than done, though. The beach was a good distance up the coast from her place in Santa Monica, but he almost had her home.

Megan watched as her neighborhood came into view. It must have been the most interesting sight she'd ever seen, the way she was glued to the window.

At last he parked. Though the spots were mostly taken up for the night with residents and visitors, at least traffic wasn't bad and he wasn't having to parallel park under duress.

Finally, she turned and looked at him. "Thank you."

Then she climbed out of the car. She looked around the foot well for a moment before seeming to remember that she'd only brought her bag with her, then she turned, walking away almost before he got the engine turned off.

"Wait." He hollered it out, then wondered if he had to. "I'm walking you to your door." He waited a beat himself when she kept walking, then tacked on, "Please."

At least she turned and looked at him. "Why?"

She had to ask? Standing on the sidewalk in Santa Monica with her bag slung over her shoulder, silhouetted in the moonlight, she was the most fascinating person he'd ever met. And she was frowning at him like she didn't believe any of it.

He was out of the car now, too, and finally standing in front of her. "Because I want to come up and talk."

Again, she said the same one word. "Why?"

He took an exasperated breath. "Why not? This is new, but it's not necessarily bad. Can't we just talk about it?"

"It *is* bad, Tristan."

She turned to walk away, and he grabbed for her, hoping to tug her back, but she was beyond his reach. Instinctively, he splayed his fingers, pushing his palms at the ground. Megan didn't see, but she almost bounced off the air in front of her.

In shock, she turned around. "Did you do that? Are you stopping me?"

He shook his head, then backtracked. "Yes, it was me. I'm

sorry, I didn't think that out. And no, I'm not stopping you, but I really, really want you to stop. Please talk to me."

"Because you threw up some invisible Spidey-web? I don't think so."

"It's gone. I'm sorry, it was a reaction." His shoulders fell, but he didn't turn away, just watched as she held a hand out behind her to test the air. Her fingers went through the space easily, the spell no longer functioning. He'd dropped it almost as fast as he'd put it up, as soon as he realized what he'd done.

She watched him as she waved her hand behind her again, feeling for resistance that didn't come. Megan took a step backward, away from him. As he watched, she took another, and a third. Then she stopped. "Why do you want to come up?"

He shrugged, hope surging just as his words failed him. "I— I mean—" *Shit.* He'd been for crap around her since day one. "What you can do is amazing. But why does it mean that you just get up and walk out? Why does my knowing what you can do mean that we're over? I don't understand."

He hoped it was English or close enough that she could follow what he meant. It felt like all the words were garbled, the tones and meanings equally unclear.

Megan seemed to grasp what he meant; she just didn't agree with him. "Because no one likes someone they can never keep a secret from."

She turned again, walking back up the street, and for a moment he was grateful they had to park two blocks away. If she'd ducked behind her door he might not even have had this chance. He ran, now, jumping in front of her.

"I don't have anything to hide." He held his arms out to his sides as if he could show her his soul in the palms of his hands.

This time the heavy sigh came from her. "Really? What about the ex-girlfriends? The fact that Yasmin thinks you're a slut? The one who put the hex on the store?"

"All true."

She rolled her eyes at him. "How often you jerk off and what you think about when you do it?"

He would have laughed, but it made him think about what he thought about when he touched himself. His breath quickened, his voice dropped out from under him and he took a step closer. "I won't hide it, but I don't think you can handle what I think about when I jerk off."

In his mind a picture gelled of Megan, naked in his shower, leaning against the large, earthy tiles, hot water sluicing over her. His hand snaking around her back, and pulling her to him, skin to skin, while the water steamed around them. He could recall the weight of her breast in his hand. In his mind she gasped, her mouth falling open as he touched her. He imagined driving into her as she clutched him, nails digging into his bare back, his arms sliding down along her wet, naked skin as he lifted her, pressed her into the wall of the shower as he drove into her.

Standing on the street, Megan stared at him.

She could see all of it. Tristan could tell. And it turned him on that much more. As he stepped forward, she sucked in a small breath, her mouth falling open just as it did in his fantasy. Just as it had when they'd been together. He remembered that. He kept his fantasies as grounded in the reality of her as he could.

Never mind that he was standing on the street in Santa Monica after midnight on a weekday. Never mind that she'd told him he didn't want her. She was wrong.

Closing the last of the small distance between them, Tristan reached for her face. Pulling her close, he tasted her, lush lips dancing beneath his, fire sparking between them the way it always did.

He felt and heard her bag slip from her shoulder and fall to the ground. Her hands clutched at his biceps, clinging to him in a way that made him only want more. He angled her head, letting them take the kiss deeper, feeling all of her pressed to all of him.

It was probably a full minute before he stepped back, her face still cradled in his hands. His breath was almost too heavy to make words, but he did. "That's why I want to come up. I want to figure out what this is between us." He sucked in air, needing it, desperately. "I won't press, I won't push, I won't ask anything of you you're not willing to give. But, please, give me this. Let's figure it out."

He could see the moment when she gave up. Her lips closed as though she was displeased with her own decision. Megan leaned over and picked up her bag then led him the last half block up the street to her building. Once inside, she took the stairs, letting him follow. Her passage through the door and up the steps so natural that it only took him a moment to realize this was her usual path and not a punishment to him for wanting to talk.

In silence, he trailed her down the hall, then waited while she unlocked two separately keyed bolts on her door and entered first before waving him in. Still not speaking, she wandered through the room, only taking a few steps before he realized she was setting her bag on the bar that separated the living area from her small kitchen. He looked around as she got into the fridge and pulled out a filtered water pitcher, then a glass.

"You want a drink?" She held up the pitcher, indicating what she was offering. Not beer.

Tristan nodded and was handed the glass of cold water she'd just poured. When she reached into the cupboard and then filled a second glass, he could see she was out of things to do to stall him.

So he opened with the most important thing. "Why does my knowing this change anything?"

"Because it changes *everything*." She almost smacked the glass onto the counter that maintained a safe space between them before she even took a drink.

"Then, help me out, because I really don't understand. You could do this since I met you, right?" At her nod, he asked, "How long?"

"As long as I can remember. My parents said I was an easy baby, always did what they wanted. So I guess even then."

"Wow." Still he didn't let that distract him. "So you've always been able to do this. Then the only thing that changed is now I know. I'm pretty weird myself. But I'm okay with this, so what's the problem?"

"The problem is that it *will* go bad." She stayed on the other side of the counter, keeping it between them like a barrier. One he didn't understand the need for and didn't want.

First, he'd been confused. So she had a unique gift? He'd been raised to appreciate what each person could do. So her gift wasn't a great singing voice—though maybe she had that, too, he didn't know yet—or something more normal. His gifts were pretty out there. So were his other family member's talents. When you added in that his sister Juliet could levitate small objects or bring back flowers from the brink of death without even using a specific spell? Well, he was used to weird.

Now, he rounded the corner on confused and went straight to angry. "You're giving up because of some prediction you don't have any right to make about me?"

She sighed. Looked away. Then sighed again. "Look, Tristan. It's not you—"

"It's *you*? Yes, it is." Well, he shouldn't have said that. But once out it was out there. Unless he was going to cast a *forget* on her, he was stuck with it. And he'd learned his lesson about casting *forgets* from his sister. His hands bunched into fists and went to his hips of their own accord.

She spoke again before he could say he was sorry.

Teeth gritting, Megan started over. "It's not you, it's

everyone. Sooner or later you'll want to keep something from me. But you'll be broadcasting it all over the place without even knowing it." She paused for effect. This time when she stopped, her voice dropped and the sadness in it made him understand she believed it because it had happened to her. "Or worse, you'll *want* me to know. You'll want me to hear your silent thoughts about how much you're attracted to some other woman or how much of a bitch you really think I am."

Still, she looked right at him. It took guts to put that out there. To tell him she was calling it off before it turned sour.

He wasn't accepting it. "I'm not like that."

"You're not *human*?" She tilted her head, questioning.

"I am, but I'm too far off the scale of normal myself to do any of that, and I have nothing to hide from you." At some point he'd set the water glass down, and now he turned his palms over to her as if to say he had nothing up his sleeves.

He'd never had a really serious relationship before. So who was he to say that they'd make it? But who was she to say that they wouldn't?

He could see she was reading his every thought. Her frown showed that she understood both the disrespect it showed him to assume he'd act one way and the pressure it put her under to throw herself out there when every piece of evidence told her things would end badly.

Tristan reached across the bar top and took her hands, gently lacing their fingers together. Then he looked her in the eyes and thought, *Come on, Megan. Give me a chance.*

CHAPTER 17

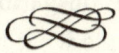

Megan stared at him. He stood calmly in her living room, staring back at her across the countertop, thinking those sinful things. It still wouldn't make a difference. She knew.

She was twenty-eight years old and she'd been here before. She'd been here with every relationship she'd ever been in. There was always that time when it seemed it would work. This would be the person who would understand her. The one who would stick.

But it never happened.

Three months and even her own mother hadn't called her.

Tristan's words were sweet, even if they weren't out loud. But he didn't know what she knew. He hadn't lived her life.

She tried again. "Best case scenario, you grow tired of me and become attracted to someone else and I get to see it in glorious technicolor."

He shrugged at her as though it didn't matter. "It could be you, you know."

"What?"

"What if you get tired of me? What if you decide you're attracted to someone else and have to cut me loose?"

"But that won't happen." Megan countered. It never happened that way.

"Why not? So I won't hear your thoughts about other men, but you think I'd be blind to it?" He shook his head. "No, rather than knowing what's going on, I'd be left paranoid and afraid and waiting for you to tell me what I already know. Honestly, a lot of relationships go that way. Why should the fact that we might actually be normal in that respect be a deterrent? I don't understand."

"No, you clearly don't. You have no idea how much it hurts to see what the man you think loves you really wants. You have no idea how awful it is to walk down the street and see that he thinks some other woman is attractive."

"Whoa." He said it as though he was stopping her, but he didn't say anything else for a minute. "You do know you're not the only attractive woman on the planet, right?"

She rolled her eyes. Of course she knew that. "No, it's when he thinks about exchanging you for her. Or worse, he sees a woman on the street and thinks about the night he was with her when he told you he was busy. Well, he was busy all right. I'm not doing that again."

"So don't. Go out with *me*."

"Tristan!" Why was he being so bull headed?

"Seriously. I watched my sisters date. There are a lot of assholes out there. And I haven't been a prize in the past, but I was always honest." He stopped then, still staring her straight in the eyes. "I'm not an asshole. I won't be one to you. And I've never felt like this before. I just want you to give me a chance."

At least he was telling the truth. While it was handy to know when someone was lying, it sucked that people did it so much. "Look, I know you want a chance. But I've given a ton of them and none have worked out. It's a guaranteed loss."

Hopefully he'd quit after that. She'd stood her ground.

He stood his. "Nope. Not buying it."

"It's the middle of the night, Tristan. You should go home. I have to go to work in the morning."

He shook his head again. "No, you don't."

"Fine. *You* have to go to work in the morning." She huffed at him, still standing behind the counter as though that would keep her safe from his persistence.

"No, I don't. I own the place." He had the nerve to grin at her. "I get it. You have a one hundred percent failure rate."

Well, that sucked to hear, but he was right. He didn't let her even get a word in edgewise.

"I can promise you I'm nothing like them. I'll bet you've never met anyone like me. So give me a chance." This time he got cocky. He leaned forward, his elbows resting on the counter as though he knew something she didn't. But his thoughts didn't broadcast anything other than his confidence.

"Tristan. I can't."

"Yes, you can." With that he grinned and lifted his hand. As she stared, he snapped his fingers.

The lights all went out.

Startled, Megan looked around. Streetlight filtered in through the windows illuminating his face and letting her know that he wasn't startled.

"The power went out." She said straightforwardly, trying to process the sudden change and his odd reaction.

"No, it didn't." He grinned and snapped his fingers again. The lights all came back on. "I did it."

"You did that?" She frowned at him. "I know you're a witch and all but you sell herbs and cast spells and mix things in a cauldron, right?"

"I do sell herbs and cast spells. I even have my great-grandmother's cauldron. But I'm the descendant of a very prominent line of witches. So I can also do this."

He snapped his fingers again, and Megan's head turned at a whooshing sound behind her. Her burners had all flared to life. She turned back to face him. "Did you really do that?"

"I did." He grinned. "Wanna see it again? Just tell me when and I'll turn it off."

"Really?" She asked, skeptically. Then before he could answer, she said, "Now."

He snapped again and the burners went off.

Megan blinked as her brain worked, trying to process what she was seeing. "It's a parlor trick."

"If you want it to be. But you know I've never been here before, so I couldn't have set anything up." He offered half a smile and half a shrug. "So it's not magnets, or tricks of light, or sleight of hand. It's me. It's what I am. So what you are isn't so weird to me."

She stared at him. Jesus, he was trying to make her more comfortable by showing her how odd he was, too. Was it working? She wasn't sure. Her mouth opened and words tumbled out. "Your grandmother used to make muffins using the blackberries from the back yard. The berries would crush in the batter and turn it purple."

"You know that?" She'd managed to shock him.

"You were thinking about them at the bakery. That the muffins weren't as good as Delilah's and that your grandmother's weren't pretty enough to be featured in the glass case, but that you wished you had them."

He nodded. "I wished I had one to give to you. So you could have that."

She nodded back at him. She'd known that, but it didn't seem necessary to say so. For a moment, Megan held her tongue, but then looked down as the water in her glass began move. It rippled up and out in circles, like in Jurassic Park and she raised her eyebrows at it as she heard Tristan laugh. As she watched, the movement in the water halted and died out.

"Can't hold it when I'm laughing." He said.

Megan was about to comment when she realized he was rounding the corner of the bar and coming into her safe space with her. She ducked out and around him, keeping Tristan from cornering her.

Or so she thought.

As soon as she cleared the edge of the counter, Tristan began advancing on her. The feeling of him entering her personal space made her heart beat faster. The thoughts he was broadcasting to her—now fully aware he was doing it—kicked the rate up even higher.

Megan couldn't catch her breath. Flashes of his imagination, wicked, sinful thoughts of the two of them moving together invaded her thoughts. She couldn't turn it off. Even if that was a skill she possessed, she couldn't have broken the contact he created as he looked directly into her eyes. He wanted her.

He wanted her in a way that no man ever had before. He knew her, knew what she could do and didn't shy away. Instead, he moved closer. Used her skill to his advantage.

Apparently, knowing she could see his thoughts turned him on, too. Whether if he was reading what his ideas were doing to her, or a combination of all of it, Megan couldn't tell. Then again, she almost couldn't remember her own name.

He was too close. Megan couldn't tell how he'd gotten there. Did he walk? Snap his fingers and erase the memory of him approaching? But now he was near enough that when she inhaled, she breathed him in. When she looked, she couldn't see the world beyond his face, and he was staring at her mouth. He was thinking about her mouth.

Though she wasn't pressed against the wall, she couldn't move back. He hadn't really blocked her in, but she felt like she was. It was her choice to move out of his way, but she couldn't do it. He wanted her. And she wanted him.

Her heart hammered as he closed the last few inches,

offering a taste of a kiss. His lips brushed hers lightly. Her chest lifted at the feeling, and the wash of his feelings assaulted her on top of her own. She was drowning. She was fighting for air. She was pressing into the kiss, demanding more.

Tristan gave more pressure, while still not reaching out, still not touching her. She could feel that he was holding himself back. Though he'd initiated the kiss, if it went any further that would be her decision. Though she knew she should pull back, say no, stick to her argument, she didn't have it in her. Not when he was kissing her that way. Pouring all his wants and needs into her.

Before she knew what she was doing, Megan snaked her arms out and around his neck. When she tightened her grip, it was all the notice Tristan needed. He hadn't been able to win her with words and reason, but one kiss, one moment of showing his need, and she was a goner.

She was hauled, almost roughly, against him. His arms braced her, his hands held her head, angling her mouth under his. No longer trying to seduce her, Tristan's thoughts ran wild. The flood of his uncontrolled desire was even harder to resist than the smoldering seduction. Megan lost her head. Had she been thinking, she would have admitted that she'd lost her heart, too. But none of that mattered now, because he was touching her.

When Tristan moved back ever so slightly, she balked until she realized he was trying to make space to get her shirt off. He'd unbuttoned it without her realizing it. It was gone before she knew it, and Megan felt her hands fighting against his to tug his shirt up and over his head. In a moment, it, too, was gone. Tristan pulled her up against him, startling her again with the hot touch of skin on skin. Her bra was missing though she didn't know when that had happened either.

His tongue fought hers for dominance, neither winning the upper hand. His fingers roamed her skin as he thought about the feel of her and she absorbed the sensations of having this man under her fingertips. It was heady knowing he reacted to her touches the same way she did.

When he stepped back once again, she understood. His hand reached out for hers. As her fingers slid into his, the nebulous thoughts of finding her bedroom solidified into ideas he had for her bed. She let him tug her down the short hallway, then tipped her head when he faced two doors, helping him not choose the bathroom. Megan felt his anticipation, his curiosity when he turned the knob, and she understood that he'd be happy with nothing more than a bed with sheets on it.

His thoughts centered on bare skin, on Megan hooking her thumbs in her underwear and stripping naked for him. He thought of her fingers deftly finding the buttons on the front of his jeans, her hands sliding inside against his skin, but he moved her backwards into the room in a dance they both knew the steps to.

Tristan traced his hands along the edge of her skirt, finding the zipper in the back and sliding it down. All the while his chest pressed against hers, his heat transferring into her the way his thoughts did.

Megan had only a few of her own thoughts in her head, but she tried to make them count. As her skirt hit the floor, she kicked off her shoes, leaving her standing in his arms in only her underwear.

She stepped back, hooking her fingers in the sides of the lace panties she'd picked earlier with him in mind. Though they weren't the ones he'd imagined, she could hear his breath suck in as he watched, transfixed.

As soon as the lace hit the floor, he walked forward, leaving her no room but to step back until her knees hit the edge of the bed in the tiny room. She had no other choice but to sink back and find herself that much closer to Tristan's imagination.

She reached for the top button on his jeans, popping it and

then each of the others as he stilled beneath her touch. Lifting her shoulders, she aimed her hands down inside his jeans, skimming her fingers along his hot skin.

Megan touched him, long and hot beneath her. His breath sucked in just as he grabbed her wrist. Pulling her hand out of his pants, he held it away from him, his eyes no longer showing heat, but shock.

His voice was harsh with anger rather than want. "No."

CHAPTER 18

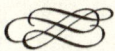

Tristan held Megan's hand away, knowing that if she touched him again, he'd lose it. He'd drop the sudden, important knowledge grabbing him and twisting his heart. "Don't."

His breath dragged in, rough around the edges. The lust that fired in his blood cooled as his thoughts collected. Megan sat still and wary in front of him. Though she tried once to reclaim her hand, he held on. He didn't want her starting back into what she was doing.

He sighed, grateful he still had his pants on, even if not completely. The naked woman in front of him was more temptation than he could stand. But what she was doing was killing him. And not in a good way. "What are you doing?"

This time she jerked her hand back escaping his grasp. Leaning back on the bed, she tried to get away, but with her legs straddling his, she wasn't able to. "If you have to ask, I'm not doing it right." She looked to the side, her expression hardening.

"No. You're doing that right." He sighed again, his air still not coming normally. She did that to him. "I'm at a decided disadvantage here."

"Told you you wouldn't like it."

And that was something he wasn't used to. He'd never met another witch as powerful as himself—at least not someone who wasn't a family member. So he'd never dated anyone with power close to his own.

Megan didn't have that, but she had something else.

His sister, Delilah, could break into his thoughts and he could break into hers. But it wasn't the constant download that Megan seemed to be getting. He'd never met—never even heard of—anyone with her gift, and he hadn't been prepared for the ramifications.

No longer trying to look like she wasn't hearing him, Megan turned the other way. "I thought it was what you wanted."

That was exactly the problem. "It is. But that's not your job."

He rubbed at his shoulder for something to touch that wasn't a naked Megan. He could have stepped back and let her move, but he didn't want her turning away, he just wanted her to understand.

"So I shouldn't do anything?" Her head tipped and she offered the words as a challenge.

He didn't bite. "I know you can see what I want. You're seeing my fantasies—"

"Hard not to." She bit off the words, now looking put out rather than turned on. "You're broadcasting them like a movie theater."

"I get that. I don't know how to not broadcast them." He sighed again. Why was this so complicated? This time he moved. Stepped back and then sat on the bed next to her.

Despite her resistance, he grabbed her hand. He laced his fingers through hers and held on tight even though she wasn't actively participating.

Tristan tried again. "I want to have sex with you."

"I thought that's what you were doing." She still didn't look at him.

"I was broadcasting my fantasies. I want to keep doing that. I don't want to hide how much I want you and what I want us to do. But you don't owe me any of it." He took a breath. "I want to be with *you*. Not with some fantasy in my head. You're better than the fantasy. I want what you want, not you giving me what I thought I wanted."

Okay, that hardly qualified as coherent, but at least he'd tried.

She was opening her mouth to speak when it hit him. "You did it at my office, too!"

She looked away again. She might as well have just said yes.

"You were playing to my fantasy then, too." This time it was Tristan who looked away, remembering the way she'd unzipped her skirt, stepped out of it in a way that had been almost identical to his imagination. He hadn't known it then, but she'd been reading his every thought and playing the role he'd set for her.

She tugged on her hand. "This is why I didn't want to do this. It doesn't work." Megan was rolling away from him, trying to get up, restrained only by his grip on her hand.

"Yes, it does." He pulled her back, closer, his untethered hand coming up to cup her head and turn her to him, for a deep kiss that he hoped said everything his inability to form sentences had missed. Her eyes said everything. Said she wanted this to work even if she didn't really believe it yet.

Holding her to him, he led the kiss, taking what she gave and returning it. For long minutes, he held her there, though his hands ached to touch her. But he had to hold back, had to let her see that she wasn't just someone to fulfill his fantasies. Besides, he hadn't lied, the reality was so much better.

When at last he leaned back, he looked at her, no ideas in his head other than his want for her. He stood, pulling her with him, and shucked the last of his clothing himself.

They stood there, naked before each other, even though

Tristan knew he was somehow all the more naked for her ability. This time when he stepped into her, there was nothing between them.

Megan kissed him back, she reached for him, touched him, stroked him even as his breath sucked in and his ribs clenched with the things she made him feel. The sensation of her thumbs sliding down his sides, brushing across his chest and grabbing his hips told Tristan that whatever he'd said worked at least somewhat. If he couldn't say what he meant, maybe he could show it.

Realizing what he needed to do, Tristan moved slightly out of reach of Megan's wandering hands and pulled back the covers on her bed. He distracted her with tiny kisses along her jaw and collarbone. He stroked her hips as he gently pushed her down onto the mattress. Letting him lead, Megan leaned backward farther and farther until she was fully laid out before him, her expression a little wary.

Tristan held himself over her. His hands occupied with holding his weight off her, he used his mouth, taking one breast then the other and gently suckling on her until her voice escaped in tiny mews that drove him nuts. He couldn't remember the last time he'd wanted a woman this way. This wasn't want. It was *need*.

He used his teeth on the side of her neck as her head tipped for better access. He was sucking on the soft skin he found there, desire shooting through him like lightning strikes when he felt her fingers squeeze on his hips, triggering a wash of images. Her hands on his dick. Stroking him, holding him, bringing him to a state of mental putty and primal physical lust.

Knowing his thoughts as she did, Megan reached for him, her fingers working magic on his sensitive cock. Her fingers stroked him, once, twice, a third time before he managed to grab her wrist again.

His mouth didn't work, his jaw clenched. This was so hard.

He wanted her, wanted her to do what she was doing, but it wasn't right. Just that knowledge dimmed his desire and he didn't want anything to do that. "Don't. Just don't."

"But you want it." She was as frustrated with him as he was with having to make her stop. "And when I do it, you make that noise. You can't tell me you don't like it."

His arm shook from where he braced his weight. His body shook from wanting her and not being there yet. The hand that circled her wrist shook from holding her back from a touch that felt like the world would explode in the best way possible. "It's not your job to fulfill my fantasies. In fact, you already did it once, and very well. So now it's my turn."

"You can't hear me." She protested, her hand still held captive.

"Yes, I can, I can hear you just fine." He looked her in the eyes, "You just have to talk to me."

For the first time, she looked embarrassed.

"Don't." He lifted the captured hand and held it above her head as he kissed the side of her mouth. "Don't be shy. I'm fully open to you, all you have to do is tell me what you want."

"I don't—" She breathed in and Tristan took advantage of the moment.

He shifted his weight, reaching for her other hand and pulling it, too, above her head.

"I haven't—" she said, offering another nebulous protest.

"Okay, then, we'll just try things out and you say 'yes' or 'no.' If that doesn't work, I'll just go by the sounds you make." He grinned at her, then looked up at the iron headboard on her bed.

The woman had odd taste in furniture, or maybe hit-and-miss was a better term. The place felt like things were missing. There was no bedside table, only a cardboard box with a small tablecloth on it, but the headboard was in place and he was grateful. Tugging her hands up, he used his own hands to mold hers, pushing her to grab onto the scroll work.

With his face down by her ear, he whispered, "No hands for you. Don't let go."

She didn't, and he didn't take a look at her face, not ready for her doubt. Instead, he moved down her body, licking and tasting as he went. He paused as he found a spot he liked, nipping at the indent of her waist, lingering further when she offered a soft intake of breath. He moved lower still, reading her thoughts not because he could hear them, but through the tension in her muscles as he got close to his goal. He read her body language as her legs first fell apart then involuntarily clamped his head, then as he worked his magic how she broke apart and turned to jelly beneath his touch.

He left her there as he searched out the jeans he'd tossed. Digging in his wallet he pulled out a condom and rolled it on. He looked up to find her watching him, her body almost fluid from her orgasm, her legs open, her face flushed, her eyes bright. She hadn't let go. Sweet Goddess, he wanted her.

He climbed onto the bed and walked on his knees until he was in position. He wanted to drag her to the side of the bed and drive into her until he came. He wanted to flip her onto her knees and pull her against him as he came. He wanted to take her sitting on the counter, from behind standing at the bar. He wanted her to ride him in his own bed. So much more than he could do right now. This one wasn't about what he wanted.

Megan was looking at him, seeing and understanding all the ways he wanted her.

"Not now." He practically growled it at her. "Now is about you. There will be plenty of time for the rest of it."

He hoped it was true. This was his chance to make it true. So he leaned over her and whispered again in her ear. "Hold on."

He meant she shouldn't move her hands, that she still wasn't allowed to touch him, but he hoped he could make her need to hold on. Shifting his hips, he entered her in one smooth stroke.

The vocalized gasp that escaped her drove him to work harder despite the need sinking its claws into him.

Each stroke pulled him closer to the edge, but he held back until he heard and felt her break under him. Then the dam that contained his orgasm cracked and he drove into the sweet, soft pressure that was Megan one last time and let it all go.

His brain stopped functioning as feeling overtook him. He grasped at her, as if he could pull them together into one being. Vaguely, he registered her arms wrapped around him.

As he settled back to earth and into his own senses, he sighed against her skin, whispering, "You didn't hold on."

"Yes, I did." She whispered back, wrapped around him, making him believe she was his.

CHAPTER 19

Megan held on tight as Tristan relaxed against her. She was on him like a vine, the very definition of clingy. The air around her was charged with their lovemaking, if she could call it that. The space smelled of sex and Tristan and a little bit of her. She breathed it in, reminding herself she shouldn't hang on so tight.

Still buried deep inside her, and shifting only slightly, he whispered in her ear. "Don't let go."

Could he hear her? It was a worry she'd never had before. It wasn't enough to make her release him, though.

After a moment he made a noise of frustration. "I have to take care of this."

So she let him go, watching as he moved naked around her small room, unconcerned with his nudity. She pointed him into the corner as he looked around for the wastebasket, then disposed of the condom.

She waited, tense, wondering what he would do.

The last time they'd been together, she'd been in his office. She'd counted him as one-and-done and walked away. Only he hadn't let her. Now he was in her bedroom and she couldn't walk away. All she could do was wait and hope he didn't do the same to her even though she probably deserved it.

He had one knee on the bed, the covers in his fist, when he stilled. "I get to stay, right?"

Trying not to let her utter relief show, she nodded. It hit her then, the horrible unfairness he was playing against. So she tried to even the field. She tried to speak, but it only came out as a whisper. "I was afraid you would leave."

He tugged the covers up and over them as he slid in beside her, curling her into him. He wrapped his arms around her and buried his face in her neck. One soft kiss almost did her in. She felt as well as heard his words.

"Haven't you figured it out yet? I'm yours."

The words washed over her, tripping her heart and making the air she breathed that much sweeter. She basked in the thought of this man saying he was hers; she rested her head on his shoulder, curling back into him. Maybe she reveled in it a little too long.

He was supple around her, his fingers offering soft strokes against her bare skin, soothing her, testing her. But then he slowed, his touch trailing off, his form stiffening behind her. She heard his worry as it followed the path of his original sweet statement.

Jerking out of his hold, she turned to face him. Her hands clasped at the face that was becoming so dear to her. He'd wormed his way into her heart even when she was determined to keep him out. She was sunk.

"I'm not seeing anyone else." She told him, watching as he nodded in response. His smile came back but only halfway, and once again she was struck by the unfair situation he'd set himself in. For her.

It wasn't enough that she wasn't seeing anyone other than him. It wasn't the same thing he'd given her. He'd screwed her up. Made her want to try. So she sucked in a deep breath and did something she'd never done before.

Megan laid all her cards on the table.

"I'm yours. I'm in. I'm crazy about you." She took another breath and even though Tristan smiled and curled tighter around her, she kept going. "You could be the death of me, you know? But I won't cheat on you and I will be honest. I've never done this before. Not like this, but I'll try. I'll try, Tristan."

"That's all I can ask." He tucked her up against him, his words and tone going sleepy now that he could let go of the worry that his feelings were one sided. In moments, he was out cold.

It had been years since Megan had slept next to a man. In fact, she probably never had. The last man she'd slept next to had really been a boy. Old enough, but not a man, not really.

Though Tristan found sleep, now she was awake. Worries assaulted her fresh. He said he was hers and he meant it, but his track record wasn't good. Did he tell every girl he dated that he was hers? Some people actually fell in love with each person they dated. They threw themselves in whole heart, and if that's what Tristan did then it was likely she was no different than the last girl. Except she couldn't cast revenge spells on his store.

What if he meant it? What if she *was* different, then it all fell apart because her ability, her gift, her curse, whatever, made a relationship so lopsided? He said it was okay, but he hadn't lived with it. It was almost three a.m., he'd now known what she could do for about three hours. What would three days look like? Three weeks? Could he possibly withstand being with her for three months?

And how much would it kill her if he walked away? When he walked away. Because what was the chance that Tristan Goodman was the one? Not good, that's what.

Her thoughts ran in bad circles while she tried to go to sleep. Eventually Megan managed to convince herself to enjoy the present, and she took a moment to enjoy the feel of muscular arms around her, of sexy man curled alongside her. Of the way he smelled, and breathed her in, and how his arms—lax from sleep—still pulled her to him.

She flung her own arm across his and was never sure when or even if sleep really pulled her under. She only knew that when she paid attention again, a hot, sexy man was nuzzling the nape of her neck. A warm hand rested on her hip, then began slowly climbing up, across her ribs, until slightly rough fingertips grazed the underside of her breast. As a thumb found her nipple, teeth softly dug into the muscle at the side of her neck.

He trailed tiny bites up under her hairline as his hand slid lower and lower until his fingers found her soft and wet and ready for him again. It took only a moment for him to make her buck in his arms. As she writhed against him, he slid one long, lean finger inside her, moving it slowly in and out, making her gasp.

Megan reached back and found him hard and ready behind her. She pushed against him, feeling him push into her hold. But even though he wanted it, he said no. He grabbed her hand and removed it. Once again, he moved it up above her head. "No, you don't get to play at being my fantasy. You just get to be you."

He tucked her hands up next to each other, holding them together, leaving his other hand unoccupied. Before she could protest, his free hand found her again. The only sound she made was a moan.

Tristan continued to work his magic on her, even as he used his knee to manipulate her. She was all sensation, the rush of his hands on her controlling her every thought, and before she knew it, she was rolled onto her stomach. He still held her hands above her head, clutched in one of his. Her knees were spread and he was positioned behind her.

When his hand disappeared, she moaned, or whined at the

loss, her hips backing up to retrieve his touch. She wasn't in control, not of him, not even of herself. If he hadn't so completely overtaken her senses, she would have been afraid to hand herself over so fully. She didn't have time to be afraid.

His odd movements revealed themselves a moment later as having put on a condom, but there wasn't time to think. He had one hand bracing her hip as he pulled her back and onto him.

As he entered her, he groaned out her name, turning her on even more, if that was even possible. She pushed back against him, trying to take him deeper. The urge was base, primal, not even a choice. She met his every stroke, whispered his name, then yelled it, as he built up the electricity between them. He was leaning over her, pressing his chest to her back, tracing circles on her skin with his clever tongue.

Picking up her pace and his, Megan strained for release. She begged him for it, harder, needed him to need her the way she needed him. When his hand snaked forward and applied pressure she moved against him until he hit the right spot and she unraveled.

With rhythmic movements against her, he came in a clench of muscles and a rush of blind thoughts of her, him, the two of them tangled together.

At last he relaxed, their moments finished. Megan waited for things to become awkward, but they didn't. Tristan didn't let it. It was as if he knew she was awkward and he wouldn't let things go that way.

She was grateful for his touch. For his sleepy thoughts that were still focused on her. For his willingness to get involved with a woman who invaded his personal space in a way most men would never allow to happen.

He disposed of the condom and crawled back in alongside her even though she could see that it was clearly morning now that her brain was processing.

He stroked her head and once again curled her into him.

Though he couldn't hear her thoughts, he seemed to have some magic of his own. He seemed to know what she needed and had no trouble meeting that need.

"Go back to sleep," he whispered.

"It's morning." Her voice sounded muzzy even to her. "Don't you have to go to work?"

"I can call in sick." She could hear the grin in his tone even if she couldn't see it on his face. "So can you."

As tempting as it was to spend the whole day in bed with him, she was growing afraid. She didn't want to crowd him. Wanted to step apart, see if things still looked the same in the harsh light of day. Reaching out to her makeshift, cardboard box night table, Megan set the alarm for ten. "That's the latest I can get online and check in. We can sleep in, but then you should go to work, too."

He was falling back asleep already, even though her answer wasn't what he wanted. But she needed a moment to regroup, to see through eyes that weren't clouded by lust. "Okay, but you call me when you finish?"

She nodded, knowing he was purposefully testing her. Though she curled back into him and felt her body falling under the pressure of sleep, she knew. The ball was in her court.

CHAPTER 20

"What crawled up your butt?" Yasmin stood, arms crossed, in his doorway. Again.

Tristan sighed. He knew the answer to the question, but he just didn't want to admit it.

"Things go south with Megan?" She asked.

So apparently it didn't matter if he said it.

"Not south." He replied, smacking his pencil onto the desk top. The sound felt good, but not good enough to make up for the loss. He sighed again. "Just . . . nowhere."

He'd said, "Call me tonight," and she'd agreed. Hadn't she? He'd given her the space she wanted. He'd waited for her to call. She hadn't. He hadn't called again. He waited the whole next day, but nothing. The third day had come and gone without word from Megan.

Vowing not to call—he didn't want to invade her space, he really didn't—he checked on her. He knew how terrible he would feel if he was sitting here being pissy if she was hurt, or in trouble. So he'd pulled out the map and the crystal on his great-grandfather's chain.

Megan was in Santa Monica. She was healthy. Her phone

worked. He even asked a generic, "Is she okay?" and the answer came back fully positive.

Nope. It wasn't trouble. It was that he'd been dumped.

Not even face to face. Actually not even dumped. She'd just . . . let go.

"I'm sorry. I liked her." Yasmin was in his office now, sitting in the not-so-comfortable guest chair.

He caved. Tristan wasn't one to kiss and tell. He wouldn't talk about Megan, but she was gone and he needed to get it out. Yasmin was a trusted friend. "She's different."

"I know." Yasmin nodded. "She wasn't your usual type."

"It's more than that. Megan can . . . she can . . ." It seemed odd to tell Megan's secret, but he was more and more confident that she was never coming back. So it didn't matter.

"She's different."

"No. Not just because of her coloring or her looks." He protested. Still protecting the woman who'd clearly left him far behind. Somehow he couldn't just push the words out. "It's . . ."

Yasmin sat, looking at him oddly. Waiting until he finally blurted it out.

"She can—she's a telepath." He felt better getting it out there. "It's not selective either. She hears everything."

Yasmin still looked at him, her sympathy showing through.

Once he started, Tristan had a hard time reeling it in. He was angry. He was hurt. He was frustrated by his complete inability to just let it go. But he couldn't. "She sees things, too. She doesn't just hear the things you think, she sees what you imagine, and seems to grasp general feelings."

Yasmin still sat there, watching him. Waiting.

Tristan stared back, wondering what she was—

"You knew!" He almost jumped out of his seat and across the desk at her. "You knew!"

She just nodded.

Tristan plopped back into his seat, all the energy suddenly drained from him. "You knew?"

"Yeah, the first night she was in here—"

"The first night!" He didn't care that he interrupted her, his brain calculating back to when she'd first been in the store.

"The first night, I suspected." Yasmin clarified. "It wasn't until a week later when she came in and touched Luke that I actually knew."

Tristan was still processing, but the mention of Megan touching Luke and something special happening jabbed him in the gut, a piercing bolt of jealousy. Completely undeserved jealousy. Luke was over the moon for Yasmin, there was nothing Megan could do to make anything happen there, but what was so special about Luke? Tristan frowned up at Yasmin.

"He'd just come in from a meet that hadn't happened; his informant hadn't shown up." She shifted in her seat with the re-telling. "When Megan touched him, she saw that the informant was dead and that the drug dealers who killed her were coming after her son. Then she passed out."

"What?" He was almost out of his seat again. How was he only learning this now? "She passed out? Here in the store?"

It seemed he could only ask questions. What he couldn't figure out was why he was asking the questions, why he didn't know these things already about the woman he'd thought was his girlfriend. He tried again, but another question came out. "So she saw the informant? Luke knew about her?"

"No." Yasmin leaned forward, almost excited to have a conspirator to talk to. "He didn't know what happened to her. Megan touched a file with info about the informant. But no one knew where the woman was. Megan didn't find her, but gave them some help. She did tell them that she was dead and that the drug runners were coming for the son as leverage against the husband. They staked out the home based on Luke's suggestion and caught a low level guy there to do the kidnapping. The son and his dad are safe now."

"So she's not just an empath and a telepath?" He was cradling his head in his hand, his elbow propped on the desk in defeat. "She's also clairvoyant?"

Yasmin waited while he sighed, realizing that she wasn't so much sharing as informing him of something he hadn't known. When she finally spoke again, it was conciliatory. "She said it wasn't common to see things like that. Mostly she just hears what people are thinking around her all the time."

"So you set her up for the *quell* knowing what it was for."

She nodded, finally grasping that he was angry about it. Yasmin had known and hadn't told him. Though he didn't really know what it mattered now, he was still upset.

"So when she came in here that first night, when she had the headache—" he put the pieces together. "That headache, was that from what she saw about Luke?"

"Yeah." Yasmin no longer looked so cocky and he pressed forward.

"When she came back here that night, you already knew what she could do?"

This time, no words, just a nod.

Did Yasmin know what had happened in his office that night? He wasn't telling. He'd had enough of getting his soul ripped out. Then again, maybe he hadn't. His mouth blabbered without his input. "Well, I only found out what she can do about four days ago." Four nights ago, but who was counting?

"I'm sorry it's not working out." Yasmin offered again. "But you can be sad without acting like you're going to bite everyone's head off."

With that, she put her hands on her legs as though she was pushing up. She stood and walked out of his office without looking back. She did close the door as if to protect the other employees from him.

He tallied receipts and took care of the books. All of it poorly. He dealt with a problem from a vendor. To be fair, the vendors knew they were working with a Wiccan shop that had a family history steeped in the religion. But Tristan didn't think they'd ever been afraid of being cast on if they missed a delivery. Not before today anyway.

Tristan.

He leaned back in his chair, recognizing the voice in his head. Delilah. He didn't need her now. He just needed to stew.

No, you don't. The voice came again. *Come over. I need adult company and you need food.*

He didn't agree, but he didn't disagree either. It was too pretty a day for his mood, so he didn't even have a jacket with him. Nothing to gather up or even do, other than telling Yasmin he was leaving. He was grateful that she hadn't left the store when she had the chance. She loved it here as much as he did. More than Delilah did. Yasmin had become family—something he and Delilah had discussed many times. Yasmin's devotion was never more evident than when she offered a slightly sad smile and said, "Go on. You need it. Don't worry about the store."

So he did.

It took nearly thirty minutes to get to Delilah's house, once he counted finding parking. That had been a bitch. One he wasn't used to dealing with because he almost never forgot to do a *parking karma* spell. The fact that he'd forgotten today, at someplace as familiar as Delilah and Brandon's house was telling of just how sour his mood had gotten.

He walked the half block under branches of overhanging trees. Sunlight filtered through. In one of the yards he passed, a young father played with small children on a swing set. In another, a cat sat on a swinging loveseat, somehow looking happier than Tristan managed. He swung open the gate in front of Delilah's house and walked right in the front door.

Brandon sat on the couch, finally comfortable with the casual ease of Tristan and Delilah's relationship. It was normal for siblings to be close. What bothered Brandon at first was that Tristan and his sister could speak to each other without talking. So while Tristan would announce he was coming, and Delilah would say, come on in, join us for dinner, Brandon wouldn't have heard a word. He would just freak out when Tristan walked right in the door. Understandably.

"Hey, Brandon." He let the screen door close behind him and looked over at his brother-in-law sitting on the couch with Ethan. For the first time, he felt a twist of jealousy.

Everything with Megan had happened too fast. He'd been smacked hard with feelings he hadn't had before and didn't know how to handle. He'd gone under, that was for sure. He knew he shouldn't grieve a relationship that had lasted only a few weeks—if he counted from when he was blindsided the first night she'd showed up in the store—but he did.

"Hi, Tristan." Brandon's friendly greeting was overrun by Ethan's squeals.

"Uncle Tristan!" He jumped up from his father's lap, causing Brandon a jerking readjustment to protect his junk from Ethan's feet.

"Jeez." Brandon wheezed out. "He has those parts. You'd think he'd know by now not to kick me in it."

Tristan laughed for the first time in several days as he scooped up his rambunctious nephew.

He was still laughing when Ethan asked, "No Megan? I like Megan."

Well, there went that happy bubble. "I like Megan, too. But Megan doesn't like me well enough to date me."

Ethan put hands of questionable cleanliness on either side of Tristan's face. "I'm sorry."

"Come on in here, Tristan." Delilah called out from around the corner.

He walked into the remastered bungalow kitchen where his sister the professional chef held court. Tristan always wondered why he didn't see visible signs of her witchcraft when it came to her cooking—maybe some dancing steam tendrils or bubbles that popped into sparkles. But no, it just looked normal, though it smelled of magick.

He gave her a one-armed hug and told her what she knew he'd come for. "Ethan is consoling me over Megan dumping me." The laughter of a moment ago had fled, Delilah's look of sadness for him not helping.

"Ethan sure liked her." She ruffled her son's hair with the back of a hand covered in flour. Or something like that, maybe powdered sugar?

Ethan looked back and forth between them, clearly making some kind of four-year-old decision, before blurting out, "Miss Megan can hear me!"

Delilah frowned at him, looking away from where she was breading chicken breasts. "She hears you?"

"Yeah, Mom. She can hear what I'm thinking." He grinned as the adults frowned.

"What are you—" Delilah was starting as Tristan spoke, too.

"You know that?"

"You know what?" Delilah was looking at both of them oddly now.

Tristan sucked it up and told his sister, not that it mattered now. "Megan's a telepath."

Tristan wasn't paying attention to Ethan as the boy patted him on the shoulder. His focus was on his sister's raised eyebrows and surprised gurgle. "Like hears all your thoughts?"

"Sees what I imagine, senses what I feel. You name it." He shrugged, because what did it matter anymore what Megan can do?

"Wow." Delilah absorbed it, but she didn't have long as Ethan piped up.

"Like me!"

"Like you, baby?" She asked, now ignoring dinner on the counter behind her.

"Yes. Megan said I'm like her. Because I hear you." He looked back and forth between them as both their mouths dropped open.

CHAPTER 21

Megan took a deep breath before she grasped the door handle and tugged open the heavy door. No magical bell greeted her, only fear that she'd miscalculated.

Entering Blessed Be was an exercise in creating her own Zen. Was Tristan here? Would he be mad at her?

The morning she'd woken up in his arms, she'd agreed to call him that night. He made her eggs in her own kitchen, kissed her goodbye, reminded her to call, and left the ball firmly in her court.

She'd done nothing with it, chickening out each time she picked up the phone.

He was right, she knew it. He'd asked her out. Pursued her. It was high time she made a move, showed him that she was really in it. Megan was crazy about Tristan, which just seemed all the more reason not to continue. Not to let things get to the point where she hated him. Or worse, to where he hated her and she was heartbroken.

Other people got heartbroken, too. She'd had a friend in high school get dumped. Hard. But "I don't want to see you anymore" just didn't offer up the same damage as being subjected to your boyfriend's fantasies about another woman. It was only worse when the man in question didn't want another woman, he wanted all other women. Anyone but her. Megan wasn't ready to let Tristan get to there. It was easier to make a clean break now.

So she stepped inside and looked around, hoping she'd run into Yasmin and not Tristan.

Megan heard Yasmin's voice from the other side of the shelves and breathed a sigh of relief. Even if Tristan was here, at least it wasn't just him.

He'd texted her the day before, even though she was the one who was supposed to reach out. The message had been simple. "You were right. It won't work out. Even if that's just because you won't allow it to."

She took turns berating her cowardice and telling herself that he was right, then reminding herself that he'd never been in it before and she had. He didn't know what it was like to crash and burn with a telepath.

A blond woman came around the corner and greeted her, "I'm Allison, just let me know if you need anything."

"Actually, I was hoping to talk to Yasmin?" Megan offered.

"I'll let her know."

Apparently, it wasn't an uncommon request and Allison went off to find her boss. It took about five minutes of wandering the aisles before Megan was greeted with a smile and a hug, both of which she was pretty certain she didn't deserve.

She heard Yasmin's thoughts flash to Tristan. "So, you know and you're still hugging me?"

Yasmin didn't remove her arm from around Megan's shoulders. The other woman treated her like an old friend, not as a freak, and without any guile or attempts to hide her thoughts. "Look, that's between you and Tristan. If I thought you were hurting him, I'd say so."

"He's pretty hurt. He doesn't understand."

"Maybe he does, maybe he doesn't." Yasmin shrugged. "It's not for me to judge. But I've seen him go through women like water. It isn't hard for me to watch him suffer a little." Her eyebrows winged up in a moment of friendly conspiracy.

"Thank you." Now Megan felt guilty that she'd come to ask for a favor. Then again, the favor was for Tristan. Well, and herself.

"What can I do for you?" As if Yasmin was psychic herself, she lifted some of the pressure off.

"So, just as you and Tristan predicted, I screwed up the *quell*." She shrugged.

"Not uncommon. You need tips? Help?"

"You offered to do it for me at one point. Is that still an option?" Megan held her breath.

Yasmin's thoughts darted to Tristan, to the fact that he was stronger at it, better than her.

Megan held out her hand, stopping the other woman. "I can't. I can't handle having him do it. Just you." She took a breath, then tacked on, "You can say no if you want to. It's okay."

"No, I'm not refusing. I just want you to get the best spell." Yasmin was thinking.

"The best one is one without your boss." Megan qualified and was happy when Yasmin understood.

The Middle Eastern beauty wandered through the store, gathering supplies and mentally making note of what she'd taken. Megan interrupted her thoughts.

"Please let me pay for what you use."

"Nope. You saved that little boy's life and probably his father's, too." Yasmin plucked another herb bundle from one of the baskets lining the shelves.

"Sure, that's possible, but no one's paying you for that. I avoid situations where I might see things or get impressions like that. So I don't mind the few times something good comes from it."

"Come into the back room." Yasmin turned the front of the store over to Allison and headed through the hallway.

Megan had been back here when she'd come back to Tristan's office that one night, but she was pretty sure that wasn't where they were headed now. Yasmin passed Tristan's open door and Megan followed, glad Tristan wasn't here until she heard him.

Megan?

He'd been at work on something and just thought he'd caught a glimpse of her through the doorway as she passed. He was convinced it was just his imagination, apparently he'd been seeing her in places she hadn't really been all week.

Should she fix it? Tell him he was right?

Later, she told herself. After the *quell*. Maybe it would work. Surely Yasmin had to be better at this than she was.

The other woman opened a door to a back room that had an old hard wood floor with a pretty grey pentagram painted on it. Salt lined the outside circle. Megan recognized the salt and the dishes in the middle and the candles at the walls from the starter kit Yasmin had given her. These were clearly much better pieces than her kit had, and she wondered if the quality of the parts made the spell work better.

"This is our beginner classroom. None of us keeps our personal altar pieces here, but it will more than suffice for a *quell*." Yasmin ushered her inside and turned to flip the sign on the door. "I know, witches should be able to sense when a spell is happening. The sign is for the beginners. They muck up all kinds of things, but don't tell Tristan I ever admitted that."

As if she would. Megan just hoped she had a chance to tell Tristan things in the future. She hoped this worked.

Yasmin sat in the middle of the circle and pulled up a wide, iron dish before she closed the salt ring. After handing Megan a bouquet of pretty and clean-smelling herbs, she lit them on fire, startling Megan. "I keep holding it?"

"Yes."

"It's on fire." Megan protested, holding the herbs away from herself. The spell had called for this but, certain she'd read it wrong, Megan had put them in a vase before lighting them. No wonder it hadn't worked.

"It's fine. It won't burn you. Hold it close." Yasmin gently grasped her hand and moved the smoldering plants closer. "You need to breathe in the smoke just a little."

Okay, another thing Megan had fudged. At least it might actually work this time.

Without leaving the circle, Yasmin turned to each of the candles, softly incanting something Megan didn't understand as each wick burst into flame. That hadn't happened at Megan's rudimentary attempt either. She wanted to ask questions, to oooh and ahhh, but she wanted the spell to work, too. It seemed wise not to interrupt.

Fifteen minutes later, they were well into the spell. Yasmin meditated next to her, directed her without words to hold the bouquet away from her, to blow it out, to wrap it in a thin, white linen and bind that with a deep blue ribbon. She tied the knot and placed the small bundle into a wide cast iron bowl in the center of the circle.

Yasmin wiped her palms together and then held them over the bundle. At first it smoked, then burst into flames from several small points. Slowly it burned as the two watched it.

Yasmin! Tristan was beyond the door, frustrated that she'd closed herself in there during open hours.

Unable to stop herself, Megan looked up at the door. He didn't want to come in and break the spell, but he was upset. She didn't want to speak and ruin the hard work.

"Tristan?" Yasmin asked her.

Megan nodded and before she could offer anything, Yasmin hollered out.

"You can come in. We're done." She smiled at Megan. "It's

okay. The spell will work. We just have to let this finish burning, but that doesn't require quiet or focus."

The door opened before Megan could say anything. Tristan stood there, ready to tell Yasmin how irritated he was but stunned by the sight of Megan in the room.

She didn't know what to say.

Tristan did. "This is my store. You're not welcome."

It was juvenile, he knew it even as he said it, but Megan heard loud and clear that he wasn't going to take it back. For a moment, she leaned back on her heels, her gaze directed to the final bits of plant burning in the iron bowl before her, rather than to the man in the doorway who hated her.

She could hear him, loud and clear, all the way from the doorway. He wanted her to go. She'd hurt him deeply and he was rightfully angry with her.

Deciding she didn't have much to lose, she finally looked up and spoke. "I came here tonight to try to patch things. I'd love to date you. So I asked Yasmin to work the *quell*. Mine didn't work."

He just stared at her, his anger not changing despite the fact that, outwardly, his expression did. "So you can't date me until you can't hear me anymore?"

She shrugged. It was harder to have this conversation than she'd thought. "Until I can't hear anyone. Until we can be like a normal couple."

It was what she wanted. When she'd screwed up the *quell* the first time, she'd thought maybe it was better not to know than to try and fail. If she didn't know, she could live with the new hope the *quell* offered. But then she'd decided to try, to see if she could make it work with Tristan.

He stood in the doorway, staring at her. Still angry.

Megan looked up at Yasmin, who was politely watching the pot and trying to stay out of a conversation that had gotten far too private for guests. She leaned over. "Can I go?"

"You should stay until it burns out. Until the last spark fades." She put a conciliatory hand on Megan's arm, clearly aware that her friend was ready to leave.

Megan looked down at the floor, wishing she could sink into it. "Does it take time to work?"

"No," Yasmin shook her head. "You're in the circle, you held it. I didn't just cast it on you. I helped *you* cast it on you."

Megan looked away. "Then I should go. It didn't work."

Yasmin stared at her. "Yes, it did."

Megan looked up at Tristan, seeing his heavy breathing, feeling his irritation wash over her, he didn't want her here. He didn't want to date normal Megan. She heard it all. "No, it didn't."

Yasmin stared hard. "Yes, it did. I've been singing Bee Gees songs in my head since I felt the spell start to settle."

"What?" Megan looked up at her. She barely noticed that Tristan did, too.

"You haven't told me to shut up." Yasmin smiled. "And, let me tell you, it's obnoxious."

Megan turned to face the man in the doorway. He was handsome, strong, crazy, and wonderful. And very angry with her. That came through loud and clear.

I wanted you the way you were.

Looking again at Yasmin, Megan shook her head. "I can't hear you. Not a single Bee Gees song. But I can still hear Tristan."

CHAPTER 22

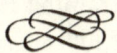

Megan made the mistake of looking at Tristan as she said she could still hear him. He was just as startled as she was. Luckily, Yasmin still had her head in the game.

Using the hand still on Megan's arm, Yasmin tugged her back toward the center of the circle. "You need to wait it out. At least it mostly worked."

That was a good point. Not hearing Tristan had been the reason for the spell in the first place, but not dealing with the usual detritus of daily thoughts around her was a definite bonus. She sat back, sorry for intruding on Tristan's time and in his store, but grateful for what Yasmin seemed to have managed to make happen.

As she looked at her friend to say 'thank you,' she found Yasmin staring at her. Hard.

"What?"

"I'm doing 'Itsy Bitsy Spider.'" She frowned as though she could force her thoughts out and at Megan rather than understanding that it didn't matter if she tried harder, Megan would hear them anyway.

Except she didn't.

"Nothing." She shook her head in wonder. Megan couldn't remember a time in her life when she didn't hear everything.

"It's the Carly Simon version." Yasmin was still staring at her.

Megan laughed, enjoying the moment and trying to ignore than Tristan was pissed. Pissed that she was here, pissed that she hadn't called, pissed that he was struck by the way she laughed. Still, she had a lifetime of training in ignoring what she heard. Making sure no one could tell what she was hearing. "What's with the seventies soundtrack?"

"Wanted to be sure you were really hearing me. Or not." Yasmin sat back as the last of the small orange dots of fire in the ashes smoldered and winked out. "I'll stop now. Apparently, I'm just annoying myself."

Megan laughed again, noticing that Tristan hadn't budged from the doorway. She wouldn't be able to get out without brushing by him.

"It's done." He said it at the same time Yasmin did. Only his tone was different, harsher, less celebratory.

For a moment, no one moved.

Then Tristan looked at Megan, but he spoke to Yasmin. "The store is closing. You should go take care of the front."

Yasmin pretty much ignored him and turned to her friend. "Hey, I want to know that you're okay before I head out." The she leaned in closer. "Okay here with Tristan."

Megan waited to hear whether Yasmin actually thought Tristan might do something to her or that she was just concerned about the conversation, but it didn't come. She took a deep breath, realizing that for the most part the room had gone silent. "I'm good."

With a nod followed by a wide smile, Yasmin stood and left the room, missing Megan's return smile. Megan stood, finally, facing Tristan. "Is there anything I need to clean up from this?"

There was an iron bowl, now with a greasy layer of hot ash, that Yasmin had pulled into the center of the pentagram for her spell. She probably couldn't touch it, let alone move it yet, but she didn't want to leave the store hanging. They wouldn't even let her pay for the herbs and linen and things they used for her.

"No." Just the one word.

It didn't matter, he was still coming through loud and clear, even though he wasn't saying anything in his head.

Understanding he wasn't going to give any ground, she pushed by him into the hallway. "I'll just be going then."

She managed to pick up her purse before she felt his hand on her arm, holding her back. "Don't go."

She didn't know what to say. He clearly didn't want her here. "Why?"

Keeping his hand on her arm, he asked another question. "So you were planning on . . . what? Calling me? If this worked out?"

She nodded. "Calling, apologizing, saying maybe it could work."

"But it can't, because it didn't work. Not entirely." His eyes were like lasers, burning into her. Nothing she could do about it.

"That's right." This time, she tugged against him, trying to see if he had enough, if he'd finally let go. She could break his hold if she wanted, but she wasn't ready to send that message. Even just this, even though he was angry, his touch felt good.

There was a pause. A moment when they simply looked at each other, his irritation, his hurt, fuzzing up the air around them.

Finally, he broke. "What have I done? I don't get it."

"It's not you—"

"Oh, don't even." He shook his head, dismissing her platitude. "What have I *thought*? What impression have I given you, that there's anything to make you think I'm not a good bet?"

But it wasn't him. It was what she knew. Glancing to the front of the store, Megan caught the voices of people talking after close. While she wanted Tristan to understand, she wasn't willing to gut herself here in the back of the store. She wasn't ready for Yasmin to hear. "Not here."

Megan wanted him to come around. She wanted him to agree that this was the right decision. It would hurt her, she knew. It felt good that he still wanted her, but Megan understood she needed to get him to stop.

"Come on." He slid his hand down her arm, grasping again when he got to her wrist.

She should have fought it, but he twisted his hand and laced his fingers through hers. He tugged her out the back door without telling anyone that he was heading out. Without letting go, he slid her into the passenger seat in his car and closed the door. He was backing out of the parking spot before she fully comprehended what she'd gotten herself into. Or allowed herself to be gotten into.

He turned down Hollywood Boulevard, heading into the lights and businesses that were just getting rolling even as his closed shop. Three different times he suggested a place they might go in and talk. Three different times she turned him down.

Each of the places was a bar, or a restaurant. She didn't want to yell her story over a beer and noise, and she didn't want to be where others could overhear it. It wasn't that kind of thing to share. They were turning up toward the canyons, into the Hollywood Hills before she realized where he was heading. He'd had enough of her saying 'no,' he was taking her to his house.

Not where she wanted to go.

He would have to drive her back to the shop, or she'd have to call for a ride, or . . . too late. They were already up beyond Franklin Avenue. Megan thought about protesting, but realized he'd probably gladly drive her home when she was done telling him the truth.

It all seemed too normal when he pulled into the narrow

drive that aimed sharply up, then leveled out with just enough space for one car. He led her in through the side door and to the kitchen, where he politely offered her a drink and she declined.

She should have told him she was making stupid decisions because on some level she was stupidly holding onto some tiny sliver of hope. Her brain didn't believe he'd be around when he knew the details. Still her heart wanted him to be. Actually, all of her wanted him to be. So at war with herself, she was doing dumb things like getting into his car and telling him her whole story. What was the point?

"I shouldn't do this." She somehow found the real words. Words to stop the charade. Even if she still wanted him. Even if part of stopping it was about never having to hear him tell her he'd had enough.

It was almost easier when she just didn't hear from him, then some sliver of her could believe it would work out.

"No. You said you'd tell me. So tell me."

"Tristan, I—"

"I drove you here. I found a place where no one can overhear." He was frustrated with her, and wasn't he always? But she could still hear him. Almost worse than her, he still held out some hope. But he was blissfully ignorant of her life. "Look. I know you don't owe me anything. But maybe you could stop showing up at my store and telling me you're going to explain if you aren't. If you really don't give a shit about me, stop looking at me like that!"

"You're right. I'm completely sending mixed signals. I'm sorry." She still didn't make a move to leave. In some part of the back of her head, she harbored a fantasy about him telling her it would all be okay. She didn't know what that would be like, what he could possibly say that would make things all right, because they weren't. They never had been.

"I grew up in a small town." She started and he waited, didn't look at her like she was dumb or off her freaking rocker, didn't even think it. She took a breath and continued. "I knew everyone, and everyone knew me."

Tristan just nodded. He'd opened a beer for himself, and she wondered if he was trying to not have to drive her home or if he just needed something to do with his hands, but he didn't say anything.

Megan took breath and continued.

"I heard everything. All the fights in marriages. All the people who stole from the gas station. All the kids thinking of suicide. All the people who'd seen the movie before, spoiling the ending. All the kids at school, thinking each other was cute, or fat, or dumb. All the teachers thinking the same thing."

"Jesus." He took a deep breath, then a drink of the beer as though it would help him swallow what she was dishing up.

"I loved being in the woods, because I was usually alone. I love the beach, because people are mostly happy." She tried to put something positive on it.

"That's why you don't want to go to the movies."

She nodded. "People think awful things. Even in the movies. Guys trying to figure out how to get in some girl's pants. One girl was pregnant and trying to figure out how to pin it on her boyfriend. She was in high school."

"That's what you listen to in the movies?" His expression turned sad.

She didn't want his pity, but there wasn't much she could do about it. "It was her father's baby."

"Good Goddess." This time he tipped the beer up and drained it. She waited him out. "What did you do?"

"What *could* I do? I was in the movies! I wasn't supposed to know that. She never told anyone. What could I possibly say? 'I overheard your worries in the movie and' . . . and what? What could I do?" Megan remembered the hurt, the worries she had for herself, could she help?

"Megan," he set the now empty bottle down. "Did you tell your parents?"

As if she could. "No. My father is the town's minister. Small town, his church is the biggest. That girl went to our church, but I couldn't tell my father."

His heart clenched for her. She could feel it in her own chest. She didn't want that. She was here now. This was L.A. not Hansen, Georgia. She wanted to forget it. Though she lived a life shut away from people, people were sometimes good. Tristan was good. Yasmin was good. Hers was still a solitary life. Not one to share. She played a harsh card. "I was nine."

CHAPTER 23

T ristan swallowed hard. He couldn't hide the revulsion her words caused.

Megan couldn't hide that she felt it.

"I knew you'd feel this way about me if I told you." She stepped back, away from his reaction.

"Feel how?" He felt his face frown. She had to know she'd legitimately confused him.

"You're horrified." She waved a hand for emphasis.

"Yes, for what you went through. Not at you." He frowned at her. Then he had an idea. A disturbing one. "What am I feeling right now?"

Angry herself, she turned away, biting off her words. "Don't test me."

"What am I feeling right now?"

She whipped back around, almost yelling. "Do you doubt me? Doubt what I can do? All I wanted was to live without it!"

"What am I feeling right now?" Tristan tried to stay calm, tried to focus his feelings at her. He was curious. Concerned. Clearly crazy.

"You're angry." She was, too. He didn't need to be psychic to feel it coming off her in waves.

"Why?" He pressed.

"Jesus, Tristan. You're mad at me. Mad at me for not being more cooperative. For not helping that girl. I know she killed herself. They buried her and no one knew she was pregnant. No one knew what her father did. I'm angry at me, too! But I can't tell people what I know!"

He took a deep breath, trying to hold back feelings that couldn't be held back. His chain of reasoning was thrown off that Megan had not only borne the knowledge that the girl was being abused by her father, but that she'd killed herself without telling anyone. Pushing that awful thought aside, Tristan refocused on the matter at hand. Neither of them could save that girl, but he still held out hope of saving the two of them.

"That's not why I'm angry."

She'd been irritated, frustrated, mad. But with those words she changed. Megan was now just confused.

"You know *what* I feel, but you don't seem to know *why* I feel it. It's just a guess isn't it?"

"Of course not." She frowned at him, her brows more furrowed than he thought possible. "I've always had this."

"I was angry that no one helped you." He said, watching her expression get even more confused.

"What?"

Another deep breath of many tonight. He figured many more were coming. "I'm angry because no one helped you. I'm angry that you were nine and you heard such things and had no one to talk to, no way to let go of what you were getting."

She stilled.

Tristan let her stand, absorbing his idea for a moment. He was just about to speak when she opened her mouth.

"You think I've been misinterpreting it all along?"

"No. I think you're probably mostly right." This time he

turned away, wishing for a pen to fiddle with, something to do with his hands. "I think when you hear what other people think, you probably mostly interpret the reasons behind it pretty well. But I'm guessing you miss sometimes, too."

Her mouth opened. Closed. Opened. Closed again. "I always believed I had everything. The thoughts, the feelings, I see pictures from people's heads. Why wouldn't I have the reasons?"

He couldn't fight the grin that spread on his face. "Because, for all your talents, that isn't one of them."

"I wouldn't call it a talent." She was at least wry, not angry anymore. "It's really more of a curse."

"It doesn't have to be."

"But it is. It's just the way it is for me." Once again she turned away.

How many times would she turn away? How many times could he turn her back before he gave up?

He didn't know, but he wasn't ready to quit yet. "Why? I'm still here. I still want . . . us." He didn't know how else to say it. He'd never had to fight for a woman like this, and he truly wasn't sure why he wouldn't just let her go. But he wouldn't. He knew that much.

"I don't trust it. This doesn't change anything. It still always ends the same."

"Maybe it doesn't!" He fought back. "Maybe you've been ducking out because someone was angry but not at you. Maybe you've been leaving rather than asking. Maybe you were wrong."

"Sure." She shot back. "Maybe when I shook that woman's hand and she was thinking about fucking my boyfriend it was an old image. Except he'd been wearing the shirt I bought him. Sure, I was wrong." She only paused to take a breath. "When my teachers thought I was so stupid, I was wrong. Or when the chem teacher held my grades hostage so I wouldn't tell that he was sleeping with the principal's husband . . . I'm sure I was wrong."

"Wait. How did they know?"

"I told you, *everyone* knew." She was exasperated. It was late, she'd done spellwork, she was probably exhausted. But she was in his house and he wasn't moving until she asked to leave.

"How?"

"Because I lived there all my life. Because almost everyone went to our church." She looked away. "Because my father never hesitated to tell anyone."

Stunned again, Tristan came to a dead stop. He hadn't realized he'd been pacing until he jolted to a halt. He searched for a reason her father wasn't being a complete asshole. "He didn't understand how much it hurt you?"

"He understood."

"*I* don't understand." Tristan had been raised with love, support, and the comfort of knowing someone understood him. "He could have helped that girl. You could have told him."

"No. You have it all wrong. He could have helped her, would have, if she had gone to him. If *I* told him, then he couldn't help her."

"That doesn't make any sense, Megan." He couldn't wrap his brain around it. How did a parent do that?

This time, she gave out. She headed to his couch and stood in front of it. After half a second, it appeared her knees just cracked and she plopped down, as though she had no other choice. Her head rested in her hands.

Tristan wanted to help, but sensed he couldn't. That even an arm around her shoulders would be more burden than relief.

Her voice, when it came, was low but steady. "You know that bible passage—thou shalt not suffer a witch to live? He thought I was a witch. He thought my 'gifts,' as you choose to call them, came from Satan."

Tristan's heart clenched involuntarily, and he wished with

everything he had that he could hide it from her. But he stayed silent.

"When I was little, he tried exorcisms. Even brought in Catholic priests. Clearly, it didn't work. I thought those were hard, but I thought I was bad, that Satan was in me, and I had to get him out.

"So I happily endured candle wax burns, starvation, being tied to the bed, and more."

He couldn't breathe. It was outright child abuse.

"Yes, it *was* child abuse. But why would I report it? I thought he loved me. I thought it was necessary. Obviously, it didn't work." A pause, a breath. Tristan was afraid it would get worse. It did.

"Then he tried to beat it out of me. Fists, belts, switches. You name it. If I mistakenly blurted something I knew, I was slapped so hard my ears rang. So I hid it. Then I was beaten for lying." She wasn't crying, but Tristan didn't know how.

He felt that sharp pressure behind his eyeballs. How had such an amazing woman come out of that?

"It was my fault they didn't have more children. It was the Satan in me that wouldn't let them have more kids. So he hated me for that. He was the minister. He was supposed to be godly, but look what he had for a daughter."

"You have to know that's not right, Megan." Tristan countered. But he understood. Even if you knew it, what you'd felt, believed, for so long left an indelible mark. Megan clearly had one.

"Sure, it's not right. But back then I believed it along with him."

"Where was your mother?" He was almost afraid to find out.

"Right there beside him. She didn't believe as strongly as he did. She didn't think it was Satan. She didn't hate me. But I hated her, because she didn't stop him."

Yeah, not the answer he'd hoped.

"They sent me to my aunt's when I was fourteen. I lived there for a year and a half. Best time of my life. She trained me to stay quiet because people don't understand. Helped me live with it. My mom got pregnant and delivered my baby sister. But then my aunt got sick—cancer—and I had to go home. It was harder after having been somewhere good."

Tristan didn't agree. She'd been accepted, but that wasn't the same as having her gifts embraced. Megan didn't comment on his thoughts. Maybe she was just ignoring him.

"I kept to myself and kept my head down. But my father didn't want me back. When I came back, he didn't try at all to save me. He just hated me."

"Is that too strong? He was your father. Did he really *hate* you?" He had to ask. Maybe things weren't as bad with her father as she thought. Maybe this was something she'd misinterpreted.

She looked up at him, looked him straight in the eye, and said, "No. He wanted me dead. He wished I was never born. That I would die. He would look right at me and think these things, knowing I could hear him."

That she didn't blink, didn't cry, didn't even have a reaction to saying those things told Tristan just how much she accepted it.

"I went away to college. Did okay, except for the boyfriend who tested me. The one who slept around and managed to hide it from me. It was a game to him. But then the economy went bad, the church didn't support my father. I went home after I graduated and got a job. Helped with my mother and my sisters." She sighed. "It was another battle. *My* money was from Satan. I couldn't even pay rent to help out. My mother and I lied. We told him her side work was bringing in more business than it was."

Tristan sensed a change in the story. "Did you stay there until you moved here a few months ago?"

She nodded. "He threw me out. Apparently I was responsible for the storm that went through. Not random weather, not global warming. Just me. He's protecting his town."

"At the cost of his daughter?"

"It's not a cost to him." She acknowledged, once again without any emotion.

"I'm glad you're here." He finally sat, next to her but just far enough away that he didn't touch her. He managed the words in a heartfelt whisper. He hurt for her. He ached. For all the teasing he'd taken in high school for being a witch, for taking the Solstice off from school for religious reasons, for his younger sister who couldn't keep her magic in her own hands, he'd never endured what Megan had. "I'm sorry he was such a horrible person."

Megan looked up at him. "He's not horrible."

Stunned, Tristan met her gaze. "How can you say that?"

"He saves people. Not just as a Christian. He finds them jobs. He's literally given the shirt off his back."

Tristan stared.

Megan continued. "He's a black man married to a white woman in the deep south. He makes sure the entire town doesn't have race issues. Hansen is the most integrated place I've ever seen, more even than here, because of him. He won't let anyone speak out against homosexuality. He began performing marriages for gay couples long before anyone else. He preaches acceptance. He visits the hospital when people are sick. He makes sure their families have food. He counsels people on drugs and in trouble. He gets them help and makes sure they never do it again, and he hugs them and tells them he forgives them." Her voice was slowly rising. "I saw him sit with a man who killed his own child in a fit of rage. He made sure the father got out of prison to attend the funeral and then he visited the man in jail every week of his sentence. He knows that's not okay, but he finds forgiveness.

"My father isn't a bad man. He's one of the best men I've ever met. He preaches love and he practices what he preaches. I hear his thoughts. He doesn't even think bad things about other people.

"The only person, he can't love . . . is me."

CHAPTER 24

Megan woke up slowly. She was warm, safe, and comfortable. It took her a few moments to come fully around, and to recognize that she wasn't at home. She wasn't even in a bed.

She was on Tristan's couch, though that didn't really describe everything. She was mostly lying *on* Tristan.

He was sprawled in the corner, Megan curled into his lap, his arms wrapped tight enough around her that she couldn't escape. As she lay there, thinking about it a little more, she decided she didn't want to.

She prided herself on being a smart girl. She was hopefully self-aware. Though according to Tristan last night, she hadn't ever picked up that she didn't understand the "why" behind a lot of the emotions. Relaxing a little into the sleeping man under her, she pondered that.

She'd left more than one relationship at the hint of problems. She'd been around often enough to know she hated when things ended, but had she cut bait too early? Maybe she had, but she was here with Tristan now. Despite hearing everything she'd spilled out, despite the fact that she could still hear him, he still wanted her.

If, or when, things went wrong, it would rip her heart out. But the last week without him had been so terrible it was obvious to her there was no surviving Tristan. The best she could do was throw herself in and hope it went well. Worst case, she could enjoy what she had and postpone the inevitable.

His arms tightened around her, even though he was fully asleep.

He'd made no moves on her last night, just quietly shifted into the corner of the couch and waited for her to cry. She didn't. She'd shed far too many tears for her father over the years. And far too many from him. Megan was done.

She might have cried for the loss of her mother and sisters, but that loss was still too fresh. She wasn't sure though that Tristan didn't shed a few on her behalf, but he didn't hate her. He didn't think her father was right. And he said he was angry for what she went through. That no one tried to help her or even gave her so much as a therapist to talk to.

Here then was what she wanted. What she'd always wanted. Someone who understood her and still wanted to be with her. Someone who didn't care that she could hear whatever his brain broadcast. She didn't want someone who thought it was a cool trick, who liked the skill more than he liked her, and Tristan was none of those. He just wanted her.

Again he shifted. He'd be awake soon and Megan decided if she was going to throw herself into it, she was going to throw herself in. She rolled, turning a little, not enough to loosen his grip, but enough to get a little closer.

He moaned in his sleep, his fingers twitching against her hip as she curled into him. His fingers twitched again and she realized her skirt had shifted, his hand was under the fabric. Had he done it on purpose? She didn't really care.

Sliding her arms up around his neck, she turned her face

into his shirt collar and began placing tiny kisses along the muscle there. She slid her fingers into his hair, ever so slightly tilting his sleepy head for her mouth to trace up to the soft, sensual spot under his ear.

This time, when his fingers twitched, it was more of a grab. He clasped her hip and didn't let go. Waking up? A soft, low moan escaped his throat and his head tipped farther on its own. Megan took advantage.

He didn't want her fulfilling his fantasies. Well, he was asleep, this was all on her.

When his head rolled back along the couch, she knew he was awake, even if he hadn't managed to get his eyes open. Pulling her hands from out of his hair, she dragged her palms down his chest, across his abs, enjoying the ridges of muscle clear even under his t-shirt. Down farther, she hit the soft denim of the jeans he liked. It was an awkward position given how she was laying somewhat sideways on him. Using her hands against his hips as a brace, she moved one leg to straddle him.

By the time she moved her hips against his, Tristan's eyes were open and he was watching her. Watching her enjoy the feel of pressure through only the thin layer of the lace underwear he was clenching the sides of.

But his head was shaking back and forth, even though he hadn't said a word, he was saying 'no.' Again.

Sitting back, still on his lap, Megan looked at him. What did he want from her? And why couldn't she tell?

"Like this?" He grinned, lifting her a little, shifting, laying her down on the couch and somehow staying trapped between her legs.

She nodded, hooking her ankles behind his butt, holding on, surprised by her fear that he didn't want her. When he kissed her, it dissolved away in a flood of her own feelings and his. Shirts peeled away. Fingers fumbled with zippers and buttons, his hands tracing down her legs all the way to her feet as he slid her skirt to the floor. When he stood, he had enough forethought to dig in his wallet for a condom before he locked eyes with her and shed his own jeans while she watched.

He stayed there, for just a moment, fully naked before her. Whether he was offering her the chance to say no or just to look her fill she didn't know. But she did understand that she would never have enough of looking at him.

He came back down onto the couch, carefully laying on top of her. She felt her breath escape in a soft sigh as they touched, skin to skin. When he pressed inside her, she pushed herself against him.

It was different, now that she'd decided. She'd given up trying to protect her heart. She'd found a way to trust in his feelings for her. Despite minor moments, like when he'd said 'no,' she was throwing herself into this.

Tristan didn't think it outright, but he sensed the change in her. She felt it. Felt it in the way he moved in her. Saw it in the way he stared into her eyes. She tried to make sure he felt it from her, too. Without thinking about it, she held onto his face, keeping him close. She pushed against him as the sensations inside her built, as her breath escaped faster and faster. His own breathing laced with heavy emotion.

"Megan." He sighed her name into her ear, turning her on more with the heat of the word and the heat of his need. "Megan."

This time she arched her back, driving against him in pure need as she came. Hard.

"Megan!" he yelled it, his own back arching, his hips still moving until the last moment, when he collapsed against her. His orgasm flooded her just as she was dropping back against the cushions, hot and exhausted beneath him.

They lay like that, tangled together, breathing heavily, relaxing into each other for a few minutes. Neither spoke a word, but neither needed to.

At last, Tristan shifted, relieving his weight off her and she took the opportunity to free herself.

"Where are you going?" He rolled off, still sleepy. Letting her go, he still trailed a hand along her arm as she stood.

"Restroom." She replied, which wasn't a lie, but she was regrouping. It was devastating being with him like that. She was so used to performing during sex, to taking her cues from what a man wanted. It was easier. When she did that, she knew she'd made him happy. She didn't neglect herself, she'd tell a man what she needed, but the idea that Tristan almost banned her from doing anything other than reacting was something unfamiliar. Dangerous.

When she emerged, she deliberately—but not quickly— gathered her clothes and put them back on.

Tristan, still languishing naked on his own couch, looked at her, wary. "I asked you to take the day off work last time, but you didn't. Is this going to be the same?"

His tone had changed while he was talking. He'd gone from sated to concerned. "Are you leaving again?"

Dressed, but without her shoes, she sat on the edge of the couch, prompting him to sit up, too. He left enough space that he didn't touch her though.

She took a deep breath, getting ready. "That's up to you."

"Really?" He didn't believe her. Megan understood.

"I can leave, walk out the door, no hard feelings—"

"No you can't. I'd have hard feelings if you did that." He interrupted. "Just like last time."

"—or we can be boyfriend/girlfriend. If that's even the right term for it." She shook her head. It hadn't sounded so silly when she thought it through. Maybe he wanted to be together but didn't want to define it.

"So we'd be exclusive? I could depend on you to return my messages? Call? Initiate some things?"

That was more than she'd expected. But everything she wanted. "Yes."

"The second one." No hesitation in his answer. None in his thoughts. "I told you, I haven't looked sideways at another woman since I first met you. You're only offering me what I already wanted. So, the second one. I can introduce you as my girlfriend? Stop telling my sister that I don't know what we are?"

Megan nodded.

Finally, he moved. His hand held her cheek, turning her face to him. He kissed her, soft, deep, undemanding. Megan kissed him back.

When at last they pulled apart, she didn't know how long it had been, but she felt better. More settled. She grinned and made an offer. "Want to take the day off work?"

She'd already sent a message saying she needed a personal day. She would have needed it if he'd said, "No hard feelings."

His grin lit up the living room. "Yes. What do you want to do?"

"Get dressed."

"Really?" He stood then, happiness radiating.

So she smacked his bare ass, "Yes. I want to go out to breakfast and if that works, I want to go see a movie!"

"What? You don't like those things—"

She watched as it dawned on him. She wanted to test the *quell*. Clearly she could still hear him, but she hadn't been able to hear Yasmin last night. She wanted to check it.

"You're still hearing me, right?" He asked, and she understood it was out of sheer curiosity, not any kind of planning on his part. When she nodded, he told her, "Because Delilah and I had a conversation about you and Ethan butted in and said you were like him."

Wow. She hadn't seen that coming. She'd learned by age three to keep her mouth shut in general. Sure, she'd screwed it up, had bad judgment sometimes, kept thinking that if she just said something it would help. It never did. "I guess he feels okay with it."

"He has family that understands. He's not afraid of what he can do." It almost sounded like censure. It almost was. But, not wanting to turn the happiness sour, he turned the conversation. "I'm hoping maybe you can help us out with him. Give Delilah tips on how to best raise him."

"Like I would know." Megan shrugged. "But I'll do what I can."

"Good. Let's go get breakfast."

"You're still naked." She pointed out. But it was a good day. "And we can't see a movie you've already seen. You'll spoil it for me."

"No worries. I haven't seen any of the new releases. I've been waiting for you."

CHAPTER 25

Tristan didn't quite know how he felt about the *quell*. It worked, for the most part. He wasn't really surprised by that. Though Yasmin hadn't been born into the craft, she was a talented witch and she worked hard at her skills. He was as surprised as everyone else that it hadn't worked on him.

Regardless of that, Megan seemed happier.

Tristan both understood it and felt it like a loss. He wasn't normal himself, but his differences had always been celebrated by his family. It felt odd to him that Megan didn't appreciate her uniqueness. He couldn't seem to make her see it, either.

He could tell her over and over that she was a good person. That her parents were wrong. That they'd abused her when she was kid—more than just the beatings and exorcisms. But she seemed to already *know* that. Making her *feel* it was a different ball game.

He wanted Megan to tell Ethan it was okay, and even good, to be the way he was. But, since she'd worked so hard to get rid of what made her her, Tristan wasn't sure what message that would send to his small nephew.

Still, he took her to breakfast and she reveled in the relative quiet of a bustling restaurant. They saw five movies in one week.

She walked backward down the street in front of him. "Oh my God, Tristan. I did *not* see that coming! Did you?"

Her grin lit up everything around her and Tristan smiled back. It was hard to argue with happiness like that. "I'm glad you enjoyed it."

To him it was just a movie.

"Yes, but to me, it was a new experience." She still heard him loud and clear, and he wasn't going to hold back his thoughts now.

"Let's go walk on the beach." He suggested.

Even though she held his hand, she managed a shrug. "I don't need to go."

A frown passed his features, Tristan could feel it. He mocked her, "It's still totally cool to walk along the beach."

"I spent so much time there because it was the only place I could just be. It's a refuge I no longer need." She tugged his hand, turning him across her street rather than down toward the water. "Let's go to my place."

They'd spent the night together three nights out of the past five. The two they'd spent apart were more about making sure they didn't move too fast, though Tristan didn't know if that was possible. He was all in—so he didn't think he could go much faster and he wasn't sure there was actually a way to slow down. It didn't matter what they did, his heart was running at breakneck speed. He couldn't control it, so he didn't try. If things went south, they would crash and burn big time, in a way he'd never experienced before, because somehow he'd made it to his thirties without ever feeling this way.

She pulled him along and he followed easily. She happily rode the elevator, yanking him close for a disturbingly arousing lip lock. Tristan was pretty sure he was being used, and he just didn't care.

Megan shoved him back against the wall of the car. "I'm not using you." Then her mouth quirked. "Maybe I am."

He would have commented but her tongue was in his mouth and somehow her ass was in his hand. He wondered how she'd made that happen when her own fingers were fisted in his shirt. Then he didn't care.

They fumbled the lock to her apartment, tumbled inside, and didn't make it past the pale, somehow tasteful shag carpet that had shown up in her place earlier in the week. She'd bought it in person, she said. She went into a shop and didn't know if the sales person was overcharging her, or thought she couldn't afford it, or just didn't like the color of her skin.

He noticed other changes as well. He noticed her spending had increased, dramatically. His, too. His creativity for their dates had hit an all-time low. He used to be a good date, he thought. He was more on his game with Megan, when they started out. But now she wanted to try every chain restaurant that existed, see every pop culture movie that came out, and hit every tourist stop in L.A. no matter how crowded. And there were a ton of chains and movies and photo ops in Los Angeles.

Still, the new carpet was fluffy and soft beneath his knees, then his back, and they'd used two condoms before they finally fell into her bed and blissful asleep.

He drove home in the morning after cooking her breakfast. Though he left her at her makeshift desk on her porch, working, he was pretty sure she was logging in late each day. He sure was.

It took a while to shower in his own place, change clothes, and drive across town again. There was a moment where he walked in the back door at the shop, when he thought no one had noticed.

"Hey, stumbling in late again?" Yasmin had to be the one opening today.

"I—" He started to defend it, then he realized he'd rushed out the door. Though he'd dressed from his own closet, he still wasn't sure he'd lined up his buttons. "Yeah. Not that late?"

"No, it's fine." She grinned. "I have to admit I've never seen a woman make you late before. I've seen you come in with no sleep, but never late. So this is interesting."

He hadn't thought of it that way, but Yasmin was right. The shop always came first. Before Megan came along. "I'm fine coming in late because I trust you."

"Ha!" She barked as she headed into the front to open the door to the public. He'd barely made it for opening. Many nights he stayed past closing. Not lately. He hadn't even brought Megan in for a beginner's class. She could use it.

It took a while to focus his thoughts back to the matters at hand. Vendors, receipts from online, making sure any returns were handled and credited. But his thoughts drifted. He worried about Megan. It was almost as if she was high. Maybe it was *exactly* like that.

Side effects of spells could be more than just the regular kind, more than upset stomach or wooziness. It could be psychological, too. Sudden release from the kind of burden Megan had carried was maybe more than he should have put on her. Or at least put on her without warning.

Then again, he hadn't put it on her. Yasmin had. Would he have done it? He didn't know.

With a sigh, Tristan realized he'd disappeared into his thoughts again. What would his sister say if the store went under? It was her legacy, too, to a certain extent. What would Yasmin say? On the upside, Yasmin was deep enough into the books that she'd never let him go under. She would save him before she let the business flounder. Especially over a woman.

But not just any woman. Yasmin understood; she'd been through a lot a while ago.

After wondering briefly about a spell that might have a Ritalin-like effect, he forced his thoughts back to the business.

He made his phone calls to vendors, checked his books, and closed them. Just after dark, he headed home. Though he wanted to see Megan, he wanted to get his head on straight.

Still, he called her. They talked. He told her the truth: he needed to show up at work on time tomorrow.

So he lay in bed, thinking about Megan. About making love to Megan. Then he thought a lot about being an idiot who wound up in this stupid bed alone. By morning, he wasn't sure if he'd slept or not. The only evidence he had that he'd actually fallen asleep was that he kept waking up. At least five times by his count.

He was conflicted. He was crazy about her. He was worried about her. He wanted her as she was, and she didn't. In the middle of the night he'd asked himself a few hard questions.

What if this was the way she really was? Maybe the telepathy had been a curse holding her back. Had he fallen for Megan herself, or had he fallen for her magic?

It took most of the day to realize he was in awe of her powers, but *she* was what he really wanted. He showed up beneath her balcony at four pm.

Are you done for today? He just stood there and thought it.

It took less than a minute for her to appear at the railing and smile down. "I'm done now. Come up."

"Nice one." A guy on the street jostled Tristan as he passed and spotted Megan calling down.

Tristan ignored him as he headed to the main door and waited to be buzzed in. He took the stairs. Despite Megan's new love of the elevator, this was what he was used to. She was standing in the doorway, waiting for him.

For the first time, he convinced her to stay in for dinner. It still involved walking down to the corner grocery, which she was more than happy to do now. They cooked, side by side, in her tiny kitchen, laughing the whole while. She chattered happily about a promotion she found out that morning that she'd snagged.

They celebrated with a bottle of mid-priced champagne they picked up for just that reason. A second round was poured before Megan declared that she had ice cream and wanted to serve it with the champagne.

"It's just so decadent. It's sinful." She grinned as she pulled out a scooper and set the carton of rich chocolate on the counter.

"Literally?" He asked with a grin.

"Yeah, I guess so." She looked thoughtful, but not upset at the thought. "My father always believed that extravagance was near to stealing from someone who needed it. We lived poor, and though we didn't deny ourselves some treats, we did refuse anything that might be called a luxury."

She said it without rancor, talking about her father and his restrictions with the ease of distance. Her words didn't hold the undercurrent of fury they'd held the first time they'd talked of her father, nor the deep sadness of the last time.

He enjoyed her enjoyment. "Then let's do this. I think we should eat it in front of the TV."

"Oh, that sounds positively awful. Yes, lets." She cleared the lone TV tray she used for a glass of water or a snack while she worked and they ate the ice cream shoulder to shoulder, watching a comedy on TV.

It felt so domestic, doing dishes, arguing over how to load a dishwasher correctly, rearranging her tray for the next day's work. They walked down the hall, hand in hand, fully clothed. They didn't make into bed without finding each other, and Tristan felt it. Deeper than he was prepared for. More intensely than he thought he could.

Later, when they were naked and still entangled it hit him.

The smell of her soap comforted him. The very sight of her

lifted him. The feel of her weight in his arms was home. He loved her.

He was in love with her.

"What?" Megan rolled over and looked at him, startled.

"I—" he faltered.

"Are you okay? Do you mean it?" She was propped up on her elbow, staring at him, more confused than he was.

"I just thought it. Give me a minute to sort it out." He stared at her.

He was in love with her. He'd once thought he'd run screaming like a scared kid if he ever had these thoughts. Instead, just the idea stabilized his heartbeat, brought the whirlwind around them to a halt.

Unsure how long he simply looked at her, Tristan let everything settle. "You heard me."

She grinned then. Wide and bright, it lit up the dark room. It lit him up, too. Then she made it even better. "I love you, too."

CHAPTER 26

"Ugh," Megan muttered under her breath. The boy standing behind to her in line was thinking about banging the girl behind the counter at the sandwich place.

Yesterday, she lifted some random thought from a sweater she tried on. That had never been the norm for her, but always a possibility. As with everything, the stronger the emotion, the more likely it was to come through to her. So Megan rarely picked up people's grocery lists when she tried on clothing. Nope, she got their dead parents. Their missing kids. The fight with the best friend.

This sweater held the remnants of a bad surprise. The woman had walked in on her husband in bed. As if that hadn't been enough, the girlfriend was the woman's boss, whom she thought was about to promote her. Worse, she wasn't sure if she was more upset about the husband or the job.

Megan's lip had curled as she put the sweater back on the rack and left the store. That sucked. She thought it just came through because the sensation was so strong. Many people believed retail therapy could help what ailed them. But they left behind some serious shit for Megan. While it didn't happen all that often, it was enough of a smack in the face when it did that it was enough to keep her out of stores.

She'd loved that sweater until she tried it on. It was the only one in her size, too. Figured.

Writing it off as an anomaly, she went about her business, but this morning the kid behind the counter at the coffee shop had touched her palm when he handed over her change and it flashed that he was trying to get a better look down her shirt. She'd sighed and stared at him like, "Really?" and he'd seemed to catch on.

Even then, it was such a normal occurrence for her that she hadn't cataloged it. Not until now, when she was bombarded by the sexual noise blaring from the kid behind her. He was a walking hormone. She wanted to tell him to keep it to himself, but the fact was he *was*. It was all her. No one else heard him. He acted respectful. Megan even stayed and watched as he paid for his sandwich. He didn't do anything but smile politely at the girl he'd just pictured under him with her knees around her ears.

It was easier to deal with in fits and spurts like this than at the normal level. But it was easier to deal with it not at all. Or only from Tristan.

She sat in the corner booth by herself. She'd planned on taking the sandwich down to the beach to eat, like she used to. But it seemed more prudent to eat in here and see if she was hearing people again.

Mostly she just heard the sounds of sandwich wrappers, drinks slurping, the chatter of voices people thought she couldn't hear with her ears. She kept her head buried in her magazine, as though she was looking at the latest shoes that were too expensive for any mortal to afford and too weird for any reasonable person to wear.

Nothing came through. Nothing odd, nothing wild, just normal conversation in the sandwich shop. Or at least what Megan assumed was normal conversation in the sandwich shop.

Two men were discussing embezzling funds from their store—but they were using their inside voices. She couldn't tell if it was hypothetical or real, so she wasn't getting anything from them.

When she finished, she didn't know anything more than when she'd sat down—except how to embezzle better—which sucked. She should have gone to the beach. She should have tried to sit and listen to the waves, to be by herself again. She'd been surrounding herself with the strangers that made up the normal population of L.A. this whole week.

Tristan was worried about her. He didn't say anything verbally, but he didn't hide it either. She told herself she appreciated that, but some days it was exhausting.

He was right. She'd been going a little nuts and decided it was time to reign it in. She had some new furniture, new shoes —though not the crazy ones from the magazine—new hobbies, and a new promotion. She needed to make sure she kept it. The promotion had been a surprise and had come on her worst attended week ever. She wasn't bad, but she wasn't her usual employee-of-the-week self either.

She'd never called in sick before when she wasn't at death's door. And she didn't think she'd ever taken a personal day that didn't have to do with rescuing her little sisters from something or getting kicked out of her house in a storm. But she'd taken one to roll around in bed with Tristan, to play tourist in her home town, to try all the things she'd never tried before.

Megan threw away her trash and headed out the door. Though she wanted to be a stellar employee at her company again, she wanted just an extra fifteen minutes at lunch. She wanted to sit on the beach and watch the waves roll in. She didn't have set hours, so it didn't really matter, but she'd always held herself to a higher standard than that.

In Hansen, she worked in the house she hated. In the house that hated her back. She left when she could, but the people in town thought she was evil. Or they were just afraid of her, afraid she would spill their secrets. Being afraid made them hateful. She'd lived with it wherever she went. Except for the months with her aunt, she'd lived with it.

The beach was as soothing as she'd hoped it would be. The sand was barely warm, the average temperature dropping just a little. Megan heard they didn't have real seasons here, just a slightly higher number of slightly cooler days. "Fall" was designated by the months and the store decor rather than any foliage or meteorological changes. Apparently, it was also designated by the sand not being almost-too-warm to the touch.

The sea smelled like salt and algae. She'd been to other beaches; this one definitely had too many people. But it was still a beach. The waves still crashed in, drowning out the other sounds. Closing her eyes, she listened.

It was quiet after a lifetime of cacophony.

It was rhythm after years of discord.

It was the simple act of digging her fingers into the sand and letting herself be.

She breathed deeply, thought quietly about Tristan and his declaration of love. One he'd never actually made out loud, but she'd heard it clearly. He'd been just as startled by his thoughts as she was. And his comment to 'let him take a minute to deal with it' showed he was getting used to her.

For the span of a few heartbeats, she let herself imagine things working out between the two of them. Would she move into his home in the Hollywood Hills? She'd met his neighbors the other day. Brandon and Bree. Of course, Brandon had introduced her to his friend who just arrived. Marco had to be Marco DeLucca, and she'd almost fainted at the hot movie star's easy handshake. That had been a moment when she regretted the *quell*. To be able to hear what that man was thinking as he met her. Lordy.

Then again, Tristan raised his eyebrows when he ushered her inside. "Am I going to lose you to the movie star next door?"

"He lives there?" She'd gushed once she was sure the neighbors couldn't hear.

"Thanks. That doesn't answer my question."

"Sorry." She was blushing. She was a small town girl from Hansen, Georgia, where her father was the biggest celebrity around. And she'd just been touched by Marco DeLucca, what did he expect? Her biggest brush with fame before that was when she'd run into Heather Locklear at the coffee shop. It took her a moment to speak clearly. "No, I will not leave you for Marco DeLucca."

His blank expression mirrored his thoughts. He wasn't convinced. Megan had taken it upon herself to convince him.

Standing from her sandy seat, she picked up the sandals she'd shed and headed up the beach. At the edge she brushed the dry sand away and slid her shoes back on before tackling the mid-level incline to her apartment a few blocks away. All the blocks were up.

She took the elevator again, still a little giddy with the joy of it. But the appeal tarnished when her companion dropped a can from her grocery bag. When Megan picked it up to return it, she brushed the woman's hand and got another flash. Her son had enlisted the month before, and she was worried.

Megan pushed her worries aside and made her way back to her laptop and back to her job. Though she sat on her porch, with traffic and waves fighting for her audio space, she didn't have to deal with other peoples' thoughts up here. Not until a knock came at her apartment door later.

Tristan. She smiled as she hopped up only just then realizing the sun was setting beyond the buildings on her left. When she threw the door open, he stood there with a bag of groceries.

She managed to wait to tell him, but after he made her

dinner, drained the last of the champagne, she broached the subject.

"So the *quell* didn't work on you." She sat on the couch as though she was being casual about it. "Is it possible that it wears off?"

Her heart was beating fast. She'd been holding it back all day, the worry that the spell wouldn't last, or that it had gone more wrong than they originally thought.

He sunk in next to her, his hand covering hers, pushing her worry just a little further until he spoke. "It does wear off. Spells don't last forever, sometimes they're really fast. You have to keep doing it, build it up."

Her relief was palpable, judging by the expression on his face.

"So we just do it again?" She asked.

He nodded, smiling softly as her concern drifted away.

"When?" What if it took too long? What if it all came back?

"Sooner is better. The spells are stronger if you pile them on top of each other."

"Tonight?" she pushed. "I have the kit Yasmin gave me, and I didn't use up all the stuff from the first attempt."

"No. Tomorrow? I can do it or Yasmin can. Whichever of us does it we'll want to use our own circle, our own tools." He looked at her. "Is it bad? Has it faded away completely?"

He didn't think Yasmin's spell should be completely gone so fast. She still heard him loud and clear.

"No, I just caught a few things here and there. I got a blast when I tried on a sweater." She explained what had happened, and curled into him as she told it. She sighed. "Then there was the old woman in the elevator."

"Well, we can do it here, but it will only be half-assed with the starter kit."

"*Quells* are hard, huh?" She smiled up at him, kicked off her shoes and buried her toes in the lush carpet.

"Not really for beginners." He grinned and followed suit. "But if we wait until tomorrow, if you can hold off touching people and taking the elevator for one day, we'll get you covered."

Their feet bumped and she enjoyed the sensation. "Am I like a diabetic? I'll need boosters every week for the rest of my life?"

"I don't know." His shrug was as nonchalant as anything. "It may build up enough to hold for a while eventually. Or you might need it every week. I've never dealt with this before."

She was nodding when he changed the topic. "If I went to the animal shelter this weekend, would you help me pick out a dog?"

CHAPTER 27

Tristan convinced Megan to go to the shelter with him before he re-did the *quell*. She'd said once that she could sense things from animals.

"Where are we headed?"

"Into the valley. I heard the shelter was overfull and there are fewer people." He grinned over at her and took her hand. Though they were sitting in traffic mid-afternoon on a Friday, they were in the canyons. Trees hung over the single line of cars, the houses were in a variety of states, some of the front doors almost within reach if Megan could stretch her hand out the window just a little farther.

"Are you going to get a dog today?" she asked him, looking across the center of the car.

Just that simple act was such a good thing. She was his girl, and this was a perfectly normal conversation.

Then it wasn't. "Not unless you talk to the dogs and find me the perfect one." He grinned.

"I don't talk to the animals. You have me confused with Dr. Doolittle." Her mouth quirked.

"That's a shame. But you can sense things, right?"

"Yeah. Some. Feelings, that kind of thing." She looked out the window as they hit the Valley floor and started sitting at stoplights. "So we're just going to look?"

"Yeah, I'm not planning to take one home. But I do have a bunch of the stuff at the house. So I wouldn't be in trouble if we did find the perfect dog." He knew how he was. He was a sucker for a stray. "I'm used to having a dog in the house. I had this small Chihuahua-Teacup-Poodle mix named Peaches."

"What?" She had to be seeing it in his head. "You had a Chihuahua?"

"A Chihuahua-Teacup-Poodle-mix." He corrected her. "My mother got Peaches just before she and Dad died. I inherited the house and the dog. Peaches was something that tied my mom to me. That dog was a little ball of anxiety. I have no idea if that was because of losing my mom or just her breed and age. The vet told me she would calm down after she turned two."

"But?" Megan prodded him, enjoying the story. Probably enjoying the thought of him testing his manliness against a tiny dog.

"She . . . well, she couldn't. She would sit, but she would buzz while she sat there. Like how your cell phone would scoot sideways when it's on vibrate. I couldn't get mad at her. She sat and she didn't get up, but she didn't actually stay in one place."

Megan was laughing. "Did you dress her?"

"Oh Goddess, no. My mother didn't either." Despite the purse-size kind of dog, his mother didn't have much of a fondness for playthings. "I think Mom just liked that she could scoop Peaches up and keep her out of places with a baby gate if she needed to."

"Are you going to get another tiny dog?"

"I'm going to get whatever size dog is right for me." His manliness wasn't invalidated by a dog. He smirked. "I miss Peaches. I miss having a dog around the house. The backyard is fenced. I didn't want to get a dog to replace her, so I waited. Now it's time."

She smiled at him. "We never had pets. My mother was such a housewife, she didn't want to have to clean anything more. So no pets."

"Goldfish?" He asked, wondering. "Pet frog?"

"Nope. Not even fish. Certainly not a frog!" Her good mood had stuck all week. He wasn't as worried as he had been. She'd done a good job of letting him know that she was aware she'd gone a little nuts, that she was pulling herself back in.

The sun was shining, the day acting like what everyone suspected every L.A. day was like. Forty-five minutes later, he was committed to a dog. And an hour after that, they were leaving Fatburger, pulling out of the parking lot as Megan lolled her head back against the seat.

"Oh, god. Those chili cheese fries had to be about a thousand calories!"

He laughed. "So what?"

"So, I'll have chili nightmares tonight!" She protested.

"What's a chili nightmare?"

"When I eat chili, I always have vivid, strange dreams and wake up a lot at night."

Tristan felt his face contort. "*What*? I've never heard of chili nightmares."

"Well, now you have. I'll wake up three times tonight at least!" She shook her head at him. "But it was worth it."

"That's good." Once again, his hand snaked across the center console. Touching her just felt normal. "Let's go get that dog."

"It's hardly a dog," she replied. "Dogs are bigger."

"Clearly, they aren't all." Tristan shrugged. The mutt had at least some French Bulldog in him, the rest was hard to tell. But, as he was close to three years old, his size was pretty much a given.

When they entered the cinderblock building that housed the

Humane Society, it was clear that the staff was nearing the end of their day. But the little brindle-and-white-patched dog sat in the office. Cleaner now, his fur colors were brighter, so were his eyes. He'd been neutered the week before when he was first adopted. But the family returned the next day, spotted a puppy and changed their minds. That sucked, but it made it easier for Tristan to claim him.

The paperwork was already signed, they just had to pick up the dog.

The woman behind the counter handed over the thin braided leash the shelter handed out with each animal. "Does he have a name? For our records."

"Redford." Tristan told her.

It was Megan who looked at him oddly. "Redford?"

He'd tossed a thank-you over his shoulder as he led the compact dog—now happily wagging his stump of a tail—out to the car. "In the back, when we were picking him out, the woman said he was no Robert Redford. But I say he is."

Megan bust out a beautiful, melodic laugh as Tristan tried to help the stubby-legged dog get up into the backseat of what he'd previously thought to be a low slung car. Redford was also heavier than he looked, which Tristan found out when he gave up trying to coax the dog and just lifted him.

"He's no Peaches, either." Megan tilted her head at the dog now seated in the middle of the back, eying them one after the other.

"No one will ever take Peaches' place." Tristan told her as he slid in the driver's seat. "You'll help me with Redford?"

"He's your dog." She looked at him sideways.

"Yeah, but I see you with him. You're communing with him. He likes you and you like him."

"Yeah, I do." She grinned.

The dog had a rough time managing his seat in the back of the car. The canyons were curvy and his compact body slid side to side with the turns. Though he seemed to think it funny while they rode, when they got out at the small lot behind Blessed Be, Redford seemed a little drunk.

"You okay, little guy?" Tristan squatted down and stroked the dog's brown-striped head until he returned to normal. When Tristan stood, leash in hand, he looked straight at Megan. "You ready for this?"

For a moment he thought maybe he should comfort her first, but though it was a big deal, it didn't bother her. She'd already put the *quell* off for almost a full day.

Though he thought she was denying herself a gift, he had to admit that he didn't fully realize what she was going through. The animal shelter visit was hard on her. She hadn't said anything, but it was clear there were a lot of bad memories for some of the animals. While it had been funny when she held up one eager puppy and commented with, "There's nothing in there. He's a sweetheart, but he's got nothing going on upstairs," it was much less so when she picked up one of the older dogs and just held him for a moment. The tears running down her face had nearly undone Tristan.

"Does he need us?" He'd asked her, thinking if this dog had been through that much, maybe he needed a home more than most. Megan had shaken her head. "He's afraid of men. You can't take him."

Though the dog had allowed Megan to touch him and even pick him up, he shied back when Tristan reached out. In another situation, he would have stopped, but he was compelled to do something. So he stroked the dog's head softly and intoned a simple *forget* on him. He didn't know how long it would last, but he'd put as much into it as he could. He would strengthen it the following week with his standard rituals.

It had all been enough that he now wondered why Megan had agreed to put the *quell* off and go to the shelter with him. Had she just not known how bad it would be? Or had she felt it was that important to hear the dog before Tristan picked him out?

The shop was open late on Friday night and, though they only headed into the back spell room, they could hear plenty of people out front. Keeping business going, he thought, good things. Libby looked down the hallway and briefly waved as they entered, then she disappeared back into the crowd in the front of the store.

It was humbling, how upset he'd been with Megan for wanting the *quell* in the first place. Now he saw more of what she was fighting every day, and he was more than willing to do it.

"Come on in." He gestured to her, casually handing over the leash and letting her find a way to keep Redford from breaking the salt circle. As Tristan headed in and out of the room, gathering his things, he heard her talking to the dog.

"Do you sit? . . . Do you do shake?" She paused after each question, then would say something else.

Though Tristan was used to people talking to their dogs, Megan didn't just talk *at* Redford, she was pretty clearly talking *with* him.

When Tristan came back into the room, he saw the dog sitting to the side, well past the boundary of the salt circle.

"He'll stay." Megan told him as she stood. "He understands not coming into the circle and breaking the spell."

If anyone else had told him that, he would have asked if they were off their meds, and he came from a family of witches. "Ready?"

She nodded.

Twenty minutes later, she took a deep breath and looked up at him with wide eyes. "I could feel it. Was I supposed to?"

"I don't know." He was putting his tools away. "It's not that you're not supposed to feel it, but every now and then someone does. I'm a pretty strong witch."

She grinned up at him from her spot on the floor. "Is that a pickup line?"

He laughed as he broke the salt circle and watched as Redford popped up from where he'd lay down patiently earlier and came rushing in to rub his nose against Megan. "Hey," he told the mutt, "You're supposed to be my dog."

"He is." Megan answered.

For a flash of a moment, he thought about Redford belonging to both of them. Of her moving into his house. In another flash, he saw them getting married.

It shocked him, the power of the thoughts, the clarity of the pictures in his brain. His immediate reaction was to look at Megan, think how he would explain it to her.

She hugged the dog close, rubbing her face against his fur. She didn't even look up.

CHAPTER 28

M egan went back to the store for the sweater. This time there were no feelings that came off it. Though whether that was because of the *quell* or because it was maybe a different sweater, she couldn't tell.

Either way, she could wear it. So she did. She was wearing it when she told Tristan what she'd figured out. "Will it come back?"

He shrugged again. "I don't know. This one is probably more powerful than the one Yasmin did. I've been at it for longer."

"So, I just got a stronger dose?"

"I think so." He shrugged again. "I don't run around doing *quells* on people all the time. So I really don't know how long it will stick."

"I can't hear you anymore." She tried to insert it casually into the conversation. Honestly, it was a weird conversation. They were easily discussing her ability—or now lack thereof—to hear other people's thoughts and his ability to alter things with spells.

His answer surprised her. "I thought so. It disappeared Friday night, just as we did it, right?"

She nodded.

It felt good, walking down the street and not being inundated by other people's ideas, anger, or more. But it felt weird, too, making love to Tristan and not being able to hear or feel him. She couldn't be unhappy about it; the benefits were exactly what she'd hoped for, even if they weren't exactly what she'd expected.

"What do you want to do today?" It was an odd question for her. She was used to knowing what he wanted. Well, she'd wanted to be normal. They were now, weren't they? They'd spent Friday night at Tristan's house, letting Redford settle in.

Tristan pulled out Peaches' old bed—a bigger bed than the small dog had needed—and Redford took to it right away. The dog bed had occupied a corner of her own bedroom last night. Redford later clenched his shortened jaw around the fleece and proceeded to drag the bed out into her living room, where he was lying in it now.

Tristan didn't really answer her. "How are you feeling?"

"I'm fine." Megan wasn't ready for his question, "Should I not be?"

"Some spells can leave you hung over, or a little dizzy." He shrugged at her. "So no morning after side effects?"

She shook her head. She hadn't felt anything of the sort. Just the weird feeling that something was missing. Megan couldn't say she missed it, though. She changed the subject. "There's a new movie out."

His head tilted as though she was a little nuts. "It's Los Angeles. There's always a new movie out." After a pause, he grinned, appearing to understand that she was making up for a lifetime of avoiding theaters. "So let's go, but after that we come back and take Redford to the dog park."

It was so normal, even though they went to a relatively early show. She had a slush the size of small country and ate popcorn for lunch and felt like a real girl.

When they returned, they found Redford asleep in his bed, but with one of each of Megan's shoes. He didn't have a single pair, just one of each of the ones he could reach, and he was curled up with them as though he was a kid and they were his stuffed animals. He didn't even have the grace to look guilty.

He let Tristan take the shoes away, and as she and her boyfriend inspected them, she couldn't find anything wrong. "I don't think he chewed them."

Tristan was turning the ones he had in hand over and looking at everything. "I think he just took them because they smell like you."

"Like my feet."

"Yeah, but like you. I understand." He offered what looked like a shy shrug. "I like the way my bed smells after you stay over." Then he looked down at the dog who was watching them take away his prizes. "I get you, Redford. I get you."

Megan laughed at both of them and even the dog seemed happier for it.

The trip to the dog park was fraught with side trips. Once again, Redford was sliding around in the back seat. It was cute until a sharp stop toppled him. A stop to the pet store revealed that other people had this same problem and wanted you to spend a lot of money on their device so you wouldn't have it, too. Tristan paid up.

Leaning in close, because she gathered that was the appropriate way to discuss magic in public, Megan whispered, "Couldn't you just put a spell on him so he doesn't slide around?"

"Sure, but this is easier." He held up the harness contraption that had a loop for the seatbelt.

"Really?" It had taken fifteen minutes and an employee to help them find one that would fit Redford's stout little body.

"Sure, now it's done. Can you cast a spell on Redford to keep him from sliding around the backseat?"

"No." Then it hit her. "Oh, so this is for when I take your dog to the dog park without you."

"You might want to." He gave her a sly smile and she wondered how much he was really thinking of the bulldog mix as *their* dog. It was a surprise that she was truly disturbed she didn't know. Not hearing Tristan was harder than she'd expected. But he kept talking, because he couldn't hear her either. "You might dog-sit while I'm out of town. But mostly, it's because spells take work and energy, and using that for something that could just as easily—and maybe more effectively —be solved by a twenty-dollar dog harness doesn't seem wise."

While they were there, Megan also learned that Redford would sit at the dog treat station and beg, and that tennis balls were incredibly expensive if you were throwing them for your dog, rather than just for tennis.

It was closing in on four o'clock when they finally made their destination. The park was several acres nestled in the folds of Laurel Canyon. The driveway was steep, and on a Sunday afternoon, that meant the place was pretty parked up.

Tristan put a leash on Redford, just to get him out of the car. Redford didn't want to move.

"Wow. It's like having a baby." Tristan commented as he tugged again on the leash. "Everything takes longer. At least until we get a routine."

Megan looked around. She'd never even known this place existed. Then again, she was still pretty new to L.A. and lived on the other side of the large city. While they waited on Redford to get his bearings—both on how to maneuver out of the car and his desire to actually go where the other dogs were—she looked around.

A sign welcomed her to the park and advised her to pick up after her dog. Another vinyl sign hung from the chain link, advertising that dogs could get vaccinated on the cheap at the park, which sounded like a pretty good deal all around to her. A nudge at her leg told her Redford was beside her and ready to go and, like a little family, the three of them walked through the double gated entry that wouldn't let dogs dash out when their owners weren't looking.

The squat dog hugged their side for the first fifteen minutes while they wandered around. Other dogs, all off leash, came up and sniffed at him. At first he was shy, then as he started sniffing back at the other dogs, Tristan leaned down and unclipped the leash with a wary sigh. "Let's see what happens."

"What happens?" She asked. "Doesn't he just play?"

"I hope so. Not all dogs are good at being social. Dog fights happen." He watched as Redford trotted off a distance and then came back, touching both Tristan and Megan with his nose before heading out for a slightly bigger loop.

It reminded Megan of her sisters when they were toddlers. They wanted independence, but weren't quite ready. They tagged in periodically, like hitting 'base' in a game, as if the person would wander off and leave them if they weren't touched.

Megan and Tristan watched the dogs for a while, then threw the ball for Redford—which, of course, turned into a game for about eight of the dogs. Then Megan saw someone she thought she recognized and when she did, she sighed and turned to Tristan.

"What?"

"I thought I recognized that guy over there. I was sure I'd met him before or something. I just couldn't place where."

His laugh punctured her embarrassment. "Did you figure it out?"

"Oh yeah. I don't know him at all. That's Noah—" she struggled for a last name. "Preston! He's in that movie coming out at Thanksgiving . . ." She couldn't think of that name either and neither could Tristan. Or maybe he could, and he just didn't tell her.

"Don't worry." He grinned at her. "That happens a lot in L.A. I've actually told people I was certain I knew them, and it turns out, they're an actor. They aren't my old friend, they just play one on TV."

By then, the sun was getting low and the park was emptying. Even Redford was dragging. Getting him up into the car was almost as hard as the first time. He was so tired, he even took the harness without complaint and was laying on the seat, passed out cold before they hit the end of the parking lot.

A stop for sandwiches and they were on their way back to Tristan's house.

Later, sitting in front of the TV, curled into Tristan, Megan figured it was the perfect day. They relaxed, played, generally hung out, and she and Tristan hadn't gotten tired of each other. In the past, she'd found out that some relationships didn't last outside of the bedroom. A whole day with Tristan, with zero sex but a lot of laughs and more, was definitely one for the books. She'd been a normal girl with a boyfriend today.

For this reasoning, she had to completely discount that her boyfriend could light candles with a flick of the wrist and that he'd found her location in a city as big as L.A. by using witchcraft. In fact, it was his ability to do these kinds of things that was why she was finally normal at all.

She'd nearly fallen asleep watching TV when her phone rang.

It was tempting to ignore it, but she didn't get that many calls since she'd moved out here. Work called sometimes, but on a Sunday evening? She didn't think so. Tristan's was the primary number in her call log, and he was sitting beside her.

Curious, she unfolded herself from the couch and rummaged in her purse to stop the buzzing. Then she scrambled to answer before the call went to voicemail.

"*Mom!*" Her heart was pounding. Tristan had looked up as she jumped for the phone, but now his gaze was sharp.

"Hi, baby." Her mother sighed out relief, as though she, too, had been afraid the call would click over.

"What's going on?" She wanted to say, *it's so good to hear from you,* but she wasn't sure it was. Why now? Why not when she'd left?

"Can you come home?" Her mother's voice was weary and Megan's heart turned over.

It wasn't until she'd heard them that she realized how much she needed the words. That she'd needed her mother to at least want her back. Her anger had carried her to another ocean, but that hadn't been as far away as she'd once thought. "Yes. When?"

"As soon as you can." Now Megan recognized another tone in her mother's voice: fear. But what was she afraid of?

"I can probably wrangle some vacation time next week." She was mentally pulling her calendar, thinking about what she could shift. It was the schedule, not the time off. She hadn't taken a vacation in several years. Where would she go? With whom? Her eyes were drifting to Tristan, considering possibilities she hadn't before, when her mother's voice cut back through her thoughts.

"Can you come earlier? We need you now."

"Mom, what happened?" Her heart stopped beating. This was her mother's way of dropping bad news. Was it one of her sisters? Was it—

"Your father's had a stroke."

CHAPTER 29

"Megan?" Tristan had tried not to interrupt her phone call with her mother, but it had been hard.

He waited, his heart hammering as she turned an odd shade of gray. Still she didn't say anything that revealed what was happening. She'd asked her mother what was wrong. Megan clearly had an answer, but the only thing she replied was that she would find a flight out tonight.

"Megan?" he asked her again. "What's going on?"

Finally, having hung up on the call, she turned to him. "I have to go home."

"Why?" His heart still stuttered, his patience the only thing holding him together. Clearly, something was very wrong.

"My father had a stroke." She spoke the words evenly, in a tone that belied the gray of her pallor and the glazed look in her eyes. She wouldn't make eye contact with him. Best he could tell, she wouldn't focus on anything, so it wasn't him.

"I'm so sorry." The words tumbled out and for the first time he was grateful that she couldn't hear him anymore. He wasn't sorry. That bastard had been nothing but bad news for his oldest daughter. Tristan closed his eyes and hugged her close.

She leaned into him, as stiff as a tree. It took a few moments before she breathed again.

When she did, all the life entered her in a rush and she pushed out of his grip. Nearly frantic, she began a verbal litany of chores. "I have to pack, but first I have to find a flight. I have to find a way to get to LAX and I need the dog taken care of—wait, he's your dog."

"And I'll take you to LAX." He answered, grabbing for her, thinking to still her thoughts, but she slipped through his fingers like quicksand.

"I'll call for a ride." She wasn't looking at him. Obviously busy making extensive mental lists, she turned away. Tristan wouldn't have it.

He gently grabbed her shoulders and turned her toward him. "Look, you have a boyfriend. Driving you to the airport in the middle of the night for any reason is what we do. I'm on it."

When she at last looked up at him, she really saw him there. "Thank you." A breath gushed out of her with the words. "I'm going to check flights right now."

"Will you wait a second?" He didn't let her go. Didn't think she was going to like it, but thought it needed to get said.

"What? I need to—"

"You need to stop and breathe and think for a minute." He looked her in the face. "Why do you have to fly out tonight? Can it wait until tomorrow?"

"No. He had a stroke. I have to go now."

"When did he have it?" Tristan asked. It was probably like getting information from a rock, she was frantic, but he had to try.

"Yesterday."

"Megan, she only called today. You can sleep in your own bed tonight and go tomorrow. Then no one will have to pick you up from the airport in the middle of the night."

She shook her head. "I'll fly into Atlanta, rent a car, and drive the rest of the way." She went on, explaining the logistics she'd somehow already worked out.

"Then it won't matter if you go tomorrow. I'm worried about you flying overnight, then driving on no sleep." His heart hurt. He hated this, and he hadn't said the worst part yet.

"I'll be fine."

He took a deep breath and tried to let go of his tension. "I will drive you to the airport, any time you want, because I support you. But I don't want you to go."

"You don't want me to be with my family when they need me?"

"The only thing they have ever done is need you! The man you are going to take care of has done nothing but make your life a living hell. Your mother didn't stop him. Shit, Megan, she hasn't called once since you moved out here, has she?"

Large eyes stared up at him, tears welling in the corners.

Shit. He'd fucked up. But he wasn't wrong.

She didn't say anything.

Tristan tried again. "Did she even call to see that you were okay? Did she call to find out where you lived now?"

"I called her. I told her when I got here. I left a message." As if that was enough.

"She called back to tell you she was glad you settled in?"

This time, the only answer was the hard set of her lips. Anger. At him, for pointing out what was real? Or maybe at her mother for not being a very good one?

"She hasn't taken care of you, Megan. You don't have to jump when she calls." He tried pulling her close. "Just sleep the night in your own bed and make your decisions in the morning."

She didn't let him pull her close. She tugged away sharply. "You don't understand!"

"You're right! I don't." He was nearly yelling. How could she want to go back to that? How could she go to take care of that man?

Even Yasmin and Delilah had accepted Megan and been better to her than her own family had. So why wouldn't she listen to him? Why wouldn't she just wait a handful of hours, and decide then?

"They're my family." The words were ground out between her teeth. "What would you do if it were your family?"

He didn't know. Tristan just sucked in a breath and tried to think. His family had never done anything like this to him. Even with all the shit that went down between Juliet and Delilah, neither had ever asked him to take sides. At her worst, Juliet had never been as bad to Delilah as Megan's father had been to her. And he'd done it since she was a child. Since she was too young to know he wasn't right. There was no answer for Megan. He shrugged.

She nodded back, understanding that he had no reference for it. "They're my family." She said it again, and he wondered if she thought saying it made it so.

"I should be your family." He said, not knowing where the words came from. Still, he'd been better to her in the past several months than her family had ever been.

Even in his thoughts, it sounded arrogant. But it wasn't. It was factual. Her family was so shitty to her that he—official boyfriend of all of one week—was better than them.

"But you're not." Her words were final. "I'll catch a ride to the airport."

Reaching out, he caught her arm. "Please don't. I want to drive you. I love you."

"You don't agree with me. You don't understand."

"I don't have to do either of those things to love you and to want to be there for you," he protested. "Let me drive you. Save the money. Don't forget to tell your work if you're missing days over this. And you should. Don't make yourself sick on top of the rest of it."

She nodded. No longer the warm, caring girlfriend of even

just an hour ago. So he waited while she packed. He spent his time gathering Redford, taking him down to the small park across the street for a bit so the dog could make the ride to LAX then up to Hollywood.

Tristan did his best to be useful. He tried to think of what he would want if he had to make the trip and she didn't agree with him. While Megan accepted his help when he specifically offered it, she didn't ask for anything, and he began to feel as though he was forcing his help onto her. Still, he and Redford made the trip down to LAX for her 4a.m. flight.

Getting out of the car, he forced more help on her by carrying her suitcase as far as he could. When she reached for it, he didn't hand it over.

"Megan."

She looked up.

"I love you. If you need to do this, then go do it. If you need me, call."

"Thank you." She sighed again and leaned into him.

"Tell me when you get in safe? And I'll call you every day." It was the best he could do. So he hugged her. Kissed her lightly, then sent her back to the family that had done nothing for her and everything against her.

Rushing back to the car he'd left at the curb, he moved Redford to the front seat before navigating his way out of the behemoth airport. He missed her already. Had he told her he loved her? Yes.

It was so hard remembering to say it. He hadn't even said it the first time. Still wasn't sure he was ready to say it, not until tonight when she'd chosen them over him and it almost killed him. He'd made a logical argument about why she shouldn't go, but he'd done it while his heart bled at the thought. He hadn't told her he felt that way. Maybe he'd forgotten she couldn't feel it herself, or maybe he'd just decided that if she couldn't feel it he didn't have the guts to say it. He didn't know. All he did know was that he was going home alone. Her apartment was empty.

Tristan rolled down the windows, letting the wind come through the car. Redford thought it was the best thing ever and perked up. It was true, having a dog was definitely a plus. He shouldn't have waited so long after Peaches. And that thing about witches and cats? Absolutely not true.

He and Redford rolled through an all-night fast food place for a real milkshake. Tristan didn't lie to himself at all, it was pure consolation. While he waited for the drink, he calculated when Megan should be landing and when he should text and ask if she'd arrived alright. He wouldn't wait for her. She was dealing with too much and he made the decision then not to read into anything.

Later, in his own bed as he was tossing and turning, he wondered if he shouldn't have had skipped the milkshake. Then he admitted that wasn't it at all. He would have lain awake no matter what he'd eaten or not eaten.

"Come on." He patted the end of the bed before he realized that Redford couldn't jump that high. Not wanting to put the dog up onto a bed he couldn't get off of, and also not wanting to invite a dog into a bed he regularly invited Megan into, Tristan pulled a blanket out of the closet and curled up on the couch with his dog.

When the light came in, he wasn't sure if he'd slept or not. Redford had—at a reasonably high decibel—but Tristan couldn't count any time he was sure he was asleep for. But he had made a decision.

He called into the shop, leaving a message on the general machine that he wouldn't be in that day. It took a bit to get his instructions across—what deliveries were expected, who should check them in, that kind of thing—but he hung up the phone satisfied things would be taken care of.

Then he rummaged through the herb closet. He hadn't done

a full makeover of the place since his parents lived here. He'd worked at it piecemeal, changing up the living room and completely re-doing the master bedroom and bathroom, but he still had his mother's linen closet and his father's herb closet with herbs his grandmother had dried and the guest room was still the same and . . .

If he wanted to keep living here, he needed to really claim the place, he thought. Then he decided maybe he should wait and see what Megan thought they should do with it. It took a moment before that thought registered and how he was starting to think of her. Having her pluck from his brain a sentiment he wasn't sure he would have shared wasn't the same as thinking she should be included in decorating his home. He would have to be sure that he wasn't thinking it just because she was gone, just because he was aware that things weren't entirely copacetic between them.

He needed to understand her.

His grandmother's herbs were dwindling. His parents had used them sparingly and so did he. Still, this was a good reason. This was a strong spell he needed. It took three solid hours of work before he was relatively certain he'd achieved it.

Though he hadn't slept, Tristan was wired and he headed out for the day. By two p.m. he was horrified.

CHAPTER 30

"Mama?" Megan walked into the hospital waiting room. She was dead on her feet but she would do her best.

"Oh, baby." Her mother jumped up and enveloped her in a huge hug.

This was what she'd come for. She'd needed her mother all this time. Megan melted into being held for just a minute, then straightened up. "I came, Mama. What do we need to do?"

She also needed to get on a schedule here, figure out how to take care of her father and mother and sisters and how much she could work during that time. She could take personal or medical leave. She had enough clothes for a week . . . Her brain churned trying to keep track of all the possibilities.

Her mother shook her head and sighed. "I don't know."

"I'll take care of it. Where are Lizzie and Ari?" Even her mother was relegated to the waiting room for the ICU. She was only allowed in a few hours a day and kicked out when the nurses came by for procedures.

"The girls can't come. They're with the Banners today."

Megan nodded. The Banners lived in the house next door to the church. The church lot was huge, but the house for the minister was tiny. They paid the taxes on the property, and a handful of the bills in exchange for the house. It suddenly occurred to her that if her father could no longer serve his function as minister to the congregation, the church might install someone else, and her mother and father and sisters might have to move out of the little house. She wouldn't consider that yet, though.

The Banners had a son who went through school a year ahead of Megan despite being just over two years older than she was. They believed Megan had at one time tried to seduce their son. It was a ridiculous thought, because at the time she would have had zero clue how to even go about such a thing. But he'd said it was her when he was pressed about the girl climbing out the window and she'd been punished, by her own father as well as the reputation. So visiting the Banners was never high on her list.

"I'll get them." She volunteered despite the resentment she felt. "Do they need dinner? Can they come see Daddy tomorrow?"

"They can't come for another few days, the doctor thinks." Her mother worried the fabric handkerchief she was holding. It had taken Megan years to figure out that her mother carried it with her because it was a Southern genteel thing, not as a tissue. The woman kept a mini-pack of Kleenex in her purse all the time. Had she just sat here, worrying all this time?

"Thank you, Honey. They do need dinner. There's chicken in the fridge . . ." She paused, gathered her thoughts, then went on explaining how to cook, not that Megan actually needed it.

"I'll get them." Megan repeated, thinking how quiet the hospital was when she couldn't hear anything. She hated hospitals; there was always someone grieving deeply and Megan always felt it. But not today. Still, she found herself looking at her mother for signs of her feelings. It was odd not to hear her mother fully.

They sat that way, in real silence for the first time in Megan's life. After a few minutes, when her mother didn't volunteer it, Megan asked, "Can I go in and see Daddy?"

Her mother's worrying stopped as she got very still. "Baby, I don't think that's a good idea."

"So he hates me that much?" Maybe it was better to speak it out loud.

"It's not that . . ." Her mother trailed off.

"Yes, it is." Megan considered getting up and leaving right then, but she hadn't come for her father. She'd come to help her mother and her sisters. "I'll get the girls then and get their food. Should I swing by the school and pick up assignments?"

"Oh, yes, that would be great." Her mother nodded completely ignoring the problem of her father. "Did you get dropped off here? Do you need a car?"

"No, Mama, I rented one at the airport." An expensive one because of the open ended return date. "I'm covered."

She didn't need anything from them except a family. After squeezing her mother's hand, she stood up to go. She wound her way out of the hospital in relative silence. Hansen wasn't big enough for the kind of high-end medical center her father needed after a stroke, so she was still a good forty minutes from home.

The school's phone numbers were still in her contacts from when she lived here. It had only been a fistful of months she'd been gone, but it felt like she was a wholly different person. Megan wondered if her mother saw that, or if she even could.

The town of Hansen was small enough that the elementary, the middle school and the high school were merely different wings of the same building. One call and one stop and she could get both her sisters' school work for the day.

The secretary was the same woman who'd been there since the year Megan graduated. It would have made sense for her not to have any real opinion about a girl she hardly knew. By that time, Megan was keeping to herself and doing a pretty good job of it. But, no, the woman behind the desk was curt, cutting Megan off several times with explanations of how wonderful her sisters were and how she—the secretary—had everything taken care of for them. Everything they needed from both days they had missed would be ready for pickup.

As if Megan should have calculated that they had missed yesterday, too. As if she was bad for being gone during this tragedy. Not that she'd known until last night.

It wasn't any better when she arrived at the Banners' home.

"Hello." Mrs. Banner opened the door with a flat expression and no welcome.

"Hi, Mrs. B. I'm here for my sisters."

There was no response from the woman other than to turn away. She didn't invite Megan into the house, just turned back inside and let the door fall almost closed behind her. Megan could hear the girls inside, gathering their things. Ari came bolting out the door, throwing herself at Megan.

"I missed you!" She wrapped herself around Megan's waist in a hug worth all the rest.

Lizzie just muttered "hello" and walked past. She stopped and pointed across the way to where Megan's rental sat in their drive. "Is that your car?"

"It's a rental." Megan answered, Ari finally extracting herself as Mrs. Banner wished the girls a good evening. She didn't say anything else to Megan.

They walked back the way Megan had come, cutting across the grass between the two houses. Megan unlocked the door with a key still on her ring despite the fact that she'd spent the last several months unsure if she would ever use it again.

The house was exactly as she remembered. It smelled like her mother's cooking and her father's cologne. Still it didn't fit the way it used to. "Come on girls. Let's get some dinner."

They cooked together, something they rarely did because

her mother so enjoyed cooking and having the kitchen as "her space." She'd made sure her daughters all knew how to make a handful of meals, then her duty was done and she would reclaim the space as her own.

The peace lasted five minutes before Lizzie decided her homework needed to be finished and left the room. Ari tried to pan roast the green beans but managed to burn them a bit, while Megan tried to supervise all of it.

The girls were in bed before Megan carried her suitcase in from the car and found that something had changed in the house. Her old room had been converted. All evidence that she had been there was gone again—just the same as had happened when she left for college.

"We'll make it comfortable for you." Her mother's voice startled her and Megan almost jumped but she was too tired.

"Jesus, Mom. You scared me. You're sneaky."

Her mother, probably exhausted herself, was pushing past her, bringing in sheets to make the bed, pulling extra pillows from the closet because Megan liked them. That at least was something, right? Megan wasn't sure.

Eventually she was sleeping in the guest bed in what used to be her own home. Her mother had checked in on the girls and Megan overheard her telling them that Daddy sent his best. The same was not repeated to Megan.

She would have thought sleep would be a hard time coming, but she woke from the depths with the morning sunlight, to a relatively busy house. The girls were getting ready for school, with Mama insisting that they go and that they let Megan take them. Soon she was out the door herself, driving the girls up to the front door and waiting in the drop-off line like a parent. When she made it back home, her mother was getting ready to leave.

"Wait, Mama."

"I need to go see your father." The woman was all nervous

energy, but Megan wasn't.

"You need to sit down and talk with me, Mama." Tugging her mother's hand, Megan pulled her to the table and sat with her. "Daddy can wait a while. You called me out here and have barely spoken to me."

"I didn't want you to leave." She looked away.

So did Megan. That was the first time she'd heard that. "It was over four months ago. You could have called me or even texted. You didn't stop it."

"There's no stopping you." A shrug, another sideways glance.

"Of course not." The old anger was boiling up. Just being here was tense. "No one had my back. If I didn't get my own shit done, no one would help me."

"There's no need to swear and that's not true." Her mother's lips pursed.

"Yes, there is and yes, it is. The Banners still think I seduced their son and Mrs. Banner will barely even speak to me."

"Didn't you?" Her mother looked startled.

"Seduce him? No!" Her mother believed that crap? Megan's heart sank. "I didn't even know at the time what that would entail."

"So why don't you tell the Banners that?"

Megan sighed. It was as useless as it had always been. Her mother loved her, in her own way. But Megan had always had to make due. "Go see Daddy. I'll take care of the girls today." Including Lizzie, who really appeared to be doing her best to not speak to her older sister.

Popping up, as though released from a physical restraint, her mother offered only a brief hug then was out the door. Megan was left at the table with her thoughts. She didn't feel good about the idea she had, but she thought it had merit, after all, Lizzie and Ari might need to go over there again. She headed out the front door, not locking it, and made her way across the grass to the Banners.

Mrs. Banner opened the door on the first knock, probably saw her coming. "Yes?"

"Hi, Mrs. Banner. I just wanted to chat for a moment." Megan smiled, but the other woman didn't smile back.

She didn't even invite Megan in. "About what?"

"About Jeremy and—"

"What could you possibly want to tell me about my son?" If she'd been cold when she opened the door, the woman was positively arctic now.

"I just wanted to say that it wasn't me in Jeremy's room that night. I don't know what you heard, but it wasn't me. It seems you've been upset with me since then." Having run out of things to say, Megan let the words trail off.

Mrs. Banner filled them. "It was my son who told me you'd been in the room. Are you calling my son a liar?"

Oh, dear God. "He was how old? Sixteen? Seventeen? It wasn't me." There. She'd given him a way out. He was just a kid. She wasn't blaming anyone, she just didn't want to live next door to people who hated her for something she hadn't even done.

"My son doesn't lie." The woman's mouth pressed into a tight line and Megan had enough.

"Yes, he does. He's also done cocaine, so my sisters won't be coming back here around you and your druggie kid. And that girlfriend he brought home last winter? He picked her up in a bar and then she asked that he pay her. So you and your lying ass son have a great life."

She turned and walked away, the triumph fading as she realized what she'd done. Her heart clenched.

Old Megan would never have done that. Old Megan stood quietly and let the winds buffet her while she fought to stay upright through the gale. New Megan told Mrs. Banner where to stuff it.

Just then her phone rang.

CHAPTER 31

Saturday hadn't gone much better than Friday for Tristan, but at least he'd managed to call Megan and see how she was doing. She'd said she was holding up fine and he was certain she was lying. He couldn't tell from the distance the phone created, but he felt it.

Then again, he didn't know what she felt from him, if she had a clue what he'd done. It didn't sound like it. It sounded like she had her hands full taking care of her little sisters so her mother could stay with her father.

It sounded perfectly reasonable until he counted up what she hadn't said: she hadn't gone to see her father. So she was there, providing care for the man, but hadn't actually spoken to him. Also, he hadn't forgotten that her mother and sisters hadn't spoken to her in months, and when they had called? It was because they needed something from her.

He was beginning to understand.

Saturday, he'd ventured out a little here and there. The grocery store seemed safe, but the woman at the check-out hated everyone going through her line. Tristan had been subjected to her vile comments about each person she waited on. This one was too fat and clearly at fault for it with what she was purchasing. That one was too old to have a baby, and was probably the baby's grandmother or someone who'd adopted. That baby didn't look like the man who was carrying him and she thought the wife had likely cheated. Tristan heard it all.

He'd taken his ice cream and gone home.

He'd tried to ignore that she thought he was hot. Then his soft but-not-interested smile earned him a scathing *He's full of himself, what an asshole* in return. He'd paid for his purchase, raised his eyebrows at her and considered calling her out for the bitch that she was.

Only no one else could hear her.

She smiled politely enough. She clearly didn't love her job, but the difference between what she showed the customers out loud and what was going through her brain was massive.

He made it to his car and through traffic up and over the hill. After yesterday he'd shopped in North Hollywood where he didn't know anyone, but it hadn't been any better. Apparently, people were crazy everywhere. Only he'd had to buy a cooler bag to get the ice cream back over the canyons and into his side of the hills.

He arrived home at noon, put the food away and made himself a sandwich. For the first time in his life he found himself grateful that bread didn't have feelings.

As soon as he polished off the small lunch, he dialed Megan again. She might not call him, but he wasn't going to hold it against her.

"Hello?" She answered absently, as though she didn't know it was him.

"Hey, just wanted to check in."

"What? Oh, hi, Tristan." He could feel her attention turn to the phone. "It's good to hear from you."

"You sound distracted."

"I'm sitting outside the local Wal-Mart waiting for my sisters to come out." She paused, then sighed. "Apparently, they don't want me to go in with them."

"Jesus, Megan. You don't have to be there."

"I do. I need to help my family. They are the only family I have."

He wanted to contradict her, but knew he wasn't in a position to do that yet. So he told her what was in his heart. "I'm sorry you're dealing with that. I wish I could help more than I can."

"Thank you." There was a brief pause again as she seemed to gather herself. "I just wanted to really thank you."

"For what? Talking on the phone? That's all it seems I'm good for." He almost laughed at the notion. Oh, she was thanking him for the *quell*, he bet.

Then he found out he was wrong.

"When I got to Los Angeles, I stopped because I couldn't go any further." Another sigh, but he waited her out. "Then I met Yasmin and you and it really made a difference."

"I'm glad." He said, but she wasn't done.

"It's worse being here now. Having seen something different. Having real friends who accepted me, rather than just putting up with the dregs I got around here."

Sweet Goddess, that was crap. And he loved her. She was stronger than he'd ever known. She could no longer hear that he was thinking that, and it wasn't the time to say so. He bit the words back.

"So I told off Mrs. Banner next door. I never would have done that. Not only did I call her to the mat for thinking I'd done something I never had, I told her what her precious Jeremy has really been up to. Needless to say, she didn't take it well." Her laugh was full of real humor even as it was tinged with regret. It sounded like she'd tried to make friends. When that wasn't possible, she'd fought back.

"Good for you. If you did it, she probably deserved it." He

wasn't usually vindictive. He'd been raised to rail against that feeling, but he felt it for Megan now.

"I want to be a bigger person than that, but I'm not. I think she's deserved it for a long time."

This time, he was the one who laughed. Just talking to her made him feel better and he could only hope that he did the same for her. A few minutes later, she spotted her sisters coming out of the store and had to hang up.

"I love you." He said it, but wasn't sure she heard him.

Deciding the shop had been neglected long enough, he packed up Redford and took a deep breath before heading out to the car. Probably the strangest thing about it was the dog.

Redford wanted to know where they were going. So Tristan found himself speaking to his new companion as though he were a person. It was almost stranger understanding that Redford understood. At least it wasn't odd to speak to the dog as though he were a person, lots of people did it. And in Hollywood, almost nothing was too weird.

"No, we aren't going to the dog park. We're going to the store."

He paused. "Like Friday night."

Again. "No, we aren't casting spells." *But I am going slightly mad.*

He kept up a conversation the whole time he was heading into the heart of Hollywood, at least it wasn't a long drive. As he parked in the back lot, he realized it was the first time he'd taken Redford out since he'd cast on himself.

Redford didn't want to leave the car because he was cautious of new places. He wasn't being obstinate, he'd been abandoned.

Tristan could not handle the things he knew. "Come on puppy." He knelt down and hugged the dog, looked him in the eye. "I will never leave you."

When he stepped back and patted his leg, this time Redford

carefully stepped down. He wasn't racing for the door, but he'd come of his own willpower.

They were heading in the back when a clear picture formed in Tristan's mind. "Cats?" he looked down at the dog.

Redford was enjoying this.

"There aren't any cats here," he told the dog, then was immediately proved wrong.

Hex and Voodoo, Yasmin's two cats, poked their little black heads around the corner from the front of the shop. Redford must have smelled them. Yasmin was busy with customers. "Oh, there are cats."

Well, shit. He wasn't sure this was okay.

Redford was curious, and the cats were, too.

"Yasmin!" He called out even though she was busy. This could get ugly fast, and he didn't think Redford would be the loser. "I brought Redford and your cats are curious."

He heard her quickly hand her customer over to Libby and come dashing back. Expecting her to scoop up her precious kitties, he was surprised by her outstretched palm and the way she quickly cast on them.

Tristan hadn't even considered spellwork. But it was almost too obvious. He raised his hand to Redford, not even asking what she was doing because it was so clear to him. He first explained to the dog that the cats were friends, then he cast the spell. He added that cats were not to be chewed on, and was surprised when Redford looked up and seemed to think it was okay, even though the dog was a bit weirded out by the feelings.

Yasmin stepped back and Tristan followed suit, letting the animals learn their way around each other. But the two humans stayed close enough to jump in if something should go wrong. A good five minutes later Yasmin backed off further.

"They seem to be getting on okay. I'm going to help in the front, if you have this?"

"Sure." He nodded up at her, then quickly looked back at the animals. Redford continued to sniff the cats and they continued to walk tauntingly in front of him, but he didn't even so much as growl.

Taking the dog into the office with him, Tristan tried to get on with his work. Though he closed the door, there was a vague hum coming from the front of the shop.

Luke showed up at the back lot and came in through that door. He was there to see Yasmin. They both worked odd hours and Yasmin said they'd missed each other for the past handful of days. Tristan was already waving and saying "Hi, Luke," before the other man passed by his barely open office door.

Libby came back and talked for a few minutes, asking if Tristan would hold the front for an hour. "Luke's here, and Yasmin's not asking, but I know she'd like to leave." Libby leaned in the now open doorway.

"I'll see what I can do." He stood up, Redford standing with him and nodding to the cats as he passed them where they'd curled up on the couch. Almost a year old now, they were still small and looked even smaller following the squat dog. They seemed to think he was their leader. Tristan almost laughed, then he held it back because he was laughing at things that cats thought.

Out front, Libby was already helping someone and Yasmin was behind the counter.

"You go with Luke." He told her even though she frowned at him. She was concerned about losing the hours and that bothered him. "Don't worry about the hours."

Yasmin had been salaried for a while, but she worked hard and made sure she was never low for hours. She frowned again, but he decided he could ease that. He'd started talking to Delilah about it a while ago, as things with Megan made him think about Yasmin being in California almost on her own. Not anywhere near as much as Megan was, but really striking out and making it. She worried about her house payment and her cats, even though Luke made a big difference with that, the concerns hadn't fully faded yet. So Tristan broke rank and pulled her aside.

His hand on her arm, it was even easier to feel her concern hop up a step. "No worries. Good news. Well, I hope. Luke, come over."

The tall, blond man also had no clue what this was about, and Tristan thought they'd be happy. "It's about your wedding present."

"Oh?" Yasmin thought he was giving her hours off, or a paid vacation.

"Delilah and I have been talking, and you both know about my sister, Juliet?" They both nodded, and he understood both were feeling a bit skittish about mentioning what Juliet had done, how she had died. Tristan let the conversation glide past that. "Well, Delilah and I inherited Juliet's shares in the store. Honestly, it doesn't feel right to us to hold them. We want to give them to you, really to you directly, Yasmin. As a wedding gift."

She was stunned. Luke was surprised, but he calculated quickly the time and effort Yasmin had invested. She started the classes; she was the one who added the online ordering option and made sure all the mail orders ran smoothly. Yasmin did it because she loved the work and she loved the store.

Tristan smiled at her. "That's why you should get Juliet's shares. You love this place, even more than she did. Yasmin, you're family." He reached out to hug her as her first fat, happy tears fell.

Then he offered a hand to Luke, which turned into a hug, too. "You're about to be family." He told the other man.

It took a few minutes for Yasmin to get herself together. She kept asking Tristan if he was sure.

"And we aren't going to change our minds either. You'll be part owner with a one-third share."

"Oh, Goddess, Tristan. Thank you. And I'll tell Delilah, too." She was talking almost in circles, so excited. He tried to follow her thoughts, but didn't even see it coming. She changed the topic so fast. "You're in love with Megan. Really in love with her." She was in awe.

"Yes." He frowned as he heard the awe she was finding, the happiness she felt for him, and the odd change of topic. Luke was just confused. "Why do you say that now?"

"Because you can hear me." She turned to her fiancé. "He cast a spell on himself to hear everyone's thoughts. Like Megan can. He wanted to know what it was like to deal with that."

"You figured it out?" Tristan asked. But then, of course she had. She was smart and she was a talented witch.

"You're answering my questions before I ask them. How has it been?" She looked at him, her head tilted. She really wanted to know.

He tried to be honest. "It's the most horrible thing I may have ever experienced."

CHAPTER 32

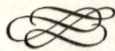

Megan stood outside the hospital room, holding her breath. A faint murmur from inside the room let her know her father was chatting with his roommate. She wasn't quite ready to interrupt.

Though she'd been in town for a week, this was the first time she was seeing her father. Her mother came every day. Even her younger sisters had gone into the ICU once before they downgraded his status and put him into a regular room.

There was always some reason why Megan shouldn't see him. He was asleep, his visiting hours had been used up by other people, he was getting a treatment, something. Today, she'd just showed up.

Her mother was at home, so Megan simply said she had an errand to run. She was the man's daughter. She'd flown across the whole country to help out and she was going to at least see him in person. What she expected to happen, she didn't know.

With a sigh at herself for balking, Megan forced herself to walk in.

She didn't know what she thought she'd find, but it wasn't another visitor. A woman from the church sat beside the bed, holding his hand. Upon seeing Megan, she jumped up, dropped her father's hand and said a hasty good-bye.

Only nodding, Megan again thought how wrong it was that people were so afraid of her. The newspaper they had been reading—Megan now understood what she'd been hearing before she walked in—lay crumpled across his lap. Despite the stroke, he sat up straight and looked relatively healthy. It had been a small one, not uncommon in a man his age with his diet and stressors. It wasn't noticeable unless you knew to check that his left hand lacked the muscle tone of his right, or that his facial expression was slightly less clear on the left side of his face.

"Hello, Daddy." Her heart beat up into her chest. She had no idea how this would go.

"What are you doing here, Megan?" His words were even, measured. His eyes, even with the stroke, were clearly narrowed, his focus sharp, probably angry.

"It's good to see you, too, Daddy." She responded, ignoring his question. But he asked it again.

"What are you doing here?"

"In the hospital or in town?"

"In Georgia." As though he owned the whole state. At least she now knew how this would likely go, but she had another card to play.

"I came back to help Mama and the girls while you were out." Her words were calm. Her voice didn't shake even though she was shivering on the inside. She wished Tristan were here.

"They don't need your help." His words were harsh. So Mama hadn't told him? Megan was surprised by this, but she shouldn't have been.

She was done lying for her mother. Megan paid bills and she and her mother said the income came from sewing work her mother had done. Megan bought her sisters school supplies and field trips and no one commented or asked where that money came from. The whole time she'd lived there after college, she'd brought home groceries each week, filling the refrigerator and no one asked where they'd come from either. She was done being silent. She had a place to go, friends to help, and better than that, she knew how to find people now.

"Mama called me and asked me to come back."

"No, she didn't." He countered, a very slight slur to his words. He would continue with therapy, she knew. Her mother had told her that, too. Had she thought Megan would just come home, help out quietly then leave when she wasn't wanted anymore?

It suddenly occurred to her that her mother must have thought exactly that. Old Megan would have done it. Apparently, none of them realized they'd created New Megan. And New Megan didn't slink away. She also didn't want to start a fight. She wanted to end one. So she didn't lash out.

"Daddy," she considered sitting on the side of the bed, but she and her father had never had that kind of relationship. She did sink into the vacated chair though. For a moment, she waited to pick up something from the woman who'd sat there before, but then remembered she was done with that, too. Tristan's spell had been more thorough than Yasmin's. It was not only wider in range, but lasting longer. She wasn't experiencing the occasional leaks in information like the first time. Tristan brushed off the better spell by explaining that he was stacking his on Yasmin's, it was the double layer that made it better. He was a stronger witch because he'd been born to it. It was fact, not brag, and the idea of it almost made her smile. Something her father couldn't take from her. She took another breath and told him.

"Mama called me the day after your stroke. I came back because I knew it would be hard on her and the girls. So I helped."

"We don't need your help." He gritted out.

She started to tell him all she'd done. To explain that she'd grown up dirt poor, her clothes all hand-me-downs from the parishioners. That sometimes she'd worried about what they would eat and that she'd saved her sisters from that. They had new clothes, wi-fi, and everything they could want because of her. But Megan held her tongue, instead, she changed the subject.

"It's gone, Daddy." She said it softly.

"What's gone?" He looked worried and she set about soothing him.

"My . . . ability." She would never call it a 'gift' like Tristan did, but after the way he passionately advocated for her skills and accepted her the way she was, she could no longer call it a 'curse' either.

"How? Really?" He stared at her. He must be thinking something terrible from the look on her face. All she could do was sit and blink back at him.

"It's really gone, Daddy."

"How did you do it?"

She'd thought he'd be happy about it. He'd done so much, spent so many years of her life trying to get rid of it, she expected him to jump for joy—or do what a man with a recent stroke would do in lieu of jumping. He should be happy he had his daughter back. Instead, he just wanted the how.

She paused. She didn't want to say she'd had a witch perform a spell. He was a big proponent of *thou shalt not suffer a witch to live*. In fact, he'd called her a witch more times than she could count. After meeting Tristan and Yasmin, Megan knew she wasn't a witch at all. Just a girl with a weird ability.

"I found a priest who fixed it." It wasn't really a lie. Tristan was clearly a master in his religion.

"No, you didn't." He growled.

"Wait." She countered. "So because you couldn't fix it, I can't either? I'm stuck forever as your demon child even though it's all taken care of? Los Angeles is a big place, Daddy, bigger than Hansen, there are all kinds of people out there."

She realized as the words fell out of her mouth that she'd told her father where she lived. Her second realization was that her mother had never asked. She'd been caught up in the worry of taking care of her husband and her two younger daughters and had never asked Megan what she'd been up to these months she'd been gone.

"It's full of heathens and whores." Her father muttered, his eyes never un-narrowing.

"You haven't ever been there. You don't know." She returned, trying to stay calm. He was good man, she reminded herself. He helped people find their way, he loved the sinners and the saints. He could love her, too.

The very thought created an odd click in her soul. He *couldn't* love her. She'd thought that now that she was "cured"— at least in his mind—he would be able to see her as a daughter. But it didn't matter. Nothing did and nothing ever would. Whatever she said, he would find fault with. Whatever the reason, her father was capable of loving other people, but was incapable of loving her.

On the heels of that thought came another. Tristan was right.

She didn't follow that idea down the rabbit hole. Instead she said to her father. "I don't have it anymore. That's my choice and I'll live with it. But I don't need you to love me or accept me. It would be great if you recognized what I've done for you, but I don't think you're capable of it."

"You little, ungrateful whore!" He didn't yell. He rarely did, but he was angry. She could see it, even if she could no longer feel it coming at her.

"No, Daddy. I was a grateful child, even when you beat me. Even when you turned me away. Even then, I bought groceries and paid bills. All of it just trying to make you love me. But you can't. You're a good man, Daddy. To everyone but me. So please understand when I call you out for being the asshole that you are."

She said it with a smile. After all, she was a southern girl. A southern girl who'd spent a lifetime learning to mask what she heard and how she felt.

He was turning red, his anger palpable, "You little—"

His hateful words were cut off by the beeping of his machines. A nurse came in, rushing through the doorway.

"Reverend Booker?" She had her fingertips on his wrist and was looking at all the numbers displayed on the various machines on stands around his bed.

Despite the fact that the nurse was there, Megan spoke one more time. "You'll be coming home in a handful of days, Daddy. I won't be there. Do not ever attempt to speak to me again. Do you understand me?"

He didn't answer, just turned red as the nurse tried to take his vitals. Instead, he spoke to the nurse. "Do you hear this ungrateful child? Coming in here while I'm sick, telling me these hateful things?"

Megan barked out a sour laugh. She was done letting this vile man dictate her feelings. She spoke to the nurse, too. "He won't tell you how he beat me when I was a kid. How he told other people I was awful. I needed my father to love me, but he's broken."

The nurse looked confused. Maybe she knew the good Reverend Booker outside of this hospital.

"Oh, he lives a good life outwardly." Megan acknowledged, a wicked part of her gleeful that her father's blood pressure was shooting through the roof. "But ask him what happened in his home. Ask him how I paid his bills for years without so much as a thank you. Despite being a good child, I was called a whore and worse. Tell her, Daddy. Tell her what you did."

Her father didn't answer. The beeping just got louder.

This time the nurse actually looked sympathetic toward her. It was the first time Megan had been around her family without the holy influence of her father's churchfolk all around. "I'm so sorry, it's my job to keep his vitals stable. I'm afraid I have to ask you to leave."

"Oh, don't be sad about asking me to leave." Megan smiled at the nurse and looked back at her father. "I'm leaving forever. You will never hear from me again. While that might make you happy, Daddy, it sets me *free*. Free of you and your asshole judgment. Free of you thinking you're better than everyone else. Goodbye."

She sauntered out the door, passing a doctor coming in, her clipboard crowding the space as Megan went by.

Each step out the winding corridors of the hospital was lighter than the one before. As she walked out onto the grass that separated the side door from the parking lot, she felt untethered. Unweighted by the responsibility of trying to be 'good' when she'd never been 'bad.'

She had never felt so free in her life. She had to call Tristan.

CHAPTER 33

T ristan's heart leapt. Megan's words were probably the best thing he'd heard in forever.

"I'm coming home on Friday," she'd said. "My father gets out of the hospital that day. I'm not helping with it. I'm staying until then, but I won't be here when he gets in. That's up to the rest of them."

It was still five days away, but it was glorious.

He was happy she was coming home. He was almost happier that she'd finally given her horror of a father the real boot. She didn't need that man in her life.

Tristan wanted to revel in the fact that now Megan had him, she didn't need her old family. Even so, he understood the old ties, the old wounds, the old needs. The other fact was, despite his feelings, he and Megan were still pretty new. He couldn't claim to fill the void left by someone who'd been in her life since birth. Good or bad, her family took up the majority of her emotional space for the majority of her life. While most of what they provided her hadn't been good, shaking that took a major upheaval.

Shucking her father and all his expectations and needs was

an amazing step. If it was the only one she ever took where her family was concerned, then she was light years ahead. He was happy for her.

Mostly, he was uplifted by her own words.

"I feel like I've been carrying weights all my life and I just dropped them. It's almost euphoric." She'd sighed happily with the sound. "The other people here in town, they're still his people. He's turned them against me. Telling them to cast out demons and more."

"Wow." It would be hard to believe if he hadn't heard the whole story, hadn't seen that she wasn't mentally ill. In fact, she was perfectly sane the whole time he'd known her. Even her odd ability was so consistent she had no trouble proving her power. Many psychics got flashes of information, often useless bits. Trying to demonstrate what they knew or could do required heavy monitoring until one thing that could be fact checked could show up. Not Megan. Two words and she had your number.

The fact that she had his number and still loved him humbled Tristan beyond words.

He told her as much, and how proud he was of her. "Your father is an epic case, Megan. I'm so sorry you had to grow up with that."

"When he kicked me out—when I came out to L.A.—he told them he was casting demons out of Hansen. He holds himself up as the shining example of what to do." Tristan could practically see her shaking her head that way she did. "He cast out his own daughter. He stood tall in the face of Satan. Apparently the fact that the beast came to him in the guise of his own child was a test. So now he's practically a saint for what he did. I'll be glad to get back home."

That last word brought another level of joy to Tristan. She called L.A. "home." After he said he loved her and hung up, he thought for a while. Had he ever been so wrapped up in someone else's happiness? Aside from his sisters, he hadn't. Sure he'd been proud of his friends' accomplishments, he'd helped people celebrate milestones, but he'd never been happy just for someone else. Not like he was with Megan.

He hadn't meant to tell her he was in love with her. He'd needed time to process it, but her ability had taken that from him. It had taken the opportunity to present it to her. But it had given him back her love sooner, too. It had given them a trust he'd never experienced before.

These past days, hearing everything bombard him from the world around him, he'd begun to understand what she went through. He'd been reduced to a fetal ball on the floor of his living room the first night and he'd barely ventured out.

While people weren't awful in general, it was simply too much to deal with. Their worries assaulted him, their fears, too, even though they didn't mean to. Yes, there were a handful of horribly rotten, wormy apples, but the main problem was just dealing with everything from everyone he passed.

By now he'd seen a movie—three actually—which had been completely ruined by everyone around him. Megan was right on that. There was always at least one person who'd seen it before. And so many people with so many theories about how it was going to go, there was little mystery to the plot. He also finally made it into a theater with only a small handful of people, and one had been fretting about all kinds of things beyond the movie. Escape from reality now depended heavily on those around him, and no longer was about his own ability to drop into the story.

Megan had endured a lot just having her skill. Being ostracized for it, too? Her own father against her? Well, Tristan held tight to a handful of words for her upon her return. The first two would be "I'm sorry." He'd had no idea what he was talking about when he told her to keep her ability, that it was a gift. He hadn't understood the family she'd been born into, none of it. And somehow she was still here. She'd still given him a chance.

His spell wasn't fading. He'd cast on himself and he'd done maybe too good of a job. Sure, he could cast again and undo it, but that took energy and time . . . and maybe he should do that. There was also the issue of his manliness. Megan had endured it for twenty-eight years. She'd endured it without knowing why she had it and with no support.

Each day he went out and dealt with it, he understood more about her. It had become a point of pride to wait it out. Plus, he wanted to hear her when she came back. He wanted to know what she was thinking. Despite all the pain the telepathy caused, their connection was better than he'd ever known. He considered whether or not they could only hear each other—if that would be better. If a spell like that was even possible.

He searched the family *Decad*—the book of spells passed down through the generations. *The Goodman Triskadel*, their Wiccan coat of arms, or plaid, so-to-speak, was embossed on the front of the leather worn smooth by generations of hands. Would one spell do it?

The herb closet yielded some of the things he needed, and there were others he set to ordering. Big batches didn't matter, he'd sell off the excess at the shop. Completing this spell would mean closing down Megan's natural ability, except to him. At the same time he would have to open his own ability. But not this wide ranging noise-signal he was getting. Just to her.

He hit the shop, put in hours at work with Redford by his side. They no longer worried about Yasmin's cats—the animals were plenty friendly now. Though Tristan continued to cast little *getalongs* on them and suspected that Yasmin did, too. He researched while he was there, pulled inventory and marked it for Yasmin, who was in charge of what was on the floor.

He bought food for dinner and dealt with the thoughts of the man behind the counter who was confident Tristan was making all the wrong choices. It was a lot of judgment about someone else's dinner, but Tristan was finding that a handful of people—even those who seemed outwardly affable—made strong, negative assessments of most everyone they came in contact with. They were often miserable human beings, but that didn't make their now-audible-to-him commentary any less hurtful.

He survived that trip, put the things in his fridge and tried to think what he would need if she wanted to be at her own place instead of his. He worked a full day the next day, then headed down to the jewelry district before they closed at five.

Megan would be home in five days. While he thought he might find something ready-made, he wanted enough time to get something ordered.

The area was close quartered. Tall buildings, almost unmarked glass doors leading into small jewelry shops that were the front of a larger more industrial organization feeding rings, necklaces, stones, and more into shops all up and down the west coast. Upstairs on another floor, designers sketched what they knew would work and experimental pieces, too. Another level was jewelers, working the designs into actual pieces and fiddling with the parts to make them more aesthetic or structurally sound. He could hear all the murmurs of brains at work just walking up to the front of the building.

A younger man said hello to him when he walked in the door, but Tristan thanked him and looked around for a moment. The owner stood in the corner and assessed him as unable to afford any of the big ticket items and handed him off to an associate. She explained the general layout of the area and asked what he was looking for.

"Do you work on commission?" He asked her bluntly. No wonder Megan couldn't deal with people. Outwardly, they were fine. The man in the suit could have left the associate with him for any number of reasons. But Tristan wasn't paranoid, he was actually hearing their thoughts.

"Well, no," she stuttered.

"But the sales totals go toward promotions and bonuses and such . . ." Tristan supplied, plucking small bits from her thoughts and putting together what he already knew.

"Well, yes." Another stammer.

"Then tell your owner that he's incorrectly sizing people up. I just happen to wear a cheap t-shirt and jeans some days. And you can wait in the corner, too, because I'm going to talk to that guy over there." He pointed back over his shoulder at the young man who'd greeted him politely and let him look. He hadn't made any judgments.

An hour later, Tristan walked out with a necklace, just as he'd intended to buy. He thought Megan would appreciate the gold scrollwork one of the jewelers upstairs had created by hand. It had small stones set in it that just happened to be both his birthstone and hers. Tristan wasn't much for the magical power of birthstones, because they varied depending on who you asked, but he thought it was a bit of a sign that the jeweler had just happened to mix those two stones.

As he walked back to the car with the small bags that had been arranged for him his thoughts turned. One bag held the necklace, wrapped and tied with a bow, stuck down in some artistic puff of tissue paper, ready to give as a gift to the woman he'd pick up at the airport the following afternoon.

The other bag had surprised even him. It had no tissue paper, and wasn't intended to be handed over as a present. It had only a small silver box that housed a velvet box that had a ring nestled inside.

Because Tristan, it turned out, knew exactly what he wanted.

CHAPTER 34

Megan woke to odd light coming through the window. By the time she fully roused she realized the light wasn't odd, just different than where she'd been the past two weeks. She was back in Santa Monica, back home.

She knew that now in her heart. Originally it had been where she was banished to. Then it was where she was carving out a space for herself. Now, it was home.

Yasmin had checked in on her while she was away, ask if she needed anything. Megan had startled at the incoming text. Her phone service texted her, people at work texted her, the delivery service texted her to let her know the guy sending up her Chinese food needed the door buzzed. But until Tristan, people had not checked in on her to find out how she was doing.

She periodically pulled up the chain of messages and re-read them just to be happy she had a real friend. She'd even promised Yasmin that they would go out for drinks when she returned to town. Like friends.

So the light here came in from a different angle than at her childhood home. There was also a bed she'd bought to her own specifications—the first one she'd ever owned that wasn't someone else's bed for her. There was a man in the bed, warm and sometimes wild, and most importantly, trusted.

"Good morning." His voice caught her unaware. Being caught unaware was still something she was coming to grips with. Her old skills would have alerted her that, in spite of his even breathing, he was fully awake. "This is wonderful."

There was a smile in his tone, so even though his head was above hers and she couldn't see his face, she knew he was happy to wake up with her there, too.

"It's so good to be back," she murmured. "I'd just hoped to go out with you last night. I need to apologize to Redford, too."

She was originally slated to get into town in the early afternoon. There were plans for the dog park, dinner, and more. Then a layover in Houston had turned into the pit-stop from hell and she'd barely arrived while it was still Friday.

"So, we'll go today. The mechanical failures of a plane are hardly your fault." He stroked her head, then down her spine, all the way to her hip—her sadly covered-in-pajamas hip. She'd been so late and so exhausted that Tristan had sensed it and put them both right to bed.

"Redford will easily forgive you," he went on, "if we take him to the dog park today. And we'll just move our dinner out to tonight." He rolled over, pushing part of his weight onto her and sinking her further into the mattress. "And these pajamas are so . . . four months ago. You should be naked."

His kiss was searing, his need palpable, his hands everywhere. Megan kissed him back, reaching for the shirt he'd climbed into bed wearing only to find that it was gone. A little lower and she discovered his boxers were gone, too. "When did you get naked?"

"When you were dreaming of me." He whispered against her skin. "I think the real question is, when are you going to get naked?"

"Now." It came out on a moan. His hands had already

decided that he pajamas were of no value and snaked under the thin top. As soon as she peeled it, he slid fingers under the waistband of the matching short shorts. She was as bare as him within a moment, but he didn't stop touching her, didn't stop kissing her, and she was right where she was supposed to be.

He played her like a harp, touching all the right places without needing direction. The intensity of their lovemaking threw her. She'd missed him. Really missed him. Tristan was looking her in the eyes as he pushed inside her, as she came apart in his arms.

When her heart rate finally re-entered the normal range, she laid small kisses along his chest. "I missed you."

"I missed you, too. So much." He was pulling her close, this time just hugging her. His words passed over her head, but into her heart. "It surprised me how much I missed you. I need you here. With me."

"I want to be here." It was so easy to be with him. He understood her as no one had and she felt comfortable with him in a way she'd felt around no other human in her life. She melted into him and almost managed to get to sleep before Redford started shuffling around like he needed to go out.

"You stay here, I've got him." Tristan was pulling away, his heat already leaving her space.

Megan was out of bed even as he slipped into his jeans. "I'm coming. I'm awake."

He didn't question her, just smiled and met her by the door in a minute, Redford patiently waiting at the end of his leash. "I've got the bags." He volunteered just before she could open her mouth and ask.

He held the door, and she passed through, then they reversed it at the elevator—working together without words, like a well-oiled machine. Or an old married couple. A small smile formed on his lips.

"What?" She asked him.

"Your buttons are one off."

Horrified and glad she was only in the elevator, she pulled the hem of her shirt out to check. "No they aren't."

"You looked."

She punched him lightly in the arm and headed first out the sliding doors and then onto the sidewalk. They got Redford into some grass quickly before continuing down to the beach where her stomach started growling.

"Breakfast here?" he pointed. There was an outdoor seating area that clearly allowed dogs.

She patted her pockets, finding nothing. She'd thought they were just walking the dog a block or so.

"I heard your stomach, and I have my wallet."

She smiled. She was becoming too normal. He was reading her like a book, but it didn't matter. The rest of the day went like clockwork. The dog park was nice—the weather beautiful and a passing migration of small, purple butterflies entertained the dogs gleefully.

Dinner was a cozy affair they were late for, because Tristan had come up behind her as she checked her dress in the mirror. She'd been wondering how it looked, if it fit well enough, hit in the right places. He'd wordlessly assured her that it did.

They went from being early and very well put-together to being late and barely passable. She'd laughed as they handed the keys to the valet. "At least you can't tell me my buttons are one off!"

He leaned in and whispered in her ear, "Nope. But I can tell you how much I want to pull the tie at your neck and let the whole thing drop."

Tristan caressed her upper back, brushing the ends of the tied fabric, teasing her until he simply whispered, "Later."

It wasn't until they ordered that he finally let her see what was in the small bag he'd brought along. "You got me a present?"

He leaned forward over the white tablecloth. "I missed you. I knew I would, but I didn't have any clue just how much until you were gone."

So she smiled at him and pulled out what looked like a jewelry box. She frowned at him. "You don't have to buy me jewelry."

"I know, but I thought of you when I saw it. So it's yours. Open it." He grinned as though he knew she would like it.

"Oh my God!" She almost dropped the box. The scrollwork was intricate, like vines intertwining to create a piece that sat just between her collarbones when she held it up. It hinted at romance and fantasy and looked expensive. "Tristan, you don't have to spend this kind of money—"

"Shut up." He grinned at her. "I know. So don't go expecting jewelry and flowers at every turn, but I wanted that for you. Wear it?"

"Oh. Yes!" She handed it to him and turned her back his way, letting him clasp it. She wouldn't have worn a halter top dress had she known she was getting a necklace. Some of the scrollwork disappeared behind the pieces but Tristan assured her he knew it was there.

Later, when they were home, they walked Redford again, this time in their nice dinner finery. Her heels clicked on the sidewalk and Tristan unbuttoned the top of his shirt. It was so comfortable. So easy. So wonderful.

When her phone beeped at her she checked it and told him. "Yasmin wants me to go out with her Tuesday night."

"You don't need my permission." His head tilted.

"I'm not asking permission, I'm just checking to be sure you didn't have something else in mind first." But he was nodding before she could finish. "I was being polite."

"Of course. No, go. Have fun."

She tapped back a message as they headed up the small incline and to the base of her building. As he held the door Tristan said, "Go, have fun with the girls. But pack a bag?"

"A bag?"

"Yes, come to my place when you're done." Another wicked grin.

"What if it's late?"

He shrugged. "So what? If you lived there and it was late, you would come in late. Want a key?"

Her hand hit her chest in awe. "A key?"

"You know, they open doors." Another grin. "You can come in late. Or come after work and surprise me with dinner?"

"I don't cook. So I don't think that's the kind of surprise you would want." But it sounded so good.

The next day while she caught up on work, he went out and duplicated keys. Not just his, but hers.

For the first time since returning, she was alone in her apartment. It felt vaguely empty without him and Redford there. For months it had been just her, and that had been wonderful. She would have thought having a man there would be stifling, oppressing, someone to answer to. Instead, it was the opposite.

Having him there set her free. Even though they stayed at his place Sunday night, it was good for her. Her mother hadn't called, but it was Monday morning before she noticed. Honestly, this was so far from Hansen, it hadn't even crossed Megan's mind.

Her mind ran circles as she drove from his house to hers. So this was her morning commute? Getting dressed to go to her own home from her boyfriend's house. So she could work on her couch . . .

But he was coming straight to her place after work. Aside from work, they'd hardly been apart. Aside from some general anxieties about the whole thing, she'd been happy with it.

Tuesday evening, she found herself packing a bag to stay over at his place. It was all a bigger step than she'd thought she'd be taking. And over drinks, she told Yasmin so.

"I'm not sure I'm ready for this. It feels like we've almost moved in together." She wasn't ready for any of it. Having friends, being normal, having a boyfriend.

"Look," Yasmin ate from the tableful of appetizers they'd ordered in lieu of a real dinner, "if you don't want to, tell him now. Don't break his heart later."

Shit. Megan was talking to the only person she could talk to, but Yasmin wasn't the right person to talk to about Tristan. "Don't worry. I know he's like family to you—"

"I told you, he gave me shares in the shop! He *is* family to me, but that doesn't change what *you* should or shouldn't do." There was a pause. "Look, I think you two are great together. Still if the speed is wrong for you, then it is. Save the relationship by slowing it down now, rather than realizing later you've felt smothered all this time. That's all."

"Is that from experience?" At a nod, Megan asked her next question. "When did you know you and Luke should move in together?"

A big laugh erupted. "Luke and I moved in together before we even kissed. But that's a story for later. Just tell Tristan you're not ready."

"But I am ready. I *feel* ready. I just think everything tells me this is faster than normal." The potstickers were delicious, and she'd thought she couldn't eat a meal of appetizers but she was finding she could eat until being stuffed and not make a reasonable dent in the food.

"Well, if you're ready, you're ready. You two should move at your own time. Faster or slower. Don't let anyone or any preconceived idea tell you what that is or should be."

Megan waited until she finished chewing the fried broccoli she'd been eating. "Then I should move in with him. Since I've come home, we function like an old married couple. We anticipate each other's moves. He understands me like no one ever has."

Yasmin was looking at her oddly. "Of course he understands you like no one ever has. Just like you understand all of us."

"What are you talking about?" Megan felt uncertainty squeeze inside her chest for the first time. The way Yasmin was looking at her . . .

"He didn't tell you?"

CHAPTER 35

Tristan had gone to bed at midnight, alone but with a smile on his lips.

Megan was out with Yasmin, having a good time obviously, since she wasn't in yet. He was actually excited that he would fall asleep and she would come in at some late hour, crawl into bed with him and wake up next to him.

At two o'clock, when he woke up briefly to find the bed empty, Tristan told himself she was fine, but texted her anyway. Just to be sure she was okay.

"I'm fine." The words that came back were brief, no tone. He frowned, but didn't want to bother her if she was still out.

"I'll see you when you get here." He'd sent back, and crawled back into bed.

When he woke up and the bed was empty, the small nagging he'd managed to squash down in the middle of the night burst into full bloom in his chest. She hadn't come.

Surely there was some reasonable explanation? Maybe she was so late that she thought it was better not to sneak in. Maybe she was . . .

Better to just ask. He called.

She didn't answer.

He messaged.

She didn't answer.

He paced and considered driving over there. What if she was in actual trouble and he left her there? That would be the worst. He called again. When she didn't answer the second time he dressed and hopped in the car. Maybe she was asleep? Well, now he had a key.

It was a weekday morning and traffic sucked. He considered panicking. He considered calling Yasmin, then realized he'd be at Megan's soon enough. But if she wasn't there or didn't answer, he would call Yasmin, her sleep be damned. He might be obnoxious, but he couldn't let Megan possibly be hurt and ignore it. Tristan didn't check in on her magickally, he just tried not to think about the things that could go wrong in a big town like this.

Her block was parked up, and despite having a key, he didn't have the clicker to her garage door. He parallel parked in the first spot he could find and rushed to the building door. Each apartment key opened the front door despite all being different. He was in and climbing the stairs before he realized just how worried he really was.

Why hadn't she showed up last night? He should have checked the garage for her car, but he was almost there. It was too early to make so much noise in the hallway but he practically ran anyway.

Without even considering knocking, he slid his key in the door and opened it wide to find . . . Megan, sitting on the floor in front of her couch talking to her computer.

With an angry hand, she waved him away and he stood still, quiet, taking a moment to process. She must be meeting with someone online. Her hand, still held up for him to stop, was likely not showing onscreen.

She smiled and chatted, answering what appeared to be a

few questions from online, though he couldn't hear any other voices. Her whole appearance was friendly, but the hand she held out to him was mad.

Megan was perfectly safe.

She'd made it home. It appeared she'd slept and even showered this morning. She'd gotten up, gotten dressed and made some early online meeting. Was she mad at him for interrupting or for something more?

He stood there for a few minutes, letting his still-pounding heart steady to a more reasonable pace. The fear that battered him on the run up the stairs morphed into something different now. Was she mad at him? Had she not come over because of something she perceived between the two of them?

"So I want you all to read this statement. It's from one of our clients. It's a bit long, so just read on your own. I'll be back online in one minute." She finished with a few more instructions, a few other clicks of the buttons, then she stood up and turned to him, glaring.

"Are you off?" He asked, confused and frightened by the cold look in her eyes.

She stared at him. "You should leave."

"Are you mad at me?" Clearly she was, he could feel it, but for some reason he didn't believe it.

She held out her hand. *Give me my key.*

It was so clear. She wanted the key back. They'd just done this. It was the first time he'd used his key to her place and she wanted it back? He shouldn't have barged in—

Give me my key. I have twenty seconds left. Her voice was clear despite her unmoving mouth.

Oh shit. His own response rung clear inside his head but she couldn't hear him. His spells had taken care of that. And his spells were what she was mad about now.

Key.

"No." He had to speak it out loud. "I'm leaving, finish your class, finish your day, then come to my house and speak to me. We'll work it out."

She shook her head. Her hand still waited, palm up, for the offending key.

He pocketed it and left. He left her there, angry at him. He left her wanting her own property back, and he'd refused to give it. Tristan headed for the stairs on shaky legs, then thought better of it. He now had problems with elevators, but falling down her staircase was a far worse prospect than meeting up with someone unpleasant or sad in the elevator.

He'd run into the building, but he was dragging himself out of it. He thought about driving into the canyons for a while, letting the air and the views take him out of his funk, or maybe steep him in it until he figured out what he needed to do.

Tristan was in the wrong here and he knew it. His intentions had been good—the best. He just had to show her that. They were too good together to let his error in not telling her what he'd done ruin everything.

He was on the Pacific Coast Highway before he realized he needed to go straight to his house. What if she finished her assignment sooner than he expected? What if she went to his home and he wasn't there? It wasn't as if he was enjoying the salt air or the sounds of the ocean intermingled with the cars. No he was stewing, and he could do that just as well at his place.

Stopping at a drive-through for a breakfast sandwich was the only thing he did to keep him from getting home as fast as possible. He hadn't eaten on the way out the door, and he wanted to be ready the moment she showed up. So he ate on the road, called in to the shop, and explained that he wouldn't be there today.

In his mind it went like this: Megan showed up. He groveled. She forgave him and they spent the day together, happy. He could reinforce the *quell* she had, or take off the spell on him. Her call—because he should have told her about it.

He was pulling into his driveway, looking for her car before he realized how far he'd come. The wrapper from his high-fat breakfast sandwich was empty even though he didn't remember eating it, and the coffee cup had only a little sludge left in the bottom. He wadded up the wrapper to toss it before he offended Delilah with his bad eating habits.

She wasn't here. A quick calculation revealed that she couldn't have made it before he did. It was impossible that she'd come and gone.

So, fed and home now, he went in and waited.

Redford paced the floor, begged for his ball to be thrown, but Tristan wasn't even willing to go out in the back yard. What if she came and he didn't hear her? Eventually, Redford went outside by himself. He'd had enough of Tristan's brooding; he wanted grass, a ball, and some time to himself apparently.

Tristan considered casting on himself to remove his new ability. He didn't even like it, except when it came to Megan. Yasmin was a neutral, so was Luke, but everyone else was a crapshoot. Libby had even been upset about something earlier in the week, and Tristan had to deal with deflecting her bad mood. He would have liked to have helped her, but it seemed he couldn't do that while he was also bombarded with every bit of anger that passed through her. Whatever her son had done, it was a doozy. Tristan hadn't asked.

He didn't want to remove the spell. He wanted to hear Megan when she showed up. Wanted to be able to tell her what she needed to hear, whether or not she would tell him. But more so, he was just afraid. Afraid she would knock or let herself in when he was halfway finished. If he was actually casting the way he needed to be—at full concentration—she could come in and out and he'd never know it.

Or she could interrupt the spell and he would wind up half-spelled. He only needed to consider Delilah and Brandon to see how badly being half-spelled could screw a person up. So he sat in his living room and waited and wallowed. He watched some truly terrible TV, then realized she was not coming as soon as her meeting finished. She must be coming at the end of her work day.

At nine p.m., after ordering Chinese delivery so he didn't have to leave the house, and eating it by himself, he admitted that she wasn't coming after work either.

At midnight, he took the fastest shower he'd ever taken, then curled up on the couch so he could hear the door if she knocked. He hugged his phone in case she called. Then he pulled Redford's bed out beside the couch for his own comfort, what little of it he could find.

In the morning, Tristan put his hand on the door and didn't feel her. He scryed to see if she'd been there. She hadn't, so he'd called Blessed Be and told them he'd be working from home again. Though this time he managed to actually do some of his work. He checked with vendors online, made calls to follow up on orders, created the schedule for the next week. And he waited for Megan to show up.

She didn't.

By Friday, he went back to work. First chance he had, he stopped Yasmin. "What happened? She went out with you and then she didn't come back."

Yasmin inhaled a slow, deep sigh as she thought about how to frame it. But as he now had Megan's ability, he didn't need it framed. "Oh."

"I didn't mean to!" She was desperate. He'd just given her the shares in the business, and she'd betrayed him.

"No, Yasmin. Don't worry about it." He could read her like a book. Now he wasn't sure he liked it. Despite that, it was comforting to know that she truly had no bad intentions. Her guilt was evidence, but it didn't make him feel better. "I know you didn't mean to. And don't worry about the business. You're family now. We will get mad at each other. Delilah and I are counting on you to fight, throw things, explain, defend yourself, and tell us when we're being fools. That's what family is. You're in. Don't worry about it."

She was in tears when she hugged him. "Oh Tristan, I'm so sorry. I don't know why you didn't tell her, but it honestly didn't even occur to me that you hadn't."

"I know. Trust me, these days, I know." He almost laughed. It hurt that Megan didn't even want to try to patch things up, but he did almost laugh.

Yasmin did, too. "You know, it's the one time I could have actively hidden something from her and I fucked it up! I'm so sorry."

"I should have told her." He admitted. He could admit it easily now. Now when it was too late.

"Why didn't you?"

Wasn't that the million-dollar question? He didn't know.

He only knew that when he saw her he'd explain everything. Only he didn't get a chance.

Megan showed up at the store the following Monday night. As she walked in the door, he was blasted with her presence. Despite the fact that his all-hearing spell was finally, blessedly beginning to fade, he heard her at full volume. "Megan!"

He didn't hide his surprise, his joy at seeing her. He should have, he realized later, but it didn't even occur to him.

Her cold reception of his warmth was underscored by the flat expression on her face. "I'm here for the beginner's class."

It was true. She still didn't want anything to do with him.

Tristan waited outside the classroom watching the students. Yasmin and Megan still interacted well. There was no animosity there, and for that small favor, he was grateful. Gods knew, Megan needed her friends.

He tortured himself by staying while she was there. Then, later, he was the last one out the back door. He locked it and drove home to his dog and his otherwise empty house.

"What would I do without you, Redford?" He asked the dog, but the answer was fading with the spell.

CHAPTER 36

Megan attended two beginner's classes at Blessed Be before she fully gave up on Tristan. He'd told her to come to him when she was ready, but she'd thought he'd be back before now. He wasn't.

It should be getting better to be without him, but it wasn't. It was worse. She thought about him all the time. She passed him each time she went to class, but she couldn't read him. That was maybe the most frustrating. Until the second successful *quell*, the one Tristan did, she'd been able to hear him. Now, with no idea what he thought or wanted, she was having trouble deciding what to do.

She was stuck in her apartment, having hit up Yasmin for company as many nights as she was willing. The woman had a boyfriend after all—a fiancé actually—and part ownership in a business. Megan hung out with Libby once. And the night before, the second week she'd attended, a handful of the beginner's class students went out for drinks afterward.

Several of them were a bit too new age for Megan's tastes. They wound up in a very philosophical discussion about abilities Megan knew first hand. Then they discussed the sexy owner of the store.

"You don't think so, Megan? I mean he's hot." Alexia had turned to her.

Farrah had joined in singing his praises and between the two of them they managed to get Megan to fess up that yes, Tristan was, in fact, very hot. She didn't tell them she'd seen him naked. Or that he'd bought her jewelry and even said he loved her.

So sitting at home with a pint of super rich ice cream wasn't her best move. It wasn't even a move. It was waiting for something that obviously wasn't going to happen. If there was going to be a move, she would have to make it herself. Would he still be willing to explain?

On a few separate occasions, Megan had thought about confronting him, but she hadn't actually done anything. This time, she put the ice cream away, and headed into her room to change into clothes. She hadn't gotten dressed all day.

Not sure if she'd finally make it out the door or not, she put on some lip gloss and stepped into sandals. Megan was in the lobby before she changed her mind. Instead of heading into the garage, she went out the door and headed for the beach.

A few blocks later her sandals came off as she contemplated what she really needed.

Sure Tristan has listened in to her thoughts, that wasn't the issue really. She'd done it to so many people herself, but she hadn't been able to help herself. She hadn't been able to turn it off. Tristan was different, though. He'd been someone who didn't hear her. He'd changed the game and not told her. He'd listened for almost a week and said nothing. She was still angry about it.

Since she turned him away, she'd been thinking about her mother and sisters more. She'd like to foster those relationships. That was easier to do when she was in Hansen with her father out of the house, but it wasn't anything she could do from here.

It wasn't anything she could do when her mother was under her father's thumb and didn't even call.

So should she call Tristan? Try to patch that up? She wasn't even sure if there could be a good reason for what he'd done.

Even though the day had been warm, the evening was cool and the sun had already been setting before she came down here. The sand was cold beneath her bare feet, wet when she dug her toes in. Just a sign she should get back home. And probably a sign that she should get in her car and go to see Tristan. At least let him give her the explanation he wanted to give her. Or tell her that he'd had enough waiting and she was too late. Maybe, just maybe, there was something he could say to make her less upset with him. And she wanted that, so bad.

She was stronger now than she'd been when she first came here. She could handle hearing that he just didn't want her and stand up to the feeling. She had a way to clear her ability and she was learning how to do it herself. Megan decided she would hear whatever he had to say and she could survive it.

Climbing the stairs like she used to, she took the long way up to her apartment. She would grab her purse, she would—

The door wasn't locked.

Slowly, she pushed it open, looking around the edge, wondering if she'd really locked it behind her when she went out.

"It's me." Instantly familiar, Tristan's voice shot straight to her heart, telling her more than she wanted to know. Making her feel more than she'd expected to feel.

"You weren't here, you didn't answer my knock." He was standing up now, talking to her, looking at least a bit contrite. "I checked the garage and your car was still here, so . . ."

She nodded at him, not really ready for this conversation. She'd thought she was ready, but she wasn't. At least this was partly why she'd given him a key in the first place. "It's okay." She paused, "Why are you here?"

"Because you didn't come to me. Even after seeing me twice at the beginners' class, at my store, you still didn't come see me." He slowly sank back onto the couch, looking dejected.

"I was angry." She shrugged.

"No shit."

It would have been funny if he hadn't seemed so beaten down. She was opening her mouth to say something more, but he beat her to it.

"You should know, it faded. I can't hear you anymore. So if you want me to know something, you have to say it. If you want to lie to me, you can get away with it."

"I won't lie to you, Tristan." But everyone did. What they said and what they thought they believed often warred with the feelings that roiled in them. Even Megan, who'd thought she was over Tristan and she could handle anything he had to say, found she couldn't handle even this. So she braced herself. "You listened in on me."

It lacked the vehemence she meant to blast him with. When faced with the man himself, her anger wasn't anywhere near as strong as it was when she could muster her righteous indignation all on her own.

"I did. You listened in on me, too, you know." He didn't say it with any heat either.

"I couldn't help it. I couldn't turn it off back then."

"You slept with me and still didn't tell me."

Her shoulders stiffened. As much as he was right, she didn't have much choice. "If I told people, I'd never have sex, or conversations. And when I did tell people, most of the people I told didn't believe me." She hated remembering it, it was still true. "If I proved I could do it, they hated me. How was I supposed to know you'd be the first person in my life to say it was okay?"

"I wasn't. Yasmin was. Luke was second. And I was there with them. You met my friends and knew where I worked and what I believed and you still didn't tell me." Now he was getting angrier. That was maybe easier to handle.

"No, I didn't. One passable experience doesn't mean I start telling everyone what a freak I am. Especially the guy I was attracted to!" This, this was the anger she'd been feeling. "I never told you I *couldn't* hear you! You couldn't hear me. There was no reason to believe it had changed. That's the lie. You lied."

"I wanted to know what it was like to hear what you did. That was all." He'd started to stand, but his will faded and he sank back down on the couch.

"And how was it?" Her hands found purchase in fists on her hips. Somehow she was still standing in the center of her living room while he tried to defend his actions.

"It was awful." The words were almost inaudible, but she heard them. With only her ears.

"I know."

"You don't know." He didn't look up. "I thought you had a gift. I acted as though it was wrong for me to do the *quell* and that I was doing you some big favor against my will. But I didn't know. I'm sorry."

"That bad?" This time she sat beside him.

"Worse." His grin was half-hearted, pained. "I saw three movies and they all went badly. I heard every thought of everyone in my store. I heard who didn't like the decor—but not just that they didn't like it. They thought it was outdated, the colors not nice. They thought Yasmin was a bitch and she's about the nicest shopkeeper you'll ever meet. They thought my grandmother's tools looked cheap and fake. I'd thought I would think people were just idiots. But it hurt. All those things. They didn't say them. I hadn't heard them before." Then he looked up. "I just wanted to know what it was like to be you."

Her heart rolled over. It was sweet in its own way, but he was missing the point. "Fine, so you did this 'Megan

Experiment.' You didn't tell me. You let me be around you for a week and you didn't tell me."

He didn't say anything. Not for maybe a full minute. Then he asked, "Do you still love me?"

She was startled, didn't know what to say. Then she did. "Yes, but it doesn't make things okay."

He ignored the second part of what she said. "I still love you. I want to be with you. I didn't mean to hurt you."

All wonderful things to hear. None of them answered her real question. "Why didn't you just tell me?"

He shrugged. "So many reasons."

"Give me one!"

"The easy answer is that I had it planned, but you got home late, then we were making love and I could hear you. Really hear you." He was looking her in the eyes now, as if staring into her soul, as if that would make her understand. "And I had already listened in without telling you. It was just easier to keep not telling you. And I liked it. I liked hearing what you thought about me. I liked knowing when you said things you weren't fully certain of. I loved that you thought I was the perfect guy, because I could anticipate you."

He'd stopped looking into her eyes, he was looking into the corner of her ceiling as though it held secrets he couldn't tap. It was only then that she realized he wore an old t-shirt and older sneakers. That he looked as if he hadn't shaved in a few days and that he hadn't slept well in a few weeks.

Her heart rolled over again as he paused, still looking away, still somewhere he could tell her these things. A place where he was both pleased by the ability and ashamed of it. Megan knew that mix of feelings far too well.

"What's the hard answer?"

Tristan looked right at her. No punches pulled. "Revenge. You did it to me. You played me like a piano. Became my dream girl, and even after I found out, it didn't matter. I was such a goner by then, I just forgave you. Some tiny part of me felt I deserved to listen in on you for a little while. And that I deserve to have you forgive me for it."

She sucked in a breath at the first hit, but as he explained it, he started to make sense. She'd been bad to him at first. She'd manipulated him, gone to Yasmin for the spell. Rather than explain or try to compromise, she'd fought his ideas. "So where does that leave us?"

Here they were, sitting on her couch, finally having it out. But she wasn't in his arms. All hadn't been forgiven.

Again he looked away. "You didn't come. Two weeks I waited for you to show up, but you didn't come."

"You wronged me." She shot back.

"And I have come to you and fought for this every step of the way!" He stood up. He towered over her, angry and hard and haggard and so handsome he took her breath. "You have never fought for us. You can't even show up! That's all I asked of you: show up. And you didn't do it."

His voice trailed off, the pain of finding her lacking as hard on him as it was on her.

Megan's voice wasn't steady, but she tried. "Tristan, I have fought for everything I ever had. I fought every day at school just to stay upright. I fight everyone around me and I fight myself. You're asking me to fight again. I've been fighting."

He walked toward the door. "I get that. I know where you came from. And trust me, I have a lot better idea now what you've dealt with. I didn't, but I do now. The thing is, no matter how much you fought in the past, no matter how hard a struggle it was to get here, I can only make up for so much. I can't be the only person fighting for us. I'm more than willing to do the majority of it, because I do know what you've dealt with, but I have to see something from you. I have to know that what I'm fighting for is real and that you really want it."

"I—"

"No, Megan." He cut her off, reached into his back pocket and put something on the table beside her door. The tiny metallic clink let her know it was the key. "I'm leaving. Obviously, I won't get over you quickly, but eventually I will. If you want there to be anything between us again, you should try to show up before I get over you."

She opened her mouth, but no noise came out. Before she could speak, he left, closing the door behind him.

CHAPTER 37

Tristan was sitting in his office with his head in his hands when Yasmin startled him. Jerking his head up, he stared at her as she stared back.

"The spell wore off?" She asked, far too casually for his bleak expression.

"Of course. Just tell me how you know." He asked, certain his eyes were bloodshot and he looked as bad as he felt.

"Only by the fact that I startled you." She crossed her arms, planting herself in the doorway. "I haven't been able to sneak up on you in quite a while. Kinda disturbing, you calling out to me before I turn the corner even. Megan tried to hide it, you flaunted it like a badge."

"Geez." He hadn't realized that. Still another way that he hadn't understood Megan. "Well, it's gone now. All of it. Her, too."

"Hence the look that screams 'embrace depression'?" She waved a hand at him, indicating his lack of care for the past handful of days. His beard was growing in, because each morning he thought about shaving it and just couldn't find the energy. He looked as bad as Yasmin had suggested, but he had zero fucks to give.

Tristan had gone out the door at Megan's hoping she'd come after him, follow him down the elevator, meet him in the lobby, stop him before he opened the door to his car. Any of it would have been fine. None of it had happened; she hadn't showed. Not the next day or the next. Hence the beard.

"Have you tried going after her?" Yasmin offered her best advice.

"I did. I told her how I felt, why I did it. Why I didn't tell her before—"

"I'm so sorry about that, Tristan."

He didn't have to be psychic to see that she felt horrible about it. "It wasn't you." He would have said more, but he'd said it before, and he didn't have the energy in him to say it again.

"I told her," he said, then started over. "I told her to come talk to me. . . . five days ago."

Yasmin frowned at him. He would have asked her to explain, but he wanted to just do the absolute minimum he had to, then go home. He hoped to curl up in a pitiful ball and try to get some good sleep. So far all he'd achieved was the curl-up-in-a-pitiful-ball part.

"Tristan," she was still frowning at him. "She's out of town again."

His head popped up. "She is? You know this?"

It was so much easier when he could just hear what she was thinking. Getting information, waiting for it, was a struggle he couldn't afford. He had stock to inventory—and in the shop that meant actually standing, walking around, and counting actual things.

"She texted me." Yasmin sighed again, as she realized that Megan had let her know she was headed out of town, but she hadn't informed Tristan. So she filled in the details she knew. "Her father's in the hospital again."

"What?"

His thoughts had walked the clear route that Megan obviously didn't want to talk to him. Despite leaving town, she still had a phone. She could have called, texted, jeez, so many options to get a hold of him and she just hadn't.

Tristan would have said he'd given up the last time she wasn't talking to him, but this time he said he'd really quit. He was getting over her. At least that's what he told himself. Still, he wanted to know what Yasmin knew.

So she sat in the uncomfortable chair and gave him what she had. "Wednesday morning she sent me a text that she was headed back to Georgia."

That thought alone made Tristan wince. Megan didn't fit in there; it was a hard journey and a difficult stay. He knew, he'd felt it from her, read it from her thoughts.

"When I asked, she told me her father was back in the hospital and they thought it was another stroke." Another sideways glance revealed that Yasmin knew far more than he did, and that she felt guilty about it. "I checked back yesterday, not a stroke but some residual neural effects. But he'll still be in the hospital for a few more days."

When Tristan offered up only a hard stare in return, she kept going.

"She'll come back before he comes home again. Probably Tuesday."

Counting out the time, he contemplated that he still knew his days of the week. Maybe because he was counting hours, wondering when he'd be whole again. Not any time soon, he figured.

Yasmin stood, indicating she was out of information. Then she stopped in the doorway, turned back and told him, "I promise I'll let you know if I hear anything else."

She was gone before he spoke. He had no idea if she heard him. "Don't."

Tristan considered yelling it after her, but he didn't.

Instead he put the thoughts aside. He counted deliveries, replacement for the seldom-sold herbs Yasmin had given to Megan for her first *quell*. He organized his folders into the file cabinets he'd cleaned out the night he'd first been with Megan. Tristan restocked the classroom, where Megan had first come with him to do the *quell*, then later brushed by him on her way into class.

Finally, he counted the ways he was an idiot and headed home.

Redford greeted him and after a thirty-minute attempt at a nap, Tristan gave up on giving up. He shaved—because he had nothing better to do and because a kind man at the grocery store yesterday had thought maybe he was homeless and tried to give him a twenty.

He showered—because he probably needed to. Though he couldn't smell himself, he also couldn't remember the last time he washed, and that wasn't good. He dressed in his good shorts, almost laughing at the thought of 'good shorts' and put on a better t-shirt and his nicer sneakers. He wasn't up for making himself decent, but he could get himself ranked higher than 'homeless.' When he looked in the mirror again, he was glad he hadn't tried harder. He still looked like crap and no nice shirt or pressed pants or silk tie could have fixed it.

"Come on, Redford." The dog trotted to his side. Tristan missed hearing the little guy's thoughts, but he wasn't about to cast that on himself again. He could cast just to hear Redford . . .

The very thought that he might regret it meant he was still nursing a hope that things would work out. Five days. Out of town. She'd talked to Yasmin but not to him. He picked up several tennis balls from the living room floor and put the dog into the car to head to the dog park.

He would leave his house. No more rushing between the shop and home so he'd be where Megan could find him if she showed up. What an idiot he was; she hadn't even been on this side of the Mississippi. He barked a laugh to himself as he and the dog sat in traffic. Redford barked back.

Maneuvering the car into one of the non-spots people took along the driveway at the park, he spotted Noah Preston and his dog again. Megan would have loved to have celebrity-sited the guy again—

Tristan cut himself off. Even in his thoughts, he wouldn't do that. Wouldn't let his brain run away with ideas that couldn't happen. Even without that, he was just this side of miserable throwing the ball for Redford. At least he could still hold up his end of fetch. He should have done it sooner. Redford didn't deserve his shit.

It didn't escape Tristan's notice that he was the one wallowing after this relationship. He'd told Megan it was her turn; she hadn't taken that turn. End of story. No one was in the wrong—or everyone was—but damn if he didn't hurt. At least he wasn't casting spells on people's businesses. He wanted to believe that made him a better person than the ex—whom he still hadn't identified—who'd done that shit to him. The thing was, whoever the spell-casting ex was, he'd chosen her. Maybe he'd walked away with no one in the wrong, but it sucked monkeys being on the other end of it.

When the dog got tired of fetch and Tristan got tired of his depressing philosophical forays, they loaded up and headed for home.

He let Redford in and then took himself out to get his favorite Thai food to go. If he had to let go of Megan, he would do it with good food. Maybe smelling it would give him some semblance of an appetite. Or not.

Reminding himself that he used to date one woman right after another, Tristan tried to calculate his time running solo. He'd told her he would get over her, he just had no idea when that would happen. Not in the foreseeable future, that was for certain.

He woke up with the dawn, after another night of broken sleep. He probably deserved it. He had definitely entered the phase of self-blame. He should have told her; he shouldn't have listened in on her.

Tristan accomplished exactly three things the next day, after which he headed home early. Then he managed to fall dead asleep for the first time since he realized Megan knew what he'd done.

So when his phone rang, he didn't wake up immediately. Hand reaching out, he groped for the phone on his nightstand before knocking it off before coming awake enough to look at the screen.

Megan.

Megan was calling him.

He slapped at the phone to answer it, scrambling to grab it, while his brain churned. Was she home? Did she want to come see him?

"Megan?"

"Tristan." Her whisper was harsh. Low.

"Megan?" His heart pounded. The tone in her voice scared him. Why would she whisper?

"I'm in Georgia. In Hansen." Her words were low again.

He nodded though she couldn't see him. His thoughts still scrambled as he searched for words.

She spoke again before he could ask, her words turning frantic. "Can you lift the *quell*?"

"Sure. When you get home—"

"Now. I need you to lift it, right now!"

CHAPTER 38

Megan's heart pounded, despite Tristan's soothing calm over the phone. She reminded herself it was her cell phone, paid for with her own money. It reassured her that no one was listening in. She wasn't confident one of the people here wouldn't pick up another line and hang up on her, or cut the line to the house.

"Stay put," he told her. "I'm on my way."

"No. I need you lift the *quell*." She was getting desperate. Not sure if she could stay in the house or if she should leave. She should probably leave.

"I'm not sure I can from this distance, but I can be there in . . ." He made some odd noise on his end of the line. She'd always disliked not hearing his thoughts, but now she hated it. She desperately wanted to know what he was thinking. It was a part of who she was. The people who hated her hadn't been wrong about that. What was Tristan doing?

What was going on beyond her bedroom door? Should she be huddled in the closet?

"Shit. Twelve hours."

It was too long. She wasn't sure what was going on, but she was sure twelve hours wasn't going to cut it.

"No." He said.

She was about to cry; he couldn't even make it in twelve hours. But Tristan's next words made her feel better.

"I can be there in six." There were more noises, sounds, keys? "I'm walking out the door now. As long as I catch this flight out of Burbank, I'll be there in six."

He wouldn't be able to lift the *quell* from his car or on the plane. "Can anything be done?"

"I'm calling Delilah and Yasmin on the way. I'll get them to do what they can from here. Where are you?"

"I'm at my mom's house." She didn't miss that it wasn't 'home' or even her 'old home.' Megan knew the difference now. She just hoped she made it back. "But I don't know if I'll be here in six hours."

Which was if everything went right.

"Keep me posted if you move. Text me the address." He sounded competent—if rushed—and it was the best she could hope for. "I have to hang up now. I hate to, but I have to call Dee and Yasmin and I have to line up a car for when I land."

"Okay. Thank you."

"Hold on tight. I'm coming." She heard his car start as background noise to his words. "I'll be there as soon as I can be. I love you."

He hung up as the words left her mouth. "I love you, too."

Fat tears rolled down her cheeks. She'd screwed it all up so badly. Oh, she'd learned her lesson. She just wasn't sure she'd live to see the other side of it.

Tristan still loved her and he'd even said it. He was coming for her. And she wished he'd heard her say it back.

She sat back on her bed and glanced at the lock on her bedroom door. It was a pushbutton in the doorknob and she was pretty sure it could be picked with a big safety pin or a bent paperclip. Hopping up, Megan pulled the old wooden chair from her desk and hastily propped it underneath the knob. She gave it a shove for good measure, then hesitated, concerned she'd break the knob off, ruining what little protection she had.

Taking deep breaths, she tried to calm herself. What should she do?

Her mother hadn't told her that people would come over.

No one had come to visit last time her father was in the hospital. They'd dropped off food for the family. Some of them handed the dishes to her, but others insisted on coming in and putting it into the fridge themselves. As though Megan's touch would ruin it.

She knew how people around here felt about her, so she'd stayed low. Helped her family. Ran her sisters to school and back. But there wasn't much she could do about being here. Everyone knew she was back. She didn't hide it. Not the first time, and not this time.

Only this time her father was upright; he was talking in the hospital; he had visitors. Megan noticed small differences this visit. In the grocery store, the girl set her change on the counter, not handing it to her like usual. Megan picked it up, not thinking much about it.

Then on the street, someone in the other car looked over at her quickly, probably recognized her, but then he flipped her off and honked before peeling out from behind her and subsequently cutting her off. Things were fine—or the standard definition of fine—when she went to pick up the girls next door. But Mrs. Banner was always rude, more so now that Megan had told her about precious Jeremy. So having the door slammed in her face while Mrs. Banner gathered up the girls and hugged each of them before handing them reluctantly to their own sister was actually normal.

Earlier, Megan pulled the girls out of school to go visit Daddy in the hospital. This time, they were tight-lipped. More than before. By then, Megan was adding it up. There was definitely a different vibe now. Here, she was used to being alone, but people had gone from uncomfortable around her to downright hostile.

Then she'd gone outside to get the mail and seen her tires. All four, flat. Upon closer inspection, it was clear they were slashed. She'd known someone was upset about her being there, but someone was always upset about her. She'd suffered the usual locker pranks in high school. She'd always written it off as one angry person at a time. She could deal with that.

It wasn't until tonight that she added things up. It was when people came over to the house while she was helping the girls with their homework that she started hearing with her ears what she wasn't able to hear in her head anymore.

"She said she can't do that anymore, but she could be lying." They whispered it loudly, as though they wanted her to hear. Then they would look her way, testing her. Only this time, she failed. She couldn't hear what they were thinking. Then again, she'd always been as good as she could be at hiding what she knew, so how were they to know she truly could no longer hear them?

Mrs. Banner and Jeremy came over while the first two church ladies were there. The Banners didn't visit while Megan was in town and the other ladies didn't leave. Mrs. Banner sat at the table opposite Megan and pulled Lizzie's math page toward her. "Here, I can help you with that."

Right under Megan's nose. It was a curt dismissal. But, not wanting to put Lizzie in a hard spot, Megan looked to her little sister, "Is this all right?"

Lizzie nodded and Megan headed into the kitchen to start dinner. It sucked, but making waves wasn't going to help anything. Her mother was falling apart. This episode was harder on her. It was becoming apparent that her father wasn't going to be his old self and the burden of that was falling to Mama.

Megan was only here to help until he came home from the hospital.

So she stayed in the kitchen, but with the open doorway she could hear a lot of what was going on. A few others showed up. Megan didn't hear the whole conversation, but she did hear Jeremy.

"She seduced me."

Unable to stop herself, Megan rolled her eyes even though no one was watching. What a dick. She pulled out a casserole when his mother added in, "She says she doesn't have it anymore. Which is the first I've heard her admit she used to have it."

Megan froze. There was no denying that they were talking about her now. And it was all negative.

Another voice chimed in. "I talked to the Reverend yesterday—I went to visit—" as though that made her a good person "—and he said she made it go away. She went out to that Los Angeles and she says she managed to cast out those demons."

At that point, she was heating the oven according to the instructions on the post-it taped to the plastic wrap that covered the dish. Megan had been enjoying the small irony of the taped-down post-it, but the voices were becoming more disturbing.

"I talked to him, too." Another voice spoke up. She recognized the voice: Mr. Russell from the choir. "The Reverend is convinced she fell in with witches. That's how she got it removed."

There was a pause, then another voice. Another she recognized, even if she couldn't quite place it. There had to be at least five extra people in there visiting her mother now, but there wasn't time to take stock. For the first time in her life, Megan had strained to hear the words coming from just beyond the big open space that led into the kitchen.

"I mean, it has to be witchcraft, right? You and the Reverend tried everything else. Didn't you?"

No answer. Her mother must have nodded. Or did she shake her head? Megan didn't see, couldn't know anymore. The fact was her mother and father had tried everything to stop whatever she was hearing. Everything except witchcraft.

"So she's a witch now?"

Megan had frozen.

Everything had changed in L.A. She'd made friends who accepted her. She'd been raised to be open-minded. Maybe she hadn't cared that they were witches because she was a freak, too. She'd been called 'demon' often enough that witches didn't seem any more horrible than her being a demon did.

They'd been nice to her. Nicer than anyone here. Which was probably how a girl raised on *thou shalt not suffer a witch to live* had wound up with one for a boyfriend.

It wasn't any big deal. Her father was just a little backward on that count. She hadn't thought anything of it—well, nothing other than not telling them about Tristan—until now.

Now they were talking about her. Now it wasn't abstract or silly. The whispers were getting scary. Still, she'd stood there in the kitchen until one of them asked, "Did the Reverend recommend we do anything about it?"

About *her*.

Her father wasn't due home for another whole day, but she needed to get out. Because despite what they were saying, it was what wasn't getting said that was most concerning.

There were no voices saying "this is ridiculous" or "Megan's not like that." Why would they? No one actually knew her or cared to know her. It had taken her years to understand that their judgments didn't have anything to do with her. They had no idea who she was.

It cut the deepest that her mother and her sisters were sitting in that same group. But she'd been telling herself it was okay if they didn't like her. It didn't matter. In the course of this one conversation, that all reversed.

Her sisters didn't speak up. Still, that she could understand. It was her mother's silence that was the most damning. It was her mother who did know her. She knew all the bills Megan paid for them; she'd wept when Megan took care of them and she no longer had to worry. She'd never said thank you, but she'd said how wonderful it was that the girls had the things Megan got for them, the supplies she made sure they had, the occasional treats. So while the words "thank you" had never been uttered by her mom, Megan had felt she was appreciated.

So this was a cold slap. Her mother said nothing. No defense of the daughter who'd done so much.

Megan had only nodded as she passed through the party in the living room. They all stopped speaking when she appeared in the arch from the kitchen. As if they didn't think she could hear their very thoughts.

She'd gone into the bedroom, only to hear the murmurs start again on the other side of the door. This time they asked, "What should we do about her?"

Do about her?

She was only here to keep house while her father was in the hospital. What should they care? But clearly, they did.

That was when she'd freaked out and called Tristan. She needed to know what they were thinking. Were they just talking crap? Were any of them serious? Would they be happy if she left? Megan thought if she could understand them, she could make a better decision. But Tristan couldn't fix things from California. So now she had to decide if she could just stay in her room here and wait for him.

She looked at her watch. It had been almost three hours since she'd come in here, two hours since she called Tristan.

By the voices, some others had joined, some had left, but the conversation hadn't changed. Still, she hadn't once heard her mother protest the horrible things they were saying.

Megan almost fell asleep. Sitting with her back to the wall, her phone clutched in her hand, the cold realization about her mother sat like a rock in her chest. Her mother had never stood up for her. All the things she'd believed about the woman, Megan had made up because she wanted to believe them. She wanted to believe her mother loved her. Maybe in her own small way she did, but Megan now knew it wasn't enough. It hadn't ever been enough, but it had been what she had, what she'd known. What she'd believed.

She didn't believe it anymore.

CHAPTER 39

Tristan drove into town as fast as he dared. He wouldn't do Megan any good if he drove off the road. He wished for daylight, wished he could pick up the phone and call her, but even a phone call on these roads was dangerous. The shoulders of the road were practically non-existent. It was taking all his concentration to hold the spell he was using to keep his tires on the pavement.

He'd called when he picked up the car in Atlanta, grateful that the large airport had rental places open twenty-four hours. During the time the agent was getting him the keys, he'd checked in. So he knew she was there, waiting. She hadn't even fallen asleep.

Tristan didn't understand all of it, but he understood enough. There were people in the house, threatening her. It was almost two a.m. and he was finally just a few minutes away. The one traffic light in town stopped him, so he took advantage of it and called her again.

Just like the last time, she answered before the first ring even ended.

"Tristan?" She sounded almost startled. "Are you here?"

"Almost. Are they still there?"

She paused. "I still hear them. Be careful."

"What's going on?" the light changed then and he pulled through, looking around. "What are they saying that has you so concerned?"

"Well—"

"Hold on." He took a sharp turn almost too late, then saw the street he needed. He didn't need to know what they were saying; he knew she was afraid. "I'm almost there."

He saw the church, large and white, gleaming in the street lights. "I'm here." He heard her sigh of relief.

She'd told him before about the church parking lot, that he should drive through to the back, but there were cars here. He parked and climbed out there in the lot, where no one would hear the door closing. He headed toward the back, noticing the little house lit up like a beacon. He slung his backpack over his shoulder, thinking about the things he'd hastily thrown into it.

As he marched as boldly as he dared up the front walk, he wondered exactly what he was walking into. He didn't have the chance to cast on himself before he left; he'd headed right out the door grabbing only the makings of an *undo*. No luggage, just the desire to get here. But now what?

He knocked on the front door, noticing that the front stoop wasn't covered, in fact, it was barely big enough to stand on. He'd have to step back—down—a step when the screen door opened out toward him.

The man who answered couldn't be anyone in Megan's immediate family. She had two younger sisters and a mother at home. Her father was in the hospital.

"Hello?" The man asked, clearly a bit confused by the stranger on the doorstep.

"I'm looking for Megan." As he spoke, Tristan immediately noticed that his own t-shirt and jeans distinguished him as an outsider. Even though the man he was looking at wore a t-shirt and jeans. Tristan was clearly different.

"The witch?" The tone had turned surly and Tristan realized he had his work cut out for him.

He wished he wasn't at a disadvantage standing a full step lower. The beer in other man's hand also indicated that Tristan was more likely fully mentally capable, but he knew not to underestimate a drunk man. He offered a frown and an honest answer. "She's not a witch."

"You one of her L.A. friends?"

"Yes." Should he say he was her boyfriend? Was he? He was still pondering what to call himself when the next question came at him.

"You a witch?"

Tristan stared at him. What was the preoccupation with witchcraft? He would bet the man had no clue what he was really asking. He was also concerned that these people had the police on speed dial. And that, should the cops come, the officers would side with the 'good church folk' they already knew. Not the newcomer from L.A. and Megan.

He tried brushing it off. "What on earth would make you think that?"

The man only stared belligerently.

"I'm here to see Megan." Tristan stared at him, stepping onto the top level of the stoop. Maybe his height would help push things his way.

It didn't.

Tristan stood for a moment longer, locked in a ridiculously stupid staring contest that was actually starting to make him nervous. Taking a deep breath, he loosened his hands from the fists they wanted to form and looked into the man's eyes. Then he snapped his fingers—spellwork at its smallest. "Bring Megan out."

"Sure." Though he didn't look happy about it, the man turned back inside and headed into the living room.

He wasn't invited in, but Tristan stepped through the door anyway and surveyed the people there. Megan's mother wasn't difficult to spot; he could see the resemblance. Same for her sisters, but there was a reasonable crowd for a family living room this late on a weeknight. Mostly, they stared at him.

He called to the back of the man heading across the room, presumably to get Megan. If Tristan had worked his magick correctly then he definitely was. "Tell her it's Tristan."

Amid murmurs in the room of "Tristan?" and "Who is that?" he saw her door open and Megan pop out expectantly.

"Tristan?" She looked beyond relieved, but then disappeared into the room again.

Tristan was taking stock—he counted about eight people total, three of them sturdy enough looking men—when she re-emerged. He wasn't sure if he was shocked that she was pulling her suitcase or not. With a moment's thought, he realized he was glad she was. He could just put her in the car and they could go.

No.

One of the men in the room was looking at him, and Tristan didn't like the vibes. He wished he could hear them. As ugly as it would be, at least he would know what they were really thinking. It hit him, this was why Megan wanted the *quell* undone. He couldn't do it yet, so he stood firm, unmoving and unmoved. He held his hand out to her.

It seemed like it happened slow motion. He saw as she walked toward him, as though he were looking through eight hostile sets of eyes. His hand stayed out to her, like any normal day. Not one in which her mother sat docilely on the couch while her daughter was virtually driven from the home she'd help support. When her fingers touched his it was the best feeling he could recall in a very long time.

"Come on." He whispered it as he purposefully turned his back on the people in the room and walked out the door, her hand firmly in his now.

She trailed the weight of the suitcase behind her. Tristan could feel it bumping over the threshold of the door, then down the steps. He wanted to take it from her, be polite, but he wanted his other hand free should anything change. His heart wasn't pounding, but he was wary.

Only after the screen door slammed behind her did she speak. "Can you lift the *quell*?"

"Yes." His answer was calm, but he was still on alert. "I'll do it as soon as we get out of town."

"Now. Can we do it now?"

They were out of the house but she still sounded frantic. "Now? Let's just leave."

"He knows everyone. I'm not sure we can make it out of town." She tugged on his hand, holding him back.

"He? Are you really that jumpy?" This time Tristan turned and looked at her. Into her worried eyes, into the fear that waited behind them.

She shrugged at him. Shook her head as though she didn't know. "I have to be. I can't hear anything. I can't tell . . ."

"Did Delilah and Yasmin's spell help?"

She shrugged, shook her head. So, no.

"Let's just get out of town." He tried again, tugged at her hand. Even though he had a backpack full of supplies to undo the spells she'd had cast on her, did they really need to do that now? "Is there a reason to think they'll hurt you?"

She blinked. Though tears didn't fall, they threatened. "They've thought about it before. My father has entertained killing me."

"*What?*" He dropped her hand and hugged her tight.

"He wouldn't do it. He only ever thought about it as a means to an end." She hugged him back, talking into his neck, but he heard her loud and clear. She pulled slightly away, looking up at him, her arms still locked around his neck, her eyes worried. "Now, he's telling people I went to Los Angeles and fell in with witches. That's how the curse was lifted."

"So you're all better but nothing here is better?" Tristan started putting the pieces together.

"I'm worse. Because before at least it wasn't my fault, not that much. Now, if I'm a witch, if I let . . ." She shook her head as though shaking off the very idea, but tears were falling now. "It's stupid, but it's worse."

"I understand." He hugged her again, just for one deep moment. "Let's get to the car, and get somewhere we can cast it, then we'll get home."

"No, *now*. I couldn't leave because they slashed my tires. It's getting worse." This time she took the lead, tugging both her suitcase and him behind her. She was already walking up to the back of one of the outbuildings as she explained. "There's a room in here. Can we be quick?"

"Should be. It's an *undoing*, they're pretty general, pretty quick." He was thinking. "I need a knife. Couldn't bring my athame on the plane."

"Athame?" The word rolled on her tongue as though she couldn't place it. She was patting under the windowsill for a key, then fitting it into the lock.

"The ceremonial knife."

"Yes, I remember from class." She was ushering him inside and looking out the doorway for anyone following them, or even maybe seeing someone back there? He wasn't sure.

Bolting the door behind them, she took the key and her suitcase along as they headed up a short flight of stairs. The place was silent, but that didn't bother Tristan, it was nearing three a.m. so he expected that. It was Megan's nerves that made him jumpy. Still, this time he carried her suitcase like a gentleman.

It turned out the room she opened the door to was a children's classroom. Crayon colored pictures of Jesus lined the walls. Small desks and tinier chairs sat in clusters around a big open space in the center.

"Is it enough?" she asked.

Enough space? He thought. Yes. But he wasn't sure about casting in the middle of a church that belonged to a people who didn't like his kind. He had a firm belief in sacred spaces.

She looked at him with a wry grin, apparently able to read him even if she couldn't hear into his head. "Does it help you to know that I gave the donation that made this classroom possible? And that I was never allowed to teach at the church or watch the children because of what they think I am?"

"Jesus." He borrowed her word. And yes, it did. He'd had enough, for himself and definitely for her. "Let's do it. I'll be as fast as I can."

Tristan opened the backpack and began laying out the pieces he needed. Then he looked up at Megan. "Knife?"

She headed out while he arranged a small circle, pouring a salt circle and setting up the small bowls he brought. He got water from the sink. Not his normal altar, especially not once Megan showed back up with a kitchen knife.

"Will this do?" She asked.

He nodded at her with the first smile he'd found in quite some time. He had a kitchen knife and sink water on the tile floor of a room he didn't belong in, but with the one woman he needed. He would do anything for her.

So he broke the salt circle and invited her in and began to cast the *undoing*.

CHAPTER 40

Megan stared at the candle flame Tristan set to flickering with a quick snap of his fingers. He didn't do the full orchestrated opening she was used to, just a quick call to each of the four corners to light the candle, protect, and guide them.

She took a deep breath in, her uneasiness following her into the church. She knew it was a sanctuary for most. The way they talked about it seemed like the same way she felt when she went hiking in the woods alone. Megan always knew if she was really alone. She would have to ask Tristan where they could go hiking near L.A. Clearly, she would have to find some balance and she hadn't achieved it by wiping out her skills.

Though she'd reveled in being 'normal,' she was coming to see that she simply wasn't normal. She wasn't herself without the sounds. It was too much most of the time, but she at least had a way to deal with it now. Maybe they could tone it down or . . . but now wasn't the time.

The people at her mother's house made her uneasy with the words she heard. Megan, more than anyone, understood what came out of people's mouths was often a toned-down version of what was in their heads. She also knew what was in their heads was often a fantasy they had no intention of acting on. And while that was true individually, it was less true in groups. Given what they'd been saying about her? She was worried.

She was so stupid. She'd believed getting rid of her ability would put her, finally, into her father's good graces. Instead, it actually made her worse. She'd told herself repeatedly that she was done with the man, but each time she came home to him, home to try again to get him to love her. Looking back, she could see the kernel of hope that stayed alive in her each time she gave up. And she never gave up on her mother. Not before.

Now, it was all dead.

Her father was never going to love her no matter what she did. And even if he could? The effort it would take her to maybe find that one thing wasn't worth it. She was too old to fight for her parents' love anymore. Not when they weren't giving it. Her mother had made her priorities clear, too. Though Megan was convinced the woman actually did love her, she was tapping out. Her mother was supposed to protect her, defend her, and she'd sat in her living room on a rent-to-own couch Megan had paid every cent of. She heated casseroles cooked with gas that Megan had paid this month's bill on. The power was on because Megan had paid that, too. And her mother had sat there on her comfy couch, with hot food and light and listened to others say Megan needed to go. To suggest she was a demon in some sort of back-woods, ultra-zealot way.

Megan was who she was. If they were afraid of her, then they shouldn't have done the things they didn't want her to know. So she breathed deeply and turned her thoughts to Tristan and the words he was almost chanting as the undid the newest layer of the *quell*.

The spell on her was now three layers deep, but as Tristan promised removing it was a relatively quick procedure.

"Can you hear me yet?" He looked at her after finishing.

Megan shook her head. "I can feel that you're anxious. I have a feeling that's separate from my own anxiety and that's yours. But I can't hear you."

He nodded, as though to confirm. He must be thinking something that would have been pretty obvious had she heard it. "I'll probably have to peel both of the spells off."

"Three. I have another one after you." That hurt. Telling him that he didn't know what was going on with her. While she had no idea how she was going to fix this, she knew she had to.

A quick nod was all she got and he walked the basics of the spell again. The corners had already been called, the candles still lit, so it took only a minute or two before she felt it.

Her breath gasped in as the thoughts and emotions hovering around her condensed into her in a rush. They were still fuzzy, she couldn't make out words or general ideas, but she had more information, now. More than she wanted.

"Again, Tristan." She almost demanded it, holding her hand out to him, wanting to grab his arm but not wanting to interrupt the spell. The second part came out on a whisper. "They're outside."

What she didn't add was that it was bad. A small mob was coming to the building. While there were no pitchforks, two of the men were thinking vague thoughts about guns. One had a mental image of protecting himself with the revolver out of his ankle holster, another thought about the gun tucked into the back of his pants. Megan barely spared a thought to wish he shot his own ass off when he reached for it.

Most of the people had only the intention of running the two of them off. That was something Megan was fully behind. She was never coming back to Hansen, Georgia. She was likely never going to speak to her family again. Her sisters would be given a chance when they were adults, but she was better off without the rest of them.

Tristan's words punctuated her thoughts. She could hear him clearly now, the chants and concentration in his head in perfect alignment with the spell he was casting. Most people had one or two thoughts going at once, but when he was casting, Tristan was as focused as a person could be. Megan didn't want to interrupt it to tell him the group had sent someone back to ask her mother for the key. Megan's heart squeezed, grateful that locking the door behind her had been such a good idea.

They had to finish up in here. The man was running across the lawn and he was going to be back soon. Once the back door was open, there was a hallway and a flight of four stairs and the classroom door would fly open.

If they came in and found Tristan mid-spell, they might shoot him on sight. People didn't understand in general, and these people had been trained to be closed-minded on this count in particular. Megan didn't discount that they were on church property. If one of the men killed Tristan, he probably wouldn't even go to jail for it. It was a small town. Everyone knew her father. Even if people didn't go to this church, they knew him, and knew him as a good man. He sat in the jails ministering to the prisoners, and he brought coffee to the cops. These men would not go down for murdering Tristan. Nor for murdering her. Her heartbeat kicked up.

This time she said it out loud. "Tristan, hurry!"

The man was running back across the lawn, triumphant. So he must have the key.

Just then, the space around her seemed to converge into her again. It was so profound she was surprised it was silent, that a flash of light didn't signal that she'd gotten it all back. Megan gasped as it hit, almost falling over. Tristan didn't reach out for her, his arms were raised to the heavens, all muscle and spellcraft, finishing his work.

The candles flared, shooting blue flames up to the ceilings and leaving scorch marks there. Then they were out, the room plummeting into darkness. But despite the light leaving, Megan's senses were full.

"They're coming!" she whispered it to Tristan as she began to reach for the things he brought, she was going to break the salt circle, too. Scatter it so it wasn't recognizable. They already thought him a witch. She shouldn't have brought him here. Shouldn't have done this. It would only mean she could hear their hate-filled thoughts as she died, or worse, as she watched Tristan die.

Wait! No!

It came to her in his voice. He'd already adapted to her hearing him again. For a shock of a moment, she remembered that he was the only person on the planet who liked that she could hear his thoughts. Her heart pounded harder at the scary idea that she'd almost lost him. That she still could.

"This is our best defense." He said that part out loud and turned away from her as she heard footsteps in the hallway.

Now facing the closed door, he closed his eyes and took a deep breath. As if he was blowing out birthday candles, he let his breath out in a *whoosh* that brought all the candles and lights to full blaze.

The footsteps outside stopped just shy of the door and Megan wondered if they were being held back by the spell Tristan was casting or if they'd just paused because they saw the lights come on.

All around Tristan the air shimmered with promises Megan wasn't sure would be kept. For the first time, she wished she was a practiced witch and could help with the spell. Instead it all fell to him. He shouldn't even be there.

Beyond the doorway, the group crept closer, the men clustered in front as though to protect the womenfolk, two with guns now drawn. Could Tristan's spell stop bullets? She didn't know. When they walked in, they would find their favorite demon cowering behind a man who was now definitively a witch. A witch in the middle of a very powerful spell.

She wouldn't cower. Megan stepped up beside him, making herself the first target, she hoped.

Then she saw the doorknob turn.

CHAPTER 41

Megan watched as the door opened. Immediately, Jeremy and another man pushed through the space, guns drawn.

Her breath sucked in, she'd never been on the barrel end of a loaded gun before. Beside her, Tristan stood firm.

"Get out of my church." Jeremy intoned. His voice was both deadly angry and wavering with his own fear.

They had to see the way the air shimmered in front of Tristan, didn't they? Megan figured they thought of witches as stirring cauldrons and trying to call dark lords, but they hadn't counted on meeting one so powerful that he could create visible change in their world with just his powers.

If she hadn't been so scared herself, she would have laughed. There were going to be some pissed pants later when they realized what they'd seen.

"We're leaving." Tristan said and started to take a step forward.

Hearing him loud and clear, Megan realized that he intended to leave all the stuff behind. He'd abandon all the things he'd brought just so they could walk out of here intact.

She took a step forward with him, but Jeremy's gun still wavered.

"Keep the gun on us if it makes you feel safer." Tristan spoke almost softly, clearly in control here. He was confident. But she'd never been in a battle of spells versus bullets. Maybe it was a good thing he couldn't hear her doubt.

He took another step forward, toward the men in the doorway. Megan followed, wondering if they'd be allowed to pass through the tiny space. If they could have gone out a back door to the classroom, all would have been well. But her father had commissioned the building for offices and classrooms. The church had spent the money as frugally as possible. Local contractors and builders loaned their time, and local inspections officers loaned their signatures despite the codes not being followed to the letter. It was just another example of the dents in her father's good-guy armor. Instead, a real good guy stood in front of her, facing bullets from her father's good-guy army.

It was time she took some control. "We're leaving. That's all we want. Just to get in Tristan's rental car and go."

Something flickered in a brain beyond the doorway, but was quickly replaced by a poor re-telling of a pretty dumb joke.

Holy crap! They'd caught on and were actively trying to shut her out. She'd look again later. "We just want to leave. Let us go, Jeremy."

She considered spilling all their secrets, but if she did that, then she and Tristan would be as good as dead. Maybe she could threaten that.

"We don't want you here!" Jeremy's words were rough, and the others behind him joined in.

"Trust me, I don't want to be here with you troglodytes."

Okay, maybe insulting the people with the guns aimed at her wasn't her smartest move, but it was done. Tristan was standing perfectly still, hands up, air still shimmering around him, but he hadn't liked it either. She couldn't apologize. She just had to go forward. Unless Tristan could erase their memories?

She pushed ahead physically as well as strategically. Tristan had the little mob on the defensive. Megan was getting out of here on her own terms. "So Jeremy, who was in your room the night you blamed it on me?"

He glared at her, his brows pinching together as he tried to block her out. She was ready and grabbed the picture that flitted through his mind. Then she grinned.

He was singing the national anthem in his head to keep her out, but he hadn't been fast enough.

"Oh say can you see . . ." She whispered at him, singsonging the words, letting him know she knew. As she watched, his chest heaved in and out. A secret he'd kept all these years now in the hands of the person he probably hated most. But that was his own doing.

Megan told him so. "You only hate me because I know exactly what you are. But I don't want to be here. I'll leave, and you'll never hear from me again."

Not the best tactic . . .

It came from Tristan. He was right. She'd gotten ahead of herself, hadn't thought it through. Jeremy now had reason to dispatch her.

Tristan breathed in slowly. Megan wasn't sure if the others noticed; she tried to keep their attention focused on her. But they saw when Tristan breathed out and the air around him moved forward, pushing them all back a step.

The doorway was open and Tristan took another step toward the loaded gun.

Grab your suitcase.

He couldn't put his hands down. He was holding firm, reinforcing his spell with every breath. Strengthening it with the extra breath he'd taken, the extra focus he'd found. He took another step forward. And another.

Megan was even with the doorway now and reached for her suitcase where she'd stashed it against the wall as she walked in.

"Keep your hands where I can see them." Jeremy jerked the gun to her while the man behind him jolted. He moved his aim to Tristan to make up for Jeremy's change.

"I'm just getting my suitcase."

"She's just getting her suitcase." Tristan repeated in an almost hypnotic voice, and as Megan watched Jeremy and the other man nodded in agreement. Was that a spell, too?

The two walked out of the room into the hallway. Megan had one hand occupied pulling the bag, but she'd drop it on a moment's notice if necessary. Now she could see all seven of the people there, her mother and sisters notably absent. "We're leaving."

Jeremy backed up a step, then another, the people behind him backing up, too. It seemed they were afraid to pass Tristan and Megan, as though something horrible might befall them if they were separated from their group with the witch and the demon in between. Well, when she thought of it that way, it kind of made sense. She kept walking forward.

"We're just leaving." Tristan said. Though they'd left the room and the candles and the salt circle behind them, Tristan's power was still evident. The others did not like it.

"Okay, leave." Jeremy said and backed up another step.

Behind him, Mrs. Banner hit the staircase and stumbled down the four steps. She landed on her feet but caused a stir in the crowd as she did it. Even Megan gasped in shock as the woman almost fell. Only Tristan stayed upright and unruffled.

Then Mrs. Banner yelled out. "Jeremy, he's using that witchcraft on you. She made me fall!"

"Bullshit." Megan was almost laughing at that. "You're just a klutz who wasn't watching—"

But suddenly everything changed. Jeremy took his mother's words to heart, he jerked the gun and pulled the trigger almost before Megan could register that he'd changed his mind. Tristan was tackling her and she hit the ground, cracking her shoulder into the cheap tiled floors.

A second and third bullet cut the air with ringing cracks before she got herself together. All the jokes and songs and nursery rhyme repetitions that had been coming to her fled in the onslaught of hate and worry and anger that assaulted her.

The ones in the back truly feared for their lives, though Jeremy and Dipshit beside him were the only ones actually trying to hurt people. The ones in the middle were about to rush, and Jeremy and Dipshit were considering pulling the trigger again.

Throwing off Tristan's protective arm, Megan acted without thinking. A lifetime of anger and hate came off her in waves she could almost see. She walked out of the range of Tristan's protective spell, all but oblivious to his mentally shouted *Megan!*

"You!" she stalked up to Jeremy and pulled the gun from his hand. He was surprised enough that she got away with it. She barely registered Dipshit turning on her, but from the corner of her eye she caught Tristan's blast of energy that sent the man flying backward into the wall. Head hit hard, he was slumping down, hand and gun gone limp, even as Megan continued what she'd started.

Using the gun as a weight—which was maybe the stupidest, but best-feeling, thing she'd ever done—she punched Jeremy in his chubby jaw. He reeled backward as Tristan reached out.

Megan watched the gun in Dipshit's hand jerk away, skitter, then slide smoothly to Tristan's grip where he emptied the magazine and the chamber before throwing it all down the hallway far behind them. Megan wasn't done.

"You don't get to do this to me anymore, Jeremy. Your mother may believe you over me, but she's just as dumb as you and just as much of an asshole!"

She couldn't recall any time she'd ever raised her voice like this. She'd been taught by her parents to be meek and good. And she'd been taught by this town, much of it by the people in front of her, to be invisible, and she'd had enough. Megan had cracked.

Mrs. Banner started to open her mouth in protest, but Megan cut her off.

"Don't even think about it, you bitch. I've had enough of you and your idiot son." She looked at the older woman, finding her through the group. As Megan stared, she watched the group part in fear, letting Megan have a clear shot. She still held the gun in her fist, not in any kind of grip to shoot anything other than accidentally, but she was too angry to fix it.

"I told you what he did. You can choose not to believe, but every single one of you knows I never lied about you. I never told most of the shit I know about this boot-licking little hick town. I didn't want to know it, but I'm stuck hearing the crap that goes through your head, old woman. And you and I both know exactly what you and your son are."

A moan came on from the floor beside her and Megan turned her head briefly to see Jeremy starting to sit up, rubbing at the jaw she'd clocked. "Don't even think about, Asshole. I know who you fucked that night and I will tell them. Give me a reason. Just give me *one*."

They all scooted back away from where she now faced Jeremy. He didn't speak, just stared up at her with rage in his eyes.

She couldn't tell if they were shocked at the foul words they'd never heard from her mouth before. Some of them were shocked that meek little Megan wasn't so meek, and that she was maybe in fact the demon they'd believed her to be. Some were just surprised that this confrontation had ended with her and Tristan standing while the seven of them cowered in the hallway of the church building.

Taking a deep breath, she started to feel the pain in her hand.

She might have broken the bones, she wasn't sure, but she didn't let it show. Instead, she turned her head, looking at each of them. As she did it, she felt a boost from Tristan as he gained his feet, holding the field around them, moving it forward to encompass her even though she'd left his side.

She turned to look at the man still sitting on the floor to her side. "Look at your friends, Jeremy. They backed up. They moved *away* from you when you were in trouble."

His jaw twitched as his gaze hardened.

"Mine flew across the country for me." Her words were intended to shame Jeremy, but mostly she shamed herself. She didn't deserve what Tristan had done. She was grateful, but knew she didn't deserve it. Still, she walked forward. She wasn't going to let Tristan suffer for coming to her rescue.

With the hand not clutched painfully around the gun, she grabbed the handle of her suitcase and pulled it. She marched through the group, watching as they parted for her. She was protected by Tristan's spell and by her own brazenness. They might still find a way to shoot her, she knew it, but she was going out with her head up. And if they didn't kill her immediately, she'd spend her last breaths telling everything she knew. She would never live long enough to tell all of it, but the mood she was in, she would crack lives open with what she could tell. So she walked for the first time in Hansen with her head held high, no longer invisible.

Tristan stood tall beside her. He thought she was both stupid and amazing, which both humbled her and somehow made her proud at the same time. She wished she was worthy of him. She hoped they made it out of this.

They made it as far as the parking lot.

CHAPTER 42

Tristan stood before his rental car, angry and dumbfounded, but he couldn't let it shake the focus that was protecting him. He'd never put his skills against this kind of violence before. His father had. Even Yasmin had, but he hadn't. He could only hope it held.

They weren't getting out of town in this car.

All four tires were slashed.

It was Megan who turned around and pinpointed the traitor. She pointed at him, making all of the others stumble back from where they'd trailed the two of them out to the parking lot.

"You did this. You did it to my car, too. Give me your keys."

"No." He responded to her demand.

"You took my car, you'll give me yours. An eye for an eye." Tristan watched as she stared the man down, a goddess under the yellow lights of the parking lot, demanding her due from faithless servants.

Poking these backwoods beasts wasn't a good idea, but if he hadn't been in love with her before, he would have fallen like a Redwood now. His hands free, Tristan turned his palms toward the one Megan had singled out. Using his focus, he pushed the man mentally, before he spoke. "Give the lady your keys and point out your car to us."

A strangled noise came out of the man's mouth as he took one shaky step forward. He dug reluctantly in his pocket and pulled out a full set of keys—house, work, probably everything given the number on there. They jangled as he held them forward, stretching toward Megan.

One of the women, the more vocal one, put her hands at her throat. "He's using witchcraft on us!" She made choking noises, drawing the attention of the small group. Tristan almost faltered at the accusation.

Megan used the opportunity to step forward and snatch the keys out of the hand of the man Tristan had pushed. She also turned to the woman, who had shunned her since third grade. "Oh, shut up, Matilda. He's not using anything on you. You're just too dumb to know the difference."

When the other woman dropped her hands and opened her mouth in protest, Megan looked at her with contempt. "See?"

Then she turned and walked toward the truck that was, of course, what this man was driving. With her back to them, knowing that he had her covered, Tristan watched as she chucked her luggage into the open flat bed. Honestly, he was surprised they made it this far with her suitcase. He'd half expected to be casting *conceals* and fleeing through the woods most of the night.

But, no, Megan walked them out of there, facing her accusers and demanding a car. Instead, they got a dirty truck. She opened the door and climbed in. Tristan waited until she started the engine before he walked backward—keeping his face and his gaze on the protesters—around to the passenger side.

He heard them whispering how he was letting Megan take the lead, letting a woman drive. He almost laughed. She knew her way around better than he did. Besides, he wanted his hands free in case he needed to cast anything on the fly. He raised his eyebrows at them before he pulled open the passenger side door and climbed in, slamming it shut in unison with Megan's door.

She had the truck in reverse and backed up just far enough to turn before peeling rubber and taking off out of the lot. She was kicking gravel around the corner onto the street when he saw the group running behind them. People on foot didn't stand a chance, so he asked her for the gun she still held tight in one hand. Though she handed it over, it clearly hurt her to release her grip.

He rolled down the window and tossed it out into the ditch they were passing. They could likely be tried for stealing the truck, he didn't want anything else on his head on that one. So he made sure he tossed it where the others could see it. Their gun wasn't getting stolen. The truck crested the hill just as a crack rang out, making both of them duck.

"Was that gunfire?" he asked Megan.

"Yeah. They're shooting at us. Idiots." Even before the words were out, her foot was on the gas, pedal to the metal, and they were over the hill and out of range before the next shot rang out. "Now they're just shooting stray bullets into their own houses."

Tristan wished he felt as secure in that assessment as she did. "What if they follow us?"

"You're right." She stayed on the gas until she approached an odd turn and took a harsh right up a long road that seemed to maybe be a driveway. She turned out the lights and waited.

Tristan reached out and held her hand, the good one. "Did you break the other one?"

That had been a hard hit. A good one, but with the gun clutched in her fingers, she'd likely done as much damage to herself as to the Jeremy guy.

"Probably." She nodded, but didn't look at him. Her head was turned looking back at the dark road.

"Can you hear that far?" He'd meant thoughts, people, but she seemed to understand.

"Only that there's at least one car coming over the hill. But I'm hearing tires. I might get an impression as they go by."

Megan managed to look calm as she watched the road behind the truck. Tristan was anything but. Inside, he was exhausted. All that spellwork took energy, all the tension and worry had been plaguing him since last evening when he'd been in Los Angeles. He'd been up since early, his usual sleep not enough for his usual day, and here he was, on the run from idiots with bullets and approaching the next morning.

Cars sped up and over the hill, two of them.

"That's them." Megan whispered, as though the speeding cars might hear a normal-toned voice from inside the truck. The only outward signal that she wasn't as calm as she seemed was the way she squeezed his hand tight enough to hurt.

He considered telling her that he might need that hand, should more trouble find them, but he held back.

The car and truck, complete with raised voices, passed behind them, never looking for a vehicle buried in the foliage of the long dark drive. Through the trees, they could make out the T in the road, both cars turning a skidded right, not bothering with the stop sign that glinted in the streetlight.

Counting under her breath, Megan put her good hand on the key and waited before cranking the engine. Just as it sputtered to life—making Tristan nervous for a moment that the engine wouldn't catch—she scrambled to hit the buttons and knobs, turning off the lights and running the truck dark.

"Is this okay?" He asked her.

"Well, if you mean, can I see? Then yes. I know my way around here well enough to go full dark, no moon." She backed out of the twisting drive with ease, proving her words. "If we get stopped by the police, that's another story."

"Good point." Tristan decided to let her handle the driving, he had work to do.

Sitting calmly and regathering the focus he'd lost in their flight from the church lot, he took three deep breaths and worked a *conceal*. So it seemed he would be working one tonight after all.

Megan felt the energy of the spell go through her, or maybe she could see it on the car. "What's that?" she asked before saying, "Oh, how does it work?"

He'd forgotten how easy it was when she was on. She just understood. Maybe that was him taking advantage of her gift, but he couldn't help but like the way they worked together. "It basically makes people see around the car, ignore it, look away at the right time. Whatever takes the least energy from the universe to make it happen."

She nodded as though what he said was the most reasonable thing in the world. Then she approached the turn and went left, away from the path taken by the hotheaded group.

The road was dark and twisted, but the pavement was relatively smooth. No traffic lights stopped their progress. Mostly they passed open fields, large southern trees, and the occasional farmhouse. The dark truck seemed to go by fully unnoticed.

It was Megan who spoke first. "This was the road I took out of town when my father kicked me out. It's less traveled and more roundabout to get down to Atlanta, so I thought it would help me get my head together. I haven't been on it since."

He almost commented, but she beat him to the punch.

"I won't be on it again. Driving this road has bookended the wildest, worst, best, and most hopeful five months of my life. Everything has changed since that night."

The words had a slightly sad but mostly infinite feeling to them. Tristan stayed silent until they hit the freeway to head into Atlanta. "We should get your hand looked at."

"No, I just want to get home."

"You can't fly with a possible break, Megan." He countered.

"I'm sure it's not broken."

"But you're only using one hand on the steering wheel."

They went back and forth until he convinced her to check into a walk-in urgent care place before they hit the airport. Then they discussed what to say. "I hit my asshole neighbor with a gun in my hand," probably wasn't the best bet. But eventually they went with a version of that. Claiming it was an abusive boyfriend, an unloaded gun, and no charges to file.

When they pulled in, they parked in front—anything else would have been weird in the empty lot. But Tristan worked a few quick spells, one not letting the car get turned in as stolen, and the second not letting the jerks claim it was stolen in the first place. They'd have to make up a story to make that work. Tristan didn't think they could sell the witchcraft angle in Atlanta. Anyway, he knew a good lawyer. They just had to get out of the state first.

Inside the clinic, they both fell asleep, dozing between visits from doctors, nurses, techs and more. Megan was x-rayed and diagnosed with three hairline fractures. Then there was more time spent finding the right brace, explaining how to use it, prescribing medication and more. Tristan managed to get two sample doses out of them, explaining that he was putting her on a plane as soon as possible. It hurt to say he was taking her away from her abusive boyfriend. *He* was supposed to be her boyfriend. But in all this mess he was just glad to be upright, even if he still didn't know where he stood.

As she signed out, lugging a good stack of paperwork, Tristan began looking up flights from Atlanta to Burbank. Now they raced to make their seats.

She had her suitcase, which was big enough to send them through every line. He had nothing but his wallet. He was still wearing the clothing he'd dressed in the day before. Even though it was now noon on the other side of the country.

They stuffed themselves into the seats and waited for takeoff. He was going to pass out as soon as the plane started moving, he knew. He didn't even try to take her hand, but when Megan reached out and clasped her fingers around his, he was grateful.

Taking his mind off things, he asked, "So who did Jeremy sleep with that he blamed on you?"

She began laughing. "You won't believe it. His cousin!"

"Ew." Now he was going to have bad dreams.

"I know. It's like he's *embracing* the stereotype."

Neither of them made it five minutes longer. Or at least that's what Tristan thought when the plane touching down jolted him awake to a mild pain in his ears. Megan hadn't even woken. She'd been more stressed than even he had and probably more exhausted. He nudged her gently. "We're home."

"Oh." She rolled her head, then fluttered those gorgeous eyes open. "Good."

He sure hoped so. Still, they didn't speak, basically dead on their feet, as the gathered her suitcase and headed out to parking where he'd stashed the car what seemed ages ago. It wasn't even twenty-four hours.

As they pulled out of the lot, he asked her, "Can I bring you home with me?"

But she shook her head.

CHAPTER 43

Megan didn't buy any new furniture. She didn't try on any sweaters—it was L.A., when was she going to wear a sweater anyway? She worked on her *quell*.

She had two big goals—heal her hand and learn to be okay by herself. She hoped to do both in the same time frame. Her hand was on a six-week schedule, or so the doctor had said.

When Tristan dropped her at her apartment that first evening, she told him what she'd planned. "I don't have a family any more. I only have me."

He'd protested of course. "You have *me*. You have my family."

"I do, and I have Yasmin and Libby. And I even got to know Mrs. Michaels across the hall." She conceded, "But your family will always be your family first. If anything happens, Delilah will side with you."

"No, she won't—"

"Yes, she will. She might agree with me, but you're the one invited to Thanksgiving, right or wrong. That's what family is." She shook her head. "I don't have that anymore. Actually, I never had that. But I finally realized it. I have to learn how to be okay on my own. Without a safety net."

It was scary just thinking about it. "I don't know how I'll feel when I get done, but when my hand heals, I'll tell you."

He hadn't agreed, but it wasn't his decision. It made her feel like crap after all he'd done for her. Still, it would be worse to be with him and then need to get out later because she'd never figured this part out. He couldn't save her. She had to know how to save herself.

Tristan sat there in his car as Megan started to get out, but he'd reached for her hand. He held her fingers, sandwiched her brace between his own palms and she felt her hand heat. "What are you doing?"

"Making sure you heal fast and well." Then the heat disappeared and he let go. He let her go. "Good luck, Megan."

She'd desperately wanted to know if he would wait for her, but it wasn't fair to ask for that. She'd used him too much already. He was a man, not a toy she could put on a shelf until she was ready to take it down and play with it.

She'd taken her suitcase and her full range of hearing up in the elevator. At seven at night, she somehow had the ride to the third floor all to herself.

She called into work to explain the emergency and the missed day. She had a broken hand to show for it, a plane ticket, and more, but no one asked. She'd been a good employee for long enough—no vacations, nothing—that it was simply fine. She worked her full time schedule the remainder of the week. Then set up a vacation for two weekends away. It was the first vacation she'd ever planned.

Megan called the shop and talked to Yasmin, got herself back into the beginner's class. Though she walked in each Monday night wondering if she'd run into Tristan, he managed to be absent every time.

"Is it normal for Tristan not to be here for this?" She'd asked Yasmin.

"There is no normal for Tristan now. Four months ago it

would have been abnormal." She smiled. "He liked to be here for the beginners' class just to be sure that I wasn't letting anyone blow up his shop. But he's not kept a steady schedule for a while."

"I'm sorry." It was all she could offer.

"Maybe you should tell him that instead of me," Yasmin offered as sage advice. It was good advice, too, but Megan couldn't follow it quite yet.

Though *quells* weren't part of the beginners' class, or even the intermediate, Yasmin helped her learn them. She wasn't the fastest student, still, she tried. So far, she'd accidentally *quelled* the curl in her hair and discovered it actually reached the middle of her back when it was straight.

Yasmin laughed at her, loud guffaws and into near tears. "I wish you could have taught me that last year."

"A hair straightening spell? I'm still not sure how I screwed that up."

"It's your head? Same general area as what you wanted?" Yasmin shrugged. "You'll have to ask Luke about the time I straightened my hair."

Megan hadn't made that mistake again. She'd made new ones. Then she took her vacation. Six days off in a row. She drove upstate to the Redwood Forest and drove through a car-sized hole in a tree. She stayed in a bed and breakfast—not the most expensive one, because of her other goals. And she hiked through the greenery. It was the first vacation she'd ever been on where she truly enjoyed everything she did. She wasn't dictated to by someone else's idea of a break. No one argued in the car, she didn't have little sisters to monitor or a father to not set off. She sat on the beach and watched the waves roll in. She went to visit the place where the seals gathered, and apparently stank up the air. She ate seafood, and read e-books to her heart's content.

Driving back down the Pacific Coast Highway—definitely

the long way—she stopped at another bed and breakfast just over an hour from home. A nice couple ran the place, the wife checking her in, smiling but wondering about a single woman. In her room with a view of the ocean, Megan watched a storm roll in and she made her decision.

Flexing her fingers, she checked her healing. Tristan had done it, almost there. She was sleeping without the brace now, her doctor telling her how impressed he was with the speed at which her bones had erased the hairline marks. One more week to check-out, then she would need to see Tristan.

She came back Sunday night, ready to hit the beginners' class Monday evening again. Tuesday, she went to Yasmin's house, like she had several times.

"Hey, Megan." Luke opened the door to the bungalow in North Hollywood, a beer in his hand.

"Off duty tonight?" She smiled and tipped her head toward the beer.

"You bet."

Yasmin said he'd been on for about two weeks straight working another case associated with the one Megan had first helped crack. A true hero, he'd never asked for her help again. Maybe Yasmin had explained, or maybe he saw for himself that first night how hard it was on her. Megan decided it was time to step up. "I can't do it all the time, but if you're stuck, let me know. I'll try to help."

His eyes widened as she passed by on her way in the door.

She shed her coat, hanging it on the rack just inside the door like the frequent visitor—and real friend—that she was. "I mean it."

"Thank you!" He closed the door behind her, then headed into the kitchen. "I won't ask much, because I have no idea how I would explain where I got the information, but thank you. Do you want a beer? Hard cider?"

She was opening her mouth to say yes when Yasmin came

down the hallway. "She can't have one until after! We can't tell what we've done if she's not fully sober."

That made sense.

"We'll all have a drink after." She declared then caught the sly thoughts the other two shared.

"Not all of us," Luke said.

"No! Yes! That's amazing."

Both of them burst into laughter.

"Did you even figure out my due date?" Yasmin asked, with a quirk to her mouth.

"No." Megan smiled. Some things didn't come through. A baby. Thoughts of her own life got pushed aside in favor of thinking about her friends. "Going to get married sooner now?"

"If we can find a place." Luke sighed and took a sip of his beer.

"How big?" Megan asked.

"His family, which is huge—what, thirty people?" Yasmin waited until Luke nodded. "My family—which is not huge. And my family here, which is bigger. And includes you." Yasmin laced her arm through Megan's, grounding her in a sense that she'd accomplished most of what she'd set out to do.

"I just stayed at this great bed and breakfast halfway up the coast. They can't sleep everyone, but you could have the wedding there. The garden is beautiful." They talked logistics while they set up the back room, Luke staying out of their way.

Two things left to do, Megan thought. A little more needed on her nest egg. She'd been socking away every spare penny, except for the much-needed vacation. And she needed her skills adjusted. Exactly what she and Yasmin were doing.

They'd been meeting weekly, casting *quells* and *undoings*. They futzed, they adjusted, they were trying to get it right. Like a patient on medication, they knew what they needed—what Megan decided was the right level to be herself and not be inundated and stuck. Tonight, they would undo last week's *quell*, tweak the spell and try again.

At the end of the evening, she had that cider with Luke while Yasmin drank a very tart homemade lemonade she'd apparently been guzzling.

"Our child is going to come out with a sour expression." Luke told her.

"I think all children come out that way." She ignored him.

It was easy being around them. Something she wanted for herself, and maybe—just maybe—still had a shot at. "Yasmin, can I ask you a favor?"

CHAPTER 44

T ristan sat in his office, contemplating his sorry existence.

"*Brrrruff,*" Redford barked up at him, also contemplating Tristan's sorry existence. Or at least that's what he looked like he was doing.

Tristan wasn't sure. He'd loved hearing Redford. Dogs were exactly as straightforward as everyone believed, or the ones he'd listened to were, but they were more complicated, too. Despite the desire to hear his pet, Tristan wasn't messing with any more of those spells. That had gotten him nothing but trouble.

Then again, right now he had nothing but nothing.

Megan's hand should have been healed two weeks ago. In spite of her promise in the car to come and tell him what she'd decided, she hadn't shown up. Maybe that was her telling him what she'd decided. It was a sharp pain to the heart, but not one to be ignored.

"It's a great irony, Redford," he told the dog, only because the door to his office was closed and he could claim he was talking to someone on the phone. "I never understood the effects of my dating habits until I fell in love with someone who couldn't fully love me back. Sad times, puppy, sad times."

"*Brrruff*," the dog answered back and put his blockhead onto his paws as he laid down.

Big changes, Tristan thought, big changes coming down the pipeline.

Delilah and Brandon had settled in and baby Julie managed to stay out of the hospital. A *sleep* spell for nights had made the whole family happier. Yasmin and Luke were having their wedding quickly, some place up on a bluff up the Pacific Coast Highway, but it didn't matter where. It mattered that Yasmin and Luke were happy and that Tristan would be happy for them, but Megan would be there.

Yasmin made no bones about it. Megan was her friend and would be invited. She'd even be staying at the bed and breakfast like most of the close family. Tristan decided to stay somewhere else.

He was the oldest of the group, and he was getting left far behind. Six months ago, he wouldn't have cared. Wouldn't have felt left, because he'd never wanted what they had. Then, bam, Megan had entered his shop and flipped him upside down. Looking over at the couch, he talked to Redford again. "I'm going to have to get rid of that couch. Too many memories."

Well, one really, but it was a doozy.

"Talking to the dog?" The voice startled him.

Yasmin was standing in his doorway, arms crossed like usual, staring at him.

"Yes, if you must know." He looked at her blankly, not pleased being caught talking to the dog, but really, what did he care? Not enough about anything lately, that was certain.

"I'm heading out." She told him. While she said that at the end of each shift, tonight it was different. She wouldn't be back for a week and half. She was heading up the coast with Luke, then Saturday everyone would gather for the wedding.

"You drive safe, okay?" He grinned, happy for her despite the hole in his own chest.

"You sure you and Redford are okay with the cats?"

He nodded at her. "Hex and Voodoo will be fine. Redford loves them. I promise not to coat them in peanut butter and leave the three of them alone. Go. Have your fun."

"I'll see you Saturday?"

"Yes." He smiled, though he thought *not a moment before.*

She didn't move. He waited. She still didn't budge.

Finally, she said, "I need a hug."

A laugh, a real one, came out of him. "I'll miss you tomorrow and Friday. But we'll be okay here." He was closing the store on Saturday so all the employees could attend. Still, he hugged her tight for a minute.

She stepped back with a smile on her face. "You drive carefully, too."

"I'll be fine. You're the ones driving the PCH at midnight." He was smiling as he said it but something didn't feel right.

"Luke is trained in defensive driving. We'll be fine—"

"Did you spell me?" It was like having a hair on his tongue he couldn't get off. He could feel it, knew it was there, but couldn't quite place it.

"Yes." She sighed and he was shocked she admitted it that fast. "It's for the wedding. You've been down. You need it."

"What? No." He shook his head. "Please take it off."

"No." That was it. Just 'no.'

"I'll take it off." He warned her even though he was having trouble finding exactly what it was. It would take effort. Yasmin was good and getting better every day. A year ago he would have believed he could shake any spell she cast on him, but now? She'd hidden it well.

"Tristan," she warned him. "It's for my wedding. Please leave it. I'll take it off you before we leave on our honeymoon."

That killed him. It was her wedding and he was acting so morose she'd cast on him. "Just tell me after the wedding so I can take it off myself?"

"I promise." Then she slipped out the door before he could say anything else. Before he could change his mind.

He'd just agreed to leave the spell in place for three days. *Ugh.* He squirmed. It didn't fit right, but he finished up his work and closed up the shop. He and Redford stopped for a milkshake on the way home, which Tristan enjoyed except for the look on Redford's face—the dog wanted some—and his growing concern that he was gaining weight. Right, no more pity milkshakes.

He walked Redford around the block when he got home, saying hello to a few of his neighbors, wondering if they thought he was as morose as Yasmin obviously did. Maybe no one else had noticed. But later, when he cracked open a beer and watched TV, he looked at the label. *Ugh.* No more pity beer either.

Yasmin was right. He deserved to be spelled.

The thought had just passed through his mind when a knock came at the door. Probably the neighbors on suicide watch. He turned to the dog as he shuffled to the door, then stopped to throw back on the t-shirt he'd peeled. "Maybe I am that bad."

He opened the door, the 'hello' dying on his lips.

She didn't say anything, just looked as amazing as the day he met her.

Tristan blinked and she didn't go away. He set the beer on the small table just inside the door, even though his mother's ghost would likely come back and kill him for not using a coaster.

Neither of them moved from where they stood.

"Yes, it's really me." She finally said, clearly reading his disbelief.

"So you haven't put the *quell* back into place." It was a stupid thing, not what he wanted to be talking about, but it was what came out his mouth.

"Actually, Yasmin and I have been adjusting it. Can I come in?"

"Sure." It was automatic. He didn't really want her inside his house. She'd been there before and was damn hard to get rid of. Instead he found himself stepping back and waving her in.

She didn't take off her coat, but she did hold up her hand. "It's healed."

"So here you are."

She nodded at him, but didn't throw herself into his arms. Didn't kiss him senseless or do anything else that would have allayed his fears. Instead she started talking.

"I've done everything on my list. I've got a nest egg just barely big enough to catch me if I fall. I've traveled, my way. I've adjusted the *quell* to fit what I need."

That one interested him, at least a little. His interest caught her attention.

"Yasmin and I have been treating it like medication. We tried different 'doses,' until we found what worked. I'm learning to cast it for myself. I haven't been all that successful yet, but I hope to be self-sufficient soon."

He didn't really care about that last part. *So you can still hear me?*

"Yes. But I'm not hearing all the other crap. I can't randomly pick up information from objects anymore. I can will it, but I can't be startled by it. That's nice. I can see a movie if I want, just not if you've seen it before." She offered half a grin.

"Why not?"

"Because I can still hear you." She smiled.

His heart kicked. *Was that on purpose?* He didn't know.

She didn't answer his mental question, just continued with her self-improvement list. "I erased my family from my phone and blocked my mom and dad's numbers."

"That's okay. Probably good." He told her. "You know it's okay to let go of the people that hurt you, right?"

"I didn't, but I do now." She looked around the house, squatted down as Redford came up and offered her a slobbery, squatty-armed hug. Little traitor. She looked up at Tristan. "I can stand on my own now, without them. Without you."

"Yay for you." His tone was as flat as it could be. Maybe she was just setting him free. Or maybe she could go now that she'd come and told him how great she was without him. His heart twisted and his eyes hurt. He wanted that beer again. "What do you want, Megan?"

"Everything."

She stood up, looking at him as she said it. As his heart leapt, he realized her mouth hadn't moved. He'd made it up.

"I want everything, Tristan. I want it with you. Not because I need something and I'm asking you to provide it, but because I love you. I'm fine on my own, but I *want* to be with you."

He heard it all, but still her mouth didn't move. She looked at him, hope shining in her eyes, a mirror of his feelings if not his confusion.

"You haven't figured it out?"

His heart skipped, turned over, stuttered.

"Yasmin did it. She cast on you for me." Megan shrugged, her lips moving with the words this time, the contents of her statements no more or less clear. "I wanted you to hear me, too. So you would know, really *know* how I feel."

She waited a beat. "So, when I tell you I love you and I want to be with you, you understand that it's coming from my feelings for you and not from fear of being alone or of anything else."

His chest felt like it opened up and his soul plummeted to his feet. Just for a moment. Just for a second of white-hot fear, before he realized she was really in front of him. Actually telling him that after all this time, she still wanted him.

"You said I needed to fight for us. Well, I will." She stood tall.

"If I owe you, if you need me to show up every day and say it again and again until you believe me, I will, Tristan."

She breathed heavily with the weight of the words she'd thrown out there, worry and uncertainty creeping into her thoughts. He could hear them, *feel* them. She was just as concerned that he would say no as he was that she wasn't real.

"You won't wake up and find me gone. Not unless you tell me to go." Her hands were curling into fists, defiant, ready to fight for him. He just needed to find words.

"I told you, you didn't have to drag me back, you just had to show up." He breathed the words out.

I did. I'm here. I'm ready.

It rang in his head. Possibly the sweetest words he'd ever heard and they weren't spoken out loud.

He should answer her, but he couldn't form a coherent thought to save himself. Instead, he grabbed her, crushed her to him. He wanted to kiss her, but he couldn't yet, he was breathing too hard, still calming the shaking at just having her back.

She wiggled in his arms and a brief flare of fear hit him that she wanted loose. But she didn't. He could feel it. She was . . . her coat hit the ground behind her. Her arms wrapped around him, her mouth found his and he sank into the feeling of finally being home. Finally being right again. Finally being better than he'd been.

It was Tristan who pulled away. "What about next time, Megan? The next time you choose them over me, or think you can't handle it?"

Her smile was understanding, even as her shoulders sank. "There is no next time. That's why I needed time to myself. They won't call. If they do, I won't be pulled. I won't doubt you, because I don't doubt myself anymore."

She stepped back, out of his arms, out of his grasp, maybe out of his reach, but her words weren't. "I understand. If you need me to keep showing up, I will. If you need six months or a year or more to believe that nothing will pull me away, then let's do it. Go out with me. Just date me. I happen to need a date for a wedding coming up."

Her grin was infectious and Tristan smiled back at her. He grabbed for her, pulling her close again, unbuttoning buttons on her shirt, speaking what few words he needed against her lips. He could read it, he could feel it, she wasn't going anywhere. What he said was, "As if I could wait any longer, when I could finally have you. Did you know I already have a ring for you? I won't let you go."

She kissed him back, her heat seeking his, her tongue chasing his, her clever fingers pulling at the shirt he'd just put back on. Her mouth was on his, but he heard her clear as if she'd said it out loud.

As if I could go. I'm completely under your spell.

EPILOGUE

"Zoe!" Rae Woodward tried to find her friend in the midst of the crowd.

"Rae?" She heard Zoe's voice but sighed as she couldn't find her.

Zoe's sister Shay had found this little B-n-B on one of her trips with her rock star husband. So for Christmas she'd given Zoe the room. Zoe had brought Rae along. They had the place for three nights, a long weekend. And she'd thought a B-n-B wouldn't be busy for spring break. What did she know?

There was a bar down the road and a beach across the street . . . even though that street was the Pacific Coast Highway.

Zoe would never have abandoned school for all of Spring Break, so they'd stayed behind and worked for the first half. They were graduating after spring quarter and both had theses to finish up. But now, the last four days were for fun. Only, where was Zoe?

Rae closed her eyes and sought Zoe out. When she opened them, she felt there was something else odd. She'd felt it a few times in Los Angeles, but it had never amounted to anything. And she brushed it off now, too.

Still, she now knew which way to go. Rae wasn't tall; she couldn't possibly see Zoe over the heads of the people crowding the downstairs at the Inn. Then, between several clusters of people, Zoe emerged, a wine glass in each hand. She passed one to Rae. "They're having a wedding."

"We came here during a wedding?" Rae asked incredulously.

"It would appear that way. Our room was booked first, and there's another room, not taken for the wedding. But everyone else . . ." Zoe looked around, able to see over heads better than Rae could. "They are sharing their wine!"

College students were not known for their lavish tastes and she and Zoe in particular were not known for having spare cash, despite some of the trends for UCLA students to be rich. The two had been paired as roommates for freshman year. By the time signup rolled around for sophomore year, they'd decided the algorithm that had put them together had known what it was doing and they stuck together. And here they were, seniors, on spring break vacation together. Or so they'd thought. Instead, they'd inadvertently crashed a wedding.

Just as she was taking a sip and thinking the wine tasted wonderful, Rae felt it again. Like someone was running their finger up the back of her brain. It didn't feel bad or weird, but it definitely said, "Pay attention."

Just then, a cheer went up. "To Luke and Yazmin!"

Zoe raised her glass with a shrug and joined the chorus of well wishers. "To Luke and Yazmin!" She hollered, even though she didn't know them.

The crowd turned as a unit and looked at the stairs.

There was a huge contingent of middle eastern looking people—the bride's family. And another huge group of dark Italians—the groom's family. Then random friends spread around. Rae had picked that much up from conversations she passed as she'd tried to find Zoe.

Thus, she was startled to see the bride and groom coming

down the stairs, smiling to the cheers of the crowd. The bride was dark skinned, curly haired, beautiful and radiant. The groom, was taller, lean, and might have even looked happier than the bride. However, he was blond, light-skinned and not at all Italian looking despite the looks of his now cheerfully crying parents and siblings.

His blue eyes scanned the room as though looking for something and she felt that feeling in her brain as he looked right at her. The groom—*Luke*—frowned and looked away before he was swept up in the tide of hugs and smiles and happiness.

Was it because she was crashing the event? Rae didn't think so. He hadn't frowned at Zoe at all. And he looked *so* familiar.

She shook it off. Free wine and all that.

The two girls finished their drinks and headed out across the street. Rae just wanted to get away and party like a Spring Breaker for a bit.

But as they climbed the stairs back up to their room late that night, they passed a picture montage of the happy couple. They looked so happy together. She could *feel* it. They *belonged*. But that wasn't what stopped Rae dead.

"You okay?" Zoe asked, now three steps up.

No, but she covered. "Go on. I just need to call Sloan."

"Okay." Zoe dragged the sound out in a way that both said she didn't believe her friend and that she was here if needed. As soon as Zoe cleared the top step, Rae pulled out her phone and started snapping pictures. Then she dialed.

"It's the middle of the night, Rae."

"Sloan," she didn't bother with any pleasantries at all. "Check your pictures. I think I might have found him!"

"What?"

"Check your pictures!" she said it again as she stared at the picture board in front of her.

"Holy crap!" Her sister, who would have gone to bed at a

truly reasonable hour and been out cold when Rae called, was fully awake now. "He looks so much like mom."

"I was thinking he looks like Grampa."

"Did you meet him? Is he the right age?" Rae could hear the excitement in Sloan's voice.

"I didn't meet him. And it's hard to guess his age, but it could be." She paused then. She knew about Aunt Emilia who'd run off at eighteen, pregnant. The family had later found out she'd died. Rae always wondered if things would have been different if her mother had stayed in Italy. As it was, Aunt Emilia had died before their mother knew any of it. Before she'd even found out her sister had a baby and the baby had been adopted out. That cousin would be their only other family.

"That baby would be thirty-five now." Sloan was doing the math, too. "But would he be in the US?"

"Do we tell Daddy?" Rae ignored Sloan's question and asked her own in a hurried whisper.

She could almost hear her sister shaking her head. "No, not until we know more. But find out everything you can!"

"You want me to stalk the groom?" Rae was incredulous, but she figured she was already doing it. She relented before Sloan could answer. "Okay, I'm on it."

There was a pause and Rae could almost see her older sister, sitting up in bed, surrounded by lush covers and wearing her silk pajamas. She knew what was coming.

"Did you feel it?" Sloan asked.

"I felt it before I saw him," Rae whispered back. After a moment of making plans, she hung up and headed upstairs.

What to tell Zoe? Zoe knew she sometimes got hunches, but she had no clue what Rae was capable of, what her family lineage had given her and her sister. The question was, was that man her lost cousin? And if so, what talents might he have?

Thank you for reading! I love romances with real love and believable characters, and I hope you found all that in these pages. I want to fall in love right along with the characters, and I do, while I'm writing it.

About Savannah

I started writing when I was eight--I hand wrote an 80-page novella that I believed to be (adult) romantic suspense. I'm proud to say, I've gotten a lot better since then. I've grown up to be a nerd at heart! I love neuroscience and people watching, and if you look, you'll find some of that in each Savannah Kade book. Most days you'll find me in my office, looking out my window at a handful of the neighbor's cows, or watching my dogs or my cat roam the backyard.

Follow me, find me, ask me questions! I would love to hear from you.
www.SavannahKade.com
Savannah@SavannahKade.com